Praise for
Guillermo Saccomanno

"A choral, savage, and ruthless work, considered to be the great Argentine social novel."

—*Europa Press*

"Like *Twin Peaks* reimagined by Roberto Bolaño, *Gesell Dome* is a teeming microcosm in which voices combine into a rich, engrossing symphony of human depravity."

—*Publishers Weekly*

"Cynical and funny: a yarn worthy of a place alongside Cortázar and Donoso."

—*Kirkus Reviews*

"By using a narrator who is not shocked, who does not look away from anything, Saccomanno shines a gruesome, graphic light on what people are willing to ignore so that their comfort remains intact."

—*Los Angeles Review of Books*

**Also by
Guillermo Saccomanno**

Gesell Dome

Guillermo Saccomanno

Translated from the Spanish
by Andrea G. Labinger

OPEN LETTER
LITERARY TRANSLATIONS FROM THE UNIVERSITY OF ROCHESTER

Library of Congress Cataloging-in-Publication Data: Available.
ISBN-13: 978-1-940953-89-2 / ISBN-10: 1-940953-89-8

*This project is supported in part by an award from the National Endowment for the Arts
and the New York State Council on the Arts with the support of Governor
Andrew M. Cuomo and the New York State Legislature.*

Printed on acid-free paper in the United States of America.

Text set in Garamond, a group of old-style serif typefaces
named after the punch-cutter Claude Garamond.

Design by N. J. Furl

Open Letter is the University of Rochester's nonprofit, literary translation press:
Dewey Hall 1-219, Box 278968, Rochester, NY 14627

www.openletterbooks.org

I curse the word love
with all its bullshit
How great is my pain

—Violeta Parra, "I Curse Heaven on High"

77

Prologue

REGARDING TERROR

The way I tell this story may be terrifying, Professor Gómez begins. And he adds: How can you narrate terror. So I won't back down, he says. Even if people criticize my story and the thoughts it provokes, I won't back down. As Martín Fierro says, "I sing what I think, which is my way of singing." I know my story makes me sound like a gaucho minstrel on the run. Because anyone who tells it straight will always be a gaucho minstrel on the run.

Attention, demands the professor. When a song is popular with the powerful, it can't be trusted. People sing it for convenience's sake. They say fear's no fool. And what about terror. Terror makes a person more cunning. Not more intelligent, more cunning. Like a fox that eludes the hunting party. But that survival skill, when it's honed, becomes madness. Terror, that's what I'm going to talk about. I'll say it again: My story's not likely to amuse, because for me there's no joy in telling it.

In more than one way, this could be the story of an act of submission. Some might say it's brave to confess to an act of submission, but it's better not to commit it in the first place. And yet, if my story strikes anyone as funny, the humor probably has its merit: terror and laughter are incestuous siblings. The fact that now, perhaps more like a confession than a tale to be told, it seems to take on a bolder tone, doesn't redeem me. I'm an old man who repeats himself. I'm over eighty. And I have nothing to lose anymore except my papers. But papers, like words, blow away in the wind.

The professor adjusts his glasses and observes the overloaded, sagging shelves of his library, the double row of books, the piles of magazines and journals stashed against the walls, the tables, the chairs. He's surrounded by folders. There's a file cabinet on the table where he sets down his pitcher of iced tea. My mouth gets dry, he says. Then he asks about words. What are they good for. To name the unnamable, he reflects. We struggle to find the exact words to explain what hurts us most, as if by naming them our suffering might diminish. In our urgency to name it, we're distracted from pain.

Because in those days terror and poverty were all around us, the professor goes on. It was impossible not to see it, not to feel it. Then there was the cold snap of '77. For anyone who doesn't know what that fatal combination, terror and poverty, consists of, I'll explain it with a smell: the smell of jails and hospitals. There's a certain smell in jails, the same one you'll find in hospitals. Ammonia and piss, blending together in a kind of sweet stench. You can smell the shakes. It's a nausea that comes from filthy bodies and sticks to your clothes. Those out-of-date clothes that you rescue from the closet at the first frost. A jacket, a coat. Camphor and cheap cologne, the smell of poverty, the smell of cold shoes, which, logically, is also the smell of fear, of followed footsteps. Because fear and hunger go hand in hand, inseparable: a poor man always walks around frightened. He'll always get the blame for some debt, some failing.

I was around fifty-six at the time. But I was afraid I'd be blown up along with the kids, the suspected young militants. Gray hair didn't guarantee your safety. My state, like everyone else's, was one of terror. The only thing available, at least for believers, was the consolation of prayer. But who was there to pray to when God gives His blessing to the rich. There were a few parish saints left. The priests who accompanied the poor in their grief, whether because of their abject poverty or a disappearance, were fired by their church superiors, that is, when they weren't shot outright. God, if He had ever existed, was dead. It was more useful to seek help from the charlatans who pretended to be miracle workers. La Difunta Correa or Pancho Sierra offered more hope. Everyone latched onto what they could just to keep going. At that time, I fell ill with fear, but in addition to my medical license, I could also fall back on some unexpected money, my mother's inheritance. Neither her house nor her store on the coast, in a province that was the start of Patagonia, was worth very much. But that money gave me some breathing room. I could hold on for a long time with no other concerns but literary ones, even if they weren't so literary. In other words, I was in a privileged situation: like a tourist in a concentration camp. It drizzled all the time. You might ask, if I was aware of everything going on around me, why I didn't get the hell out of there. One explanation might be that I was paralyzed by terror. But it seems more reasonable to say that I was surviving by guiltily waiting for punishment. I still think so today. The drizzle continues.

The professor grows silent. His mouth is dry; he needs more tea. He stands, walks to the kitchen and after a while returns with a fresh pitcher. He sits, adds a half-teaspoon of sugar to his glass, a heavy glass, stirs, drinks, and after pushing the glass to one side, rummages in the file cards, removes one, looks at it, and puts it back again.

And I still don't know the answer, he reflects. Why I didn't get out. Instead of answers, more questions.

Enough preamble. Let me tell you the story.

Part One
THE GREAT DAMAGE

1 The place was in an underground strip mall downtown. The inscription, in gilded letters on the black-painted window, read:

DOCTOR JOSEPH LUTZ

MENTALIST

Your blue-and-white energy is very low, he said to me as soon as I walked in. He said it barely turning toward me, as if I had always been there:

When it's that low, he went on, the energy becomes negative.

Lutz was digging around in a small cabinet, rummaging among protractors, loupes, compasses, and other instruments. Finally, he found a pendulum, picked it up and made it swing. Then, holding it in his hand, he deigned to look at me:

Your astral body is in the gutter, he said.

Lutz was an albino whale, with the mug of a little boy. Tall and pot-bellied, he hardly fit in his studio, that narrow little underground den in a strip mall on Calle Esmeralda, crammed with a small table upholstered in black leatherette, two facing chairs, and bookshelves all around, a place overflowing with books and magazines specializing in the esoteric. From treatises on Hermes Trismegistus to the works of Villiers de L'Isle Adam, and passing over Éliphas Lévi, just one glance at the authors and titles of the works was enough to realize that Lutz's thing was the study of the Great Mysteries. Lutz obsessively repeated that phrase, the Great Mysteries, the subject of his research.

Since we were in a basement, every so often the walls shook when the subway went by. The piles of magazines wobbled and at one point collapsed. And whenever Lutz got up to look for a book on astral calculations, an encyclopedia of prophecies, a treatise on exorcisms, his own movement made the place quiver with a temblor like the subway's. Lutz leaned more to the left than to the right when he moved, an imbalance caused by a limp that he tried to conceal. A bullet to the leg in '58, he explained. But he also suffered from gout. Sickness screws you up worse than a war injury, he said. His eyes were translucent, like a blind man's. I remember there was something in his expression, the expression of a person who's seen something he shouldn't have. But also, now that I think of it, I could be exaggerating: I've always been impressionable.

Lutz frequently quoted Swedenborg and Blake. From the start, he wanted to be considered a psychic, rather than a mentalist, despite what the sign on his shop said. A psychic explores beyond the world of the senses, he explained to me on one of those afternoons when I had the urge to consult him. If Lutz had printed "mentalist" on the sign, it was to distinguish himself from those who abused the word "psychic." Joining this category was a highly varied fauna that included neighborhood *curanderas*, astrologists, Tarot experts, and numerologists who predicted the outcome of the football lottery. His specialty, psychic readings, had depth. Nothing phony about it, Gómez, Lutz told me. Because he had studied it for a long time before giving up Jungian ideas and launching himself headfirst into the study of the Great Mysteries. More than once Lutz bugged me with his ethereal theories, tripping up my Criollo-style Marxism and an Argentine Freudianism that I had often armed myself with in order to explain the inexplicable. But deep down, my magical thinking remained intact, always alert, ready to emerge from its siesta and turn me into the victim of superstitious naïveté. Lutz had sized me up from the get-go and wasn't about to lower himself in a discussion of the evil eye, indigestion, and shingles, beliefs that might have had their own validity, but which, far more than the mere superstitions of poor folks, represented an aspect of the Great Mysteries that the masses could understand. Lutz didn't deny that a religious medal and a stamp could be more effective for simple souls than any psychological interpretation, but he wasn't ready to condescend with such banalities:

I'm not into reading the lonely hearts section of women's magazines, Gómez, said Lutz, toying with the pendulum. Try to understand. Flesh is always hard to digest. And I didn't come to this planetary juncture to go around solving the vaginal ravings of maids and secretaries. What I do is serious investigation, Gómez. For the initiated. The psychic realm contains unfathomable depths.

Lutz's gaze dissolved into a bilious gray.

You're fucked up, he said.

The pendulum had stopped swinging. And Lutz kept staring at me. When Lutz looked at a person, it seemed like it wasn't his eyes that were focusing directly, but rather some point higher up, on his forehead. The third eye, I thought at the time. No sooner had I met him, no sooner had I entered his subterranean shop, than I began to feel his hypnotic influence. No matter how hard I tried to avoid falling prey to suggestibility, due to the condition I was in when I descended into his lair, I already felt a certain draw. Just being in poor spirits is enough to make a person think he's run into hard-core psychics like Gurdjieff around any corner, I thought. But there was also the possibility that Lutz was one of those and that I was too absent-minded to take him seriously.

I tilted my chair backward. I corrected him:

Worried, rather.

We're all fucked up, he said. It's understandable, with the drama that's been brewing around here, Lutz sighed. I agree, youth versus age. But also the eternal drama of occult forces. Krumm Heller, better known as Maestro Huiracocha, prophesied what was to come. With you I can be frank, Gómez. Because I can sense an initiate in you. Nobody gets involved in matters concerning the Cosmic Mystery if they don't have the thirst for knowledge. Wisdom, the Great Wisdom. The verb that must become flesh. The ancients—now they really understood it. Excuse me if I'm overwhelming you with my knowledge, but when you're a Child of Truth, you don't have anyone to discuss these matters of mystery with. It's not easy to identify those of us who are into this thing. And yet cosmic energy has conspired to bring us together, and that's how you happened to walk into this strip mall, come downstairs, stop in front of my studio, and then—I know: when you read the sign in the window, you must've felt the radiation.

Suddenly he fell silent. He irradiated me with his gaze.

I feel the vibration, he said. You've got death in your soul. It's understandable.

2 There was nothing magical about how I ended up in Lutz's hole-in-the-wall. I'll try to explain bit by bit.

I was bumbling along, rolling downhill. At twenty we believe in passion; we tremble. We allow ourselves the luxury of suffering for love since we have an arsenal of spasms at our disposal. The most trivial, sentimental foolishness thrills us or plunges us into despair. Our emotional repertory seems inexhaustible. But when we least expect it, when we pass fifty, the operatic mechanism of seduction gets corroded, and we stumble around at an age when passion gives way to indolence. Then we appeal to various resources to recover a feeling that has vanished: with each lust-at-first-sight pickup, a second-hand enthusiasm. And yet I can't do without that giddiness, so I went searching for it at night, when the city became a no-man's-land. There were few assaults. With a couple of pesos in my pocket, I would go out into the street and walk aimlessly, meandering. I would stroll along Santa Fe in search of quick comfort. A fast fuck and *chau*. If I had no luck, there were always the public bathrooms at the bus terminals. A major one was located at the 3 de Febrero terminal, near the race track. My age, dark gray suit, glasses, a few gray hairs, black moustache, I felt, made me look respectable. More than once I was stopped by a police or army barricade. There wasn't a single night when a green Ford Falcon didn't spot me, marking me. The guys would give me the once-over, and since I didn't try to dodge their gaze, they continued on their way. I had gotten used to running into patrol cars, Federal police vans, carriers, armored cars. A blackout was the sign of an operation in progress. Sometimes a helicopter flew overhead. Other times, while crossing a street, I saw a display of uniforms half a block away. They would yank a family out of a house, a building, and force them into a truck, hitting them with the butts of their rifles. The city remained deaf to the sirens, the orders, the screams and sobs of the children. There were nights when the shooting and explosions deafened me. Early one morning, passing by an empty lot, I saw some guys pull a group of blindfolded young boys and girls from their vans and shove them against a wall. I heard shutters slamming. I hid. Curled into a ball, I hid. Then, the explosions. Finally, the van's engine. And silence. In the stillness, I left my hiding place and walked toward the open lot. They were so young.

In spite of the terror, at night I walked and walked like one possessed. It would still be a while before I was diagnosed, early one morning at a hospital emergency room, with obsessive wandering syndrome. I would come to like that diagnosis, those three words: obsessive wandering syndrome. But it would still be a while till I was diagnosed. Now it was April, and I went walking through the nights and the cool early morning till the first signs of daylight. It seemed unlikely, as I said, that a respectable-looking citizen would be loaded into a green Falcon. More likely that a gang of bums would drag me to an open space, a construction site, as they did early one morning around Dock Sur.

The giddiness had just eased up when the cramp attacked my legs. Now I could return to my apartment and collapse. All I needed was a quick nap to be ready for action again, teaching my class. Although I was sleeping less and less, I didn't feel exhausted. But I was beginning to notice some anxiety and clumsiness in my gestures, and then a lethargy to which I reacted with an unexpectedly rapid heartbeat, small memory lapses, stumbling, all signs I hadn't noticed before. It was then, when I turned fifty-six, anticipating my approaching decline, that I consulted the inevitable *I Ching*. The oracle replied: "The concealment of the light." The power of darkness controlled everything. Light had been violated. But finally evil, because of its essentially stupid nature, would end up destroying itself. And while this prediction had its share of optimism, it was no great consolation. Like more than one depressive, I looked for solace in Taoist texts. I started going to the Kier Bookstore, as if that establishment were the anteroom to nirvana.

Bodhi was twenty-something. He was beyond skinny; he looked emaciated. In his gestures you could see an unaffected fragility, his delicacy. I met Bodhi one March afternoon at the bookstore. He adopted that nickname after Bodhi Dharma, though any queen hearing the name would have thought *body*. The boy was looking for The Hermetic Circle, the correspondence between Hesse and Jung. A pickup, a fast fuck, I thought, would help me endure my anguish. But the sensual attraction was displaced by a mutual courtesy. He always addressed me with the formal *usted*. I was moved by the spirituality the kid exuded because, let's look at it this way, he was slightly over twenty, and I, an old man, fiftyish, considered his mystical arguments childish illusions. Who, in a bout of depression, hasn't swallowed a bellyful of Orientalism? The esoteric can turn out to be an illusion of exile. Breathing the ether, you could forget what was happening right under your nose.

Any way you want to look at it, Bodhi smiled at me with the sweetness of an altar boy. Nothing is accidental. This meeting wasn't.

Bodhi opened the book and read to me:

"Nothing happens by chance," Hesse says. "This is the hermetic circle."

The kid inspired a feeling in me that, I have to admit, wasn't physical appetite. In his gullibility there was a kind of purity. And purity isn't something you can buy at the corner kiosk.

I can see it in your face, Bodhi said to me. You're damaged.

The conviction with which the boy said it disturbed me. It was the conviction of a pure soul, a saint who has come to reveal a truth. The physical attraction I had felt when I met him turned into the descent of an angel. It's true that for a moment I thought Bodhi was possessed, one of those many sallow, scrawny types, overfed on Lobsang Rampa, who latched onto an Orientalist dream to escape from reality. In a few minutes, I said to myself, the boy's gonna go all Hare Krishna on me.

You must be a vegetarian, I said.

I am, he replied.

He didn't seem to pick up on my sarcasm. And if he caught it, he let it slide. He regarded me with a self-sufficiency that wasn't devoid of pity. He made me feel ashamed of my condescending tone. Suddenly my desire vanished, and what I felt for the kid was envy of his principles, his confidence in his mystical convictions, as he admonished me.

When someone is damaged, he can't find peace, he said. He blames his pain on other people's incomprehension, he locks himself up inside, he weeps over the lack of love. He becomes a tormented soul.

Forgive me, I said. Maybe I misjudged you.

Forgive you for what, he said. You didn't insult me. No, you're the one who's punishing yourself. Maybe you need to touch bottom. As soon as you touch bottom, you'll search for the light.

I thought you were . . . I said. But I didn't finish the sentence.

The hermetic circle, Gómez, he said. Believe or explode.

And what if I don't believe.

If you don't believe it's because you still haven't penetrated the darkness. Like the swimmer who jumps off a diving board: he needs to touch bottom in order to rise to the surface. Then the truth will be revealed to him.

We went into a bar on Calle Libertad. I ordered a coffee and gin on the rocks. Bhodi asked for a pitcher of water. And this struck me as a detail that revealed his personality. Captivated, I wondered if the virginal character suggested by each of his minimal gestures might be a symptom of repression and stupidity. A simple exchange of glances in the bookstore had been enough to reveal that the two of us liked one another, but now, as the conversation and the afternoon went on, I started to wonder if the boy was a madman or a genuine saint. With the first swig of gin, I grew bold enough to prod him:

Tell me, kid, have you lived your entire life in a test tube?

Bodhi launched into his story. My father was an anarchist, he said. And my mother was a spiritualist. They never got along. For him, going against management meant not working. He always came back to the house drunk. "House" is just an expression: we lived in a tenement near Barracas. We got by with what my mother earned as a nurse at Tornú Hospital. We all slept in the same room. The double bed, a crooked dresser, a couple of chairs, a little heater, and my cot in one corner. On winter nights, when my father came home drunk, he pushed my mother out of bed and forced me to lie down next to him. That's how he initiated me in vice. A few minutes ago you were thinking that maybe I was a virgin. Don't ask me how, but I knew you were thinking that about me. When a person has had transcendent psychic experiences, he acquires very keen perceptions. I remember the darkness of those nights, the red-hot coals in the heater, my mother's sobs, and my father's rough hands all over me. Till one night my mother stood her ground. She was waiting for him with a syringe. As soon as my father walked into the room, she surprised him from behind and stuck the needle into his neck. There must've been a really powerful drug in that syringe. My father barely had time to let out a shriek, turn around swearing and walk out to the patio, clutching his throat. He fell like a stone. Then, the ambulance. They took him to the Municipal Hospital. Since all the tenants came out in defense of my mother, she was released from the police station immediately. It was a little after that when she started going to spiritualist meetings. She came back from those meetings uplifted: she wore a grateful smile. I was very small when she took me to Luna Park, to the Basilio Science School meeting. My mother

19

always said that Perón was a divine being. We owed him the possibility of divorce and the acceptance of spiritualism. Thanks to my mother, I was initiated into the Great Wisdom. Excuse me if I'm talking too much. Maybe I'm boring you. All it takes for me to communicate is for someone to show me his sensitive side. Just like I knew what you were thinking about me a few seconds ago, I know that now you're sincerely moved.

Two possibilities, I thought: Bhodi needed a psychoanalyst or a confessor. I asked him why he was telling me his story, why me:

I learned that if you want someone to open up his heart, first the emissary has to open his own. You need to open up your heart. You need help.

And you, angel boy, are my emissary.

My derision bounced right off him.

I'm not the emissary, he said. You're the one who's been chosen by the circle.

You don't say.

The circle is closing, he said.

Afternoon was winding down. The first shadows. The first lights. We turned onto Avenida Santa Fe. On this side of the city you were somewhere else: there were stylish shops, elegant women, men in smart suits. Even those who were dressed casually looked like they were strolling through the Windsor Castle gardens. Here the kids were not only blonds, but heirs. Me and my resentment, I chided myself. But by recalling Evita I was able to assuage my bitterness. If violence was the midwife of history, I thought, Evita was the bitch who had managed to cut those assholes down to size. Though the snobs had gotten even. "Long live cancer," they had painted on walls when she developed it in her uterus. I looked at Bodhi. Out of the corner of my eye, I looked at him. What had he done with his pain, I asked myself. The theosophical jackass was walking along, lost in thought. His spirituality was the refrain of a frightened child, singing in the darkness to settle his nerves.

We were walking along the sidewalk of San Nicolás de Bari when two green Falcons stopped a few yards away. The cops got out in a rush, wielding rifles and pistols. A clicking of weapons, shouts. Some of them had long hair and headbands. The one in charge was a massive, dark-haired guy in sunglasses. I thought they were coming after us. But no. They dispersed, blocking the path of two women. Two women, one who looked like the mother and the other, the daughter. Both women ran back toward the church, trying to climb the stairs and enter the sanctuary. They didn't make it. They were caught before they got there. The cops seemed more interested in the daughter than in the mother.

I remember the girl. Tiny, short hair, a little blue coat. All four of them grabbed her and beat her viciously. They stuck their fingers in her mouth to make her spit out the pill. The mother tried to shake them off, crying for help, till one of the guys hit her on the back of the head with the butt of his Ithaca. The girl was cursing. They grabbed the mother by the arms, threw a hood on her, and shoved her into one of the cars. The girl was dragged down the stairs. Her head started to bleed as it struck the steps. They seized her by the ankles and the hands, and they put a hood on her, too, and shoved her into the other car. No one interfered. Then, the slamming of the Falcons' doors. The screech of tires.

We walked on without a word. Bodhi's silence angered me more than my own. In his self-absorption there was a kind of superior attitude. He probably had an airtight explanation for what we had seen. I preferred not to ask him, not to listen to his thoughts. Bhodi was the same age as the girl who had been kidnapped. Maybe his muteness was easier to tolerate than the esoteric arguments he would use to explain what had just occurred.

We were making our way along Charcas, near Callao. I felt like smacking him. I couldn't take any more of this young snot whose meekness cloaked a know-it-all quality that wore me down. That's all I need, I thought. For some young kid to give me advice on how to live. That's what I got for not having enough self-control to stay in my apartment, concentrating on my papers and on a journal where I spilled all my solitary anguish. As if writing could bring relief.

You're suffering because of the internal chaos we live in, Bhodi said. And he sighed:

When you can't take it anymore, consult my Master.

Bhodi handed me a card.

Lutz, he said. He's my Master, my spiritual guide.

Saying good night, Bodhi extended a cold, bony hand. I took another look at the card and was still looking at it when Bhodi vanished into the darkness. I turned onto Ayacucho. The shadows of the trees added to the nocturnal gloom. That street was a tunnel.

3 The odor of burnt hair stank up the building in those days. As soon as you walked in you noticed the smell. The lobby, the staircases, the halls, the elevator. You could smell it everywhere. Not everyone could identify that smell, but I could. For me it was unmistakable. That smell came to me from my childhood. In the place where I was born, a village in Patagonia scattered among cliffs, there was a neighbor, a friend of my mother's, who was a nurse as well as a *machi*. She gave injections, but she also cured the evil eye and indigestion. She assisted at childbirths and drove away spells. When she burned hair, it was because the evil she was fighting was powerful.

Whenever I came home at night, I would sniff to see where that odor was coming from. But I couldn't manage to figure it out. I've lived in this building forever and I know almost all the tenants, except a few renters who move in and out. It was built in the thirties, and some of its first occupants still live here, retired old fossils who spy through the peephole before opening the door to anyone who rings their bell. Every time new tenants arrived, I would hear the old folks say that they needed new blood in the building. The expression affected me. Yes, I'm impressionable. And back then, that winter, I was even more so.

Ever since I moved into this apartment, I've had few dealings with my neighbors. My solitude was already populated with too many voices to complicate it with the choral novel of alliances. I've always felt I had little discretion. It was in those days, when the smell of burnt hair started to become noticeable, that a young man with the air of a born winner moved into the apartment next door. I would run into him entering or leaving the building, with his slicked-back hair and toothpaste-ad smile, his impeccable suit, tie, and executive briefcase.

I'm your neighbor, he said one morning when we got into the elevator together.

He spoke with an upper-class accent, as if he had a potato in his mouth.

Gonzalo del Solar, he introduced himself. I work in marketing. For Gillette.

Pleased to meet you.

The smell, he said. Where's that smell coming from?

Work, I said. Someone's having work done.

I'll have to ask Ramón, said Del Solar. Every super is also a secret agent.

Don't worry about it, I said. There are lots of old folks here. And more than one of them is nuts.

I have to admit that Del Solar had a certain bearing. Besides, he looked me straight in the eye. But if this was a pickup line, I wasn't about to bite. All I needed was to lose the respect the other tenants had for me.

That morning, before taking his leave, he said to me:

Anything you need, I'm at your disposal, he smiled. No matter what time it is.

He had left my hand impregnated with his Eau Sauvage cologne. No sooner did I take my hand away from my nose, I could smell the burnt hair again. The odor had become almost palpable.

Ramón the super. A crafty old fox from Santiago del Estero. He must have been around fifty, also, but he looked younger than me because, like he said, with half-breeds—including me—you can never detect their age or their grubbiness. Ramón lived in a tiny apartment on the ground

24

floor, behind the elevator. Here the smell of barbecued meat covered up the odor of burnt hair. The walls were aquamarine blue, with a predominance of vinyl, River Plate team banners, trophies from *truco* championships. There was a diploma from a union, certifying completion of a course in San Cayetano, with a dried little olive branch, the inevitable portrait of the Blessed Ceferino, a photo of the General on his pinto horse. Signed, with a dedication to Compañero Ramón. Ramón had hooked up with a woman from La Rioja ten years his junior. They had a son: Juan Domingo. The kid had started school and was in first grade when the mother fell in love with a merchant marine. Ramón complained: he had never done anything to let the woman down; he'd satisfied all her whims. But she dumped him anyway. The husband and the son. Ramón took great pains in raising the boy, a sad-eyed, chubby little kid who was bumbling his way through elementary school. I don't want Juancito to turn out like me, he said. I want him to be somebody. Two afternoons a week the kid went to an English language institute. The language of the future, Ramón said. When Juancito came home with bad grades, Ramón slapped him. If he didn't study English, he'd end up a super like his father, he told him.

His ambition to become block leader frustrated, Ramón attempted to be a leader in the building. One morning, as he was spilling buckets of water on the sidewalk, I asked him about the smell.

Some crazy old bat must have had a spell cast on her, professor. Nothing to worry about.

Ramón tried to change the subject:

I think the new guy smells even worse, he said. Del Solar.

Why, I asked. He seems like a pretty nice guy.

What if he's a subversive, he baited me.

He looks like a movie star, I said. Not a subversive.

Subversives dress to look like us, professor. They said so on TV.

I don't have a TV, Ramón.

What country are you living in, professor. You can't trust everybody.

Well, anyway, it's no business of mine. I don't like to stick my nose in other people's lives. To each his own.

Now Ramón was swabbing the floor of the marble entryway:

But what happens if it turns out he has explosives, he said. He'll blow us all up.

Why do you think Del Solar is a subversive, I asked.

He hasn't given me the keys yet, Ramón said. And I have everyone's keys.

You don't have mine, I reminded him.

Ramón looked at me thoughtfully. You're right, he said.

He winked at me slyly.

Maybe you're one, also.

And he backpedaled:

Don't be offended, he said. You're different. But it's just that there are many leftist professors. Why wouldn't you be one of them.

I stood firm. I had to stand firm now.

I'm a Peronist, Ramón.

They call themselves Peronists, too. The infiltrators.

I'm going to make you a copy of the keys, Ramón. I turned to leave. Remind me if I forget.

If I find out about the smell, I'll let you know, he said.

Ramón's mistrust made me feel a certain solidarity with my neighbor. But at the same time, I was still doubtful, trying to figure out to what extent Ramón's suspicions might be well-founded. On the one hand, Del Solar struck me as an inoffensive social climber. On the other, I understood Ramón's resentment: he couldn't stand my neighbor's status. It made him an enemy. The smell of burnt hair persisted. And Del Solar and I continued greeting one another in the elevator. As days went by, Del Solar seemed more and more like a dandy than a guerrilla fighter. Though it was also true that there were plenty of social climbers in the guerrillas' ranks. I wondered if it would be a good idea to inform

Del Solar of Ramón's suspicions. When everyone is suspicious, the guy who inspires the least suspicion becomes the guilty party. And that just might be Del Solar's case, with his winning smile. Ramón's suspicions, I reasoned, were mere resentment.

Just the same, I started paying attention to the sounds coming from his apartment. I felt embarrassed when I found myself holding a glass to the wall. Sometimes you could hear laughter from the other side. All I had to do to make it stop was bring the glass a little closer to the wall. The neighbor was laughing at me. I tried to concentrate on preparing my class on *Facundo*. Again, laughter. The intrigue was more powerful than my concentration. I put the glass against the wall once more. No sooner did I do it than the laughter ceased. The laughter of a madwoman.

One night, I tiptoed out into the hall, barefoot. I carefully sidled over to the door of the adjoining apartment. You could hear the laughter from outside. When I thought of what the neighbor would say if he caught me in the act, I felt ashamed. Regardless, I went on toward his door and pressed my ear against it. The laughter dissolved into an abrupt silence. In the distance a siren wailed. I quickly retreated. I locked myself back in my apartment.

Around that same time Del Solar came to me with the business of the damage.

One morning, before I left for school, the doorbell rang. It was Del Solar. He was pale. He had lost his smile. He apologized for what he was about to ask me. Because he didn't know how to ask it, he said. He didn't like to get involved in his neighbors' personal lives, he hurried to add. But I seemed like a trustworthy guy; maybe I would know something about it.

Something about what, I pressed him.

If I had any idea, Del Solar asked, who in the building was screwing around with voodoo.

27

Then he showed it to me. Impaled on the tip of a ballpoint pen he held a dead, dried-out toad.

Witchcraft, he said.

I didn't know what to say.

I'm not superstitious, he said nervously. Someone in this building has a thing for *Rosemary's Baby*.

I advised him to take the matter seriously. Report it to the super, I told him. Ramón had to know who was burning hair and was involved in witchcraft. That's what I told him. Because I thought that by becoming an informer Del Solar would alleviate Ramón's suspicions that he was a guerrilla. A guerrilla, I imagined Ramón would think, wouldn't resort to swearing just because someone had stuck a toad on his doorknob. A guerrilla, in those days, surely had other things to worry about.

The next morning at dawn, when I returned home from one of my nighttime excursions, as I got out of the elevator I saw light coming from the apartment next door. The door was ajar. I approached cautiously. And peeked in. Chairs flipped over, shards of ceramic vases, a broken lamp, scattered clothing, records, and papers strewn everywhere. A poster of the Biennial of the Di Tella comic book had been torn off one wall. I felt a chill in the air. And it was because the double door to the balcony was open.

I had palpitations. I shut myself back up in my apartment. I wondered who to call, to notify. Ramón was the least likely person to go to for help. I poured myself a shot of whiskey. I needed more to control my tremors.

I went to bed with my clothes on. And in the morning, when I awoke with cramps, I tried to convince myself that what I had seen next door was a nightmare. I barely had time for a shower, a shave, a coffee, and then off to class. I needed to hurry. I didn't want to find out if what had happened was for real.

When I opened my apartment door, I found a toad hanging from the outside doorknob. Now the smell of burnt hair was suffocating.

4 Lutz seemed surprised by my story. He sat up straight, making the chair creak, and fixed those watery eyes on me. Though as I said, his eyes didn't focus on mine, but rather higher up, toward my forehead. He folded his hands over his belly, lacing the fingers. Until then I hadn't noticed his hands: small, chubby, and white. For a few, interminable seconds, which would have lasted an eternity if I hadn't spoken, he remained in that position. An Albino Buddha.

What, I asked.

What, he repeated.

I've told you, I said.

Calm down, said Lutz.

I don't want to be my neighbor's toady, I said.

Lutz let the joke pass. Emotionless, his eyes on my forehead, his hands with their interlaced fingers. He had all the time in the world. He made it clear that he had explored abysses before, and mine was mere foolishness. After a long pause, he purred:

You're really fucked. Pay attention. And be discreet. Because not everyone has the sensitivity to understand the Great Mysteries, I'm telling you. And it wouldn't be smart for you to go around blabbing it either, not these days.

According to Lutz, both reincarnations and curses from beyond the grave figured among the Great Mysteries. Secrets are my thing, Gómez, he said. And for your information, not just anyone can plunge into these black depths and pop right on back to the farm as cool as a cucumber to drink mates. The influence of those powers extends to our own days. Not to mention our nights. Watch yourself. You have to take precautions. Especially if you're damaged.

I'm not damaged, I muttered.

You don't have to be a psychic to see it. When a guy goes around like you, with a low astral body, his energy in the gutter, he's in danger.

I didn't need Lutz to tell me that. The street, the city, the country, without a doubt, were not safe places. But it wasn't wise to shut myself in, either. They could kick your door down in the wee hours. Until the end of that fall, the most terrible thing for me had been loneliness. Sometimes I blamed myself for my neutrality toward what was going on around me, a neutrality that seemed too much like indifference and egotism: how could suffering over the lack of love not be a frivolity while terror bled from every crevice of ordinary events. For many, perhaps the majority of people, it was business as usual. If a military raid shook the night with explosions, gunshots, shrieks, and babies' screams, the neighborhood soothed its conscience by thinking there must have been a reason. And tomorrow would be another day. But even when I was neutral, I never quite got used to terror. Night after night, as though escaping without knowing from what, I would leave my apartment and hit the streets.

Lutz had his theory for what was happening. And the explanation was the Great Damage.

I have a confession to make to you, Gómez. In my youth I was part of the Nationalist Alliance. I got into brawls. In order to pay for my philosophy classes, I would pick up a few pesos through contraband. Since the cops were after me, too, I had to split to Rosario for a while. When the gorillas took power, I was hiding in a brothel by the Paraná River. It was a romantic time in my life. When the military defeated him, remember, Perón took off on a Paraguayan gunboat bound for Asunción. In Rosario rumor had it that the Leader would disembark at the port and fight to reclaim his government. The night the gunboat was due to sail past Rosario, the people were supposed to spill out on the banks. Alerted by the expectation that the gunboat would leave the Río de la Plata, the military moved the General to a Paraguayan seaplane. That night in Rosario, you could hear the murmur of the crowd, the quiet footsteps down to the Paraná to greet the gunboat that would never weigh anchor at that port. Imagine, Gómez, the lowered voices and the sound of those cautious footsteps in the night. I returned to the capital and formed part of the Peronist resistance. I planted guns out of sheer idealism. I wanted the Justicialist Revolution. If I stole weapons it was because the revolution seemed Peronist. I joined up with El Gordo Cooke. That's how I woke up. A Lenin, that Gordo. But the General, no matter how much he yakked about Mao, was tipping the scale to the right. It took me a while to wise up. Till I had the revelation. Why do you think Perón was part of a brotherhood with the name of Brother Pablo? Come on, Gómez, tell me why Brother Pablo authorized sects. It wasn't only for the pleasure of screwing the candle-suckers. Why did the planes that bombed the Plaza in '55 have the motto "Christ Conquers" on their fuselage. Why did Evita's body disappear. Why are images of the tyrant and the woman with the whip forbidden. The General of the Nation, now with no glory and no nation, is nothing but a small-time local boss from the Pampas, enjoying the dead calm of a banana republic. He has no shortage of bit players or coal miner mutts sniffing around between his legs. The man doesn't seem too depressed by his exile: he still has that slicked-back hair and the Gardel smile. He wears white guayaberas and white shoes, too. A spiritualist dancer, former performer of *vidalitas* who wanders around the tropical cabarets wiggling to the beat of the cha-cha-cha, picks up the General. Later, the General and his concubine settle down in a mansion in Madrid. Meanwhile, back home, we "shirtless ones" take up guns and shoot the shit out of one another. The General glimpses the possibility of returning and staking his claim. To prevent the boys from riddling one another with bullets and for some wise guys to establish a Peronist regime without Perón, the General sends the dancer as a messenger of unity. A former police corporal with pretensions of becoming a tango singer, a guy who's also into the Zodiac, comes on to the broad. Imagine that trio, Gómez: the military officer and promoter of sects, the ever-watchful astrologer, and the spiritualist stripper. Together the cop and the concubine manage to fill the General's skull with their esoteric blather. The cop becomes his majordomo, but everyone who visits the General nicknames him "the Sorcerer." The Major Arcana advise you to conspire, the Sorcerer tells him. In Madrid, Ava Gardner lives in the mansion next door. It drives the diva crazy to see the General step out onto his balcony every morning, throw open his arms, and rehearse speeches to imaginary throngs. You can hear the sound of the sprinklers. But to the General, that irrigational ssh-ssh sounds like the clamor of the Justicialist Party masses. It seems the Old Man (because now the General plays the Wise Elder and allows himself to be called the Old Man) wants revenge. He'll teach them a lesson that'll explode in their ears, he threatens. The bomb-throwing youths come to see him: back home the military forces that organized the coup, the magnates, and the bankers are ruining the economy; workers and students have spontaneous protests, throw Molotov cocktails, go on strike, and join the guerrilla movement. The kids are confused: they think Brother Pablo is Fidel. And the Old Man takes advantage of their confusion, goading them to keep up the shooting. He will return to his country. The Old Man will return. The military calls for elections. The Old Man wins by fraud. Now everyone wants to get into his good graces. And he, like Vizcacha, that sly old varmint in Martín Fierro, does business with all of them. He promises to be the great peacemaker who will unite the Argentineans. The Old Man enjoys hearing people talk about his glorious return. And he also enjoys trying on his general's uniform again, riding his trusty horse, having his photo taken for posterity, dying like a Roman soldier. Nothing modest about his desire. The Old Man returns. The masses mobilize to greet him. A human tide rushes in to welcome his homecoming. A huge celebration. Flags, drums, smoke from *choripanes* cooking and rug rats on their parents' shoulders. But before the plane can land, the left and right wings of the movement fight over the president's box at Ezeiza Airport. A battle erupts. Right-wing snipers hide in the trees. The guerrillas fire back from below. The protesters stand in the middle of the crossfire. The lefties who fall prisoner to the right are tortured at the airport hotel. The Slaughterhouse. The Old Man can't ignore the fact that his second-in-command, the Sorcerer, is writing an essay called *The Cow*, an esoteric continuation of Esteban Echeverría's *The Slaughterhouse.* Evita's remains are brought home and transferred to the country house in Olivos. Neither can the Old Man fail to notice the Sorcerer's juggling as he beds the *vidalita* singer on top of Eva's coffin. That way the slut can absorb the magnetism of the deceased. I'll tell you something else: Daniel is the esoteric name that the Sorcerer hides behind. The signs turn into facts, my dear friend. The young people don't give up their guns. A labor leader, the Old Man's right-hand man, is rubbed out. The blood splatters on the Old Man. Now he wants to discipline the young people. He puts the Sorcerer in charge of everything. The Sorcerer recruits shooters and torturers from the Ministry of Social Welfare. He appoints his Lady Wife, the stripper, vice-president. The little lambs grow uneasy. In Plaza de Mayo, they ask him: What's going on, General? Why is the people's government full of gorillas? The Old Man reprimands them from the balcony. All he wants now is to die in peace with that glorious music—the roar of the people shouting his name—in his ears. What's going on, General? Why is the people's government full of gorillas? The kids pick up their posters. They've slipped through his fingers, and now they're slipping away from the plaza. They leave an enormous void. The oligarchy and the military rub their hands: they're preparing for a great barbecue. The fascist trade unions go after the left-wing youth. Political enemies are burned to a crisp in syndical ovens. The Sorcerer's thugs toss the stiffs' bodies onto the road. The Old

Man is beset by age and illness. At last he kicks the bucket. His Lady Wife assumes the presidency. An outpouring of public grief. Even the cops and military officers who watch over the coffin are sniveling. Crows flutter above the holy innocents crying in the streets. The blackest crow is the economist with his court of Chicago-educated swindlers. They're prepared to hock the country with declarations of famine. The scene is set for the *danse macabre*. The church prelates call for divine punishment in their prayers. And the exorcism is the crucifixion of an entire nation. Signs, Gómez. Pay attention to the signs. The Great Damage is nothing new. It's part of the thunderbolts that announce the catastrophic changes coming to this planet. The Age of Aquarius, my ass. What's happening now is that the Great Damage is showing signs of its arrival. The Evil One has awakened from his siesta. The Great Damage is here. And it'll be here for a long time. Let's hold on tight because you don't fuck with mysterious forces. Those Christ Conquers people know it. That's why they're bugging everyone again. The guys in uniform, at the Service of the Evil One, are attacking power. The Great Damage is showing signs. For those candle-suckers in power, young people are the Antichrist incarnate. The military is the Holy Inquisition. Torture, for them, is an exorcism. Read what the military junta has to say in this afternoon's *La Razón*: "A terrorist is not only someone with a revolver or a gun, but anyone who spreads ideas against Western, Christian civilization." The Great Damage includes these people and those people, and it includes all of us. You and I, Gómez, even if we're not directly involved, we're not on the sidelines, either. And once the Evil One's work has deployed all its terrible power, it will affect generations of our countrymen. Armageddon, hah! Compared to what's coming, it's peanuts. Don't ask me for more, Gómez. In these times knowledge is dangerous. And talking is even more dangerous. I'd better stop now. Let's get to what brings you here.

Lutz breathed heavily. He was staring right at me, apparently waiting for me to speak. But I remained silent. After a pause, he leaned backward, dug around in the desk drawer, and pulled out the pendulum. He lifted it, swinging it before my eyes.

Lutz nailed that gaze of his to my forehead:

Don't say anything, he said before I could react. Anyone can see the anxiety in your face. You've come to consult me because you're going through a rough patch. You feel like your nerves are shot. Sometimes you're tempted to give up on everything. Purgatory. You feel like you're the victim of a conspiracy. Sometimes you have the feeling everybody is plotting against you. It might be a fellow teacher a school, a colleague. It might be a friend. A neighbor. No doubt you've also thought about a girl who hates you for some reason. Female hatred is always frightful. That's why it's so profitable for the witches in the neighborhood: they never lack customers who want to fuck up some unwitting sucker who thought he was a Don Juan. It's a fact these days that damage can strike from any direction. The other guy is suspicious. And we are too, for others. We're all suspicious characters. But this business of yours, Gómez, with your vibrations. Your thing is out of the ordinary. I can tell from the vibrations. Your damage is inscrutable. And it's just beginning. I can't save you, either. Warn you, at best. How can I promise you anything these days. If you want some advice, get the hell out of here. Don't give it another thought. Beat it. You've still got time.

The pendulum swung back and forth. I had palpitations; my hands were clammy and cold. I wondered what I could ask him. A tremor rattled the place. Now the pendulum went wild. I had the impression that two trains were passing one another in the subway tunnels. But the tremor, accompanied by a deafening roar, drowned out the subway noise. An earthquake, I thought. Now I was overheated. My heart beating out of control. The planet was cracking open. I felt a galloping in my chest. I saw reality tilted, askew.

Get the hell out, I repeated.

Your low astral body, Lutz said.

I was about to say something, but Lutz beat me to it:

I ought to split, too, he said. Any minute now I'll be killed. I'm on two lists. Right wingers and lefties all consult me. A Montonero's sister and a general's wife. It's not like I have a crystal ball, they come to me from both sides. When I least expect it, I'll get caught in a roundup and take a bullet for vagrancy.

Lutz gave me a wink.

That'll be five pesos, Gómez, he said. I'm giving you a discount, considering the damage, which is considerable.

It was late. The shops in the strip mall were closing. I went up to the street, into the night. It had cooled off. Traffic was backed up on Esmeralda. I walked amid exhaust fumes and horns honking. I could detect the sound of a siren getting closer and closer. Two green Falcons advanced and braked among the buses and cars. The thugs inside had their weapons out. They banged on the buses with the butts of their rifles.

After the Falcons left, the engines and honking sounded muffled. I walked down toward Lavalle, mixing in with the crowd. In the doorway of Discos Broadway were some taxiboys. I chose the straightest-looking one. The kid took me to a by-the-hour hotel on 9 de Julio.

Then I went on toward Constitución. I ate a pizza at Tren Mixto, and after a bottle of red wine I had enough courage to prowl around the platforms of Constitución Station and pick up another kid. I was with four that night.

Dawn was breaking when I returned to my building. I looked to both sides. I inserted the key. I entered. The elevator produced a slow, ominous rattling. I opened the gate, pressed the button, and slid the gate shut. The elevator went up as slowly as it had gone down. It stopped. Agitated, I held my breath. I was frightened.

The door of the apartment next to mine was now closed. As was my own.

No one was waiting for me. No one had come for me.

Stiff with cold, I felt sticky, dirty. I could smell the combined perfumes and odors of the four kids on my body. I lit the water heater; I stripped. I turned on the shower. The tiles fogged up. I couldn't see the soap for the steam.

5 Even though it was May, that morning of my fifty-sixth year it seemed like summer, the professor recalls. Some storm clouds and a sticky heat hovered over the city. The sky was a mouse-gray canvas. A perfect time for passions to condense and for horniness to boil over. Animal urges were in the air. And let's not even talk about those co-ed classrooms. It was hard for me to hide my predilection for male youths over eager young ladies. The odor—because it's an odor, not a perfume—of those boys and girls, enveloped in a whiff of hair, sweat, breath smelling of gum and cigarettes. A classroom's like a cage, I thought. When I walked into the classroom, the first one I noticed was Esteban. Later, during the class, it was a struggle for me to stop staring at him. I tried to get back to our discussion of Sarmiento. But Esteban distracted me.

Just by reading his quizzes you could see, expressed in his nervous handwriting and clear ideas, the solidity of his views. A blond lock of hair always dangled over his forehead, a lock that he constantly tossed back with a shake of his head. He shuffled his moccasins as he walked. He wore a rictus of superiority. The kid was trying to demonstrate that he was miles ahead of the rest. If something annoyed him, he would explode in a burst of rage, a sort of wildness. Those qualities explained why Paloma, who looked like a David Hamilton model, was his girl-friend. Paloma's expression said: I'm here, but not altogether. It said that to everyone. Except Esteban. Because Paloma couldn't keep her eyes off him.

That morning I was teaching *Facundo*, by Sarmiento. I dared to continue teaching it from Hernández Arregui's perspective. Although I was a teacher of English literature, for the last few years, given the anticolonialism that rocked the country, I had started concentrating on Argentine literature. What defines our national character, I would ask the kids, civilization or barbarism? Sarmiento, with that social climber's instinct of his, proposed a firm hand in applying republican ideas. He was the provincial instrument of select minorities, a real Sepoy, according to Hernández Arregui. Just look at how Sarmiento viewed the natives: he called them Bedouins and Tatars. Patagonia? A marketplace for ostriches and eggs. Overcome by a sense of my own genius, I told the kids about those notations Sarmiento had made in his travel journals, the painstaking records of his expenses, among them, what he spent on orgies.

On ne tue pas les idées

And I, a *cabecita negra*, a half-breed, nationalistic and a man of the people as I presented a revisionist reading of *Facundo*, wondered about the nature of my desire. Why did I lust after a blond ephebe when I descended from Indian raids. How was I any different from the author of that book, which was as violent as my desire. The half-breed who goes for anything blond. Once more, in the name of beauty, I betrayed my origins, my memories of provincial life, a store lost in the southern desert of the Patagonian coast, a single mother.

With the chalk still in my hand, I turned toward the class.

What is the terrible shadow behind this essay, I asked.

Terrible shadow of Juan Domingo, I shall evoke you, said Esteban.

Laughter filled the room. Not even I could resist the temptation.

Then, suddenly, the cops. Rushing in, weapons at the ready. They entered the classroom. In plain clothes, armed. And the joke was over. There must have been thirty of them. More guys waited outside. Their Ithacas were aiming at the class. Silence.

Echagüe, the corporal shouted.

And he pressed the Ithaca to my head:

Echagüe, he repeated.

I bit my lips. I didn't feel up to heroism. Besides, I was the teacher. I was prepared to teach by my example. I wasn't going to rat out the boy. I felt the barrel against my neck, my throat.

Esteban stood up. He was aiming a revolver. The girls started to scream. The boys threw themselves on top of them, trying to protect them. The pigs blocked the door. Panic erupted and the classroom was thrown into chaos. Esteban stood there, alone, in the middle of all those bodies lying on the floor. The girls shrieked hysterically. The cops aimed at Esteban, and Esteban aimed back at them. The whole class on the floor. Esteban hesitated. Or else he wanted to buy time. The girls never stopped crying and screaming. With the first shot there would be a massacre. Esteban lowered his weapon.

The cops jumped him. They forced his mouth open. They beat him with the butts of their weapons, dragged him across the schoolyard. His blood stained the tiles.

That's how they took him away.

The class was in tumult. I tried to find Paloma. I didn't see her. It wasn't easy to calm everyone down. I made them go out to the school-yard, to get some fresh air, to breathe. They pushed and shoved as they fled. I looked for Paloma among the stampede. She wasn't there. Then I had a bright idea: I went to the cloakroom. Don't ask me at what point the girl found an opportunity to hide. She was inside, among rolled-up maps and slides, huddled in a ball, weeping, trembling, clutching a pendant, a little metal hand, that talisman of countryfolk.

I helped her get up.

The first thing I thought to say to her was:
It'll be better if you get away from here, honey.
The poor thing had soiled herself.
I took her to the bathroom and waited outside the door. Then I walked her to the curb and hailed a taxi.
Don't even think of coming back, I said.

The student centers had been dissolved, and you could smell the anxiety among the school authorities. It was in the air: terror was on the roll call lists. The military issued an announcement: First we will eliminate the subversives, then their accomplices, then their sympathizers, and finally all those who are indifferent or lukewarm. Nobody had the nerve to go to the nearest police station to file a complaint or to present a writ of habeas corpus as Esteban's parents later did. No agency was willing to take on a kidnapping. And this was true in Esteban's case, as well.

Paloma didn't return to school. Nobody in the classroom, no girl, no boy, had the nerve to sit at those two desks.

The final blast of summer gave way to a storm. The temperature dropped every day. Coats, wraps, and heavy sweatshirts were resurrected in the streets. Now, in addition to the cold, there was drizzle, a drizzle that wouldn't go away for a long time. But the bad weather was the least of it.

Soon no one at school would remember Esteban. During a free hour I went to see what was left of him in a file at the secretary's office. I had to dig through cardboard boxes and stacks of folders tied up with twine. Esteban was listed as a former student who had lost his regular status due to absence. I jotted down his address.

And one rainy afternoon I went to visit his parents. They lived in Barrancas de Belgrano, in a house near the station. The father came out to greet me, a guy around my age who maintained a cool distance for the duration of my visit. The tragedy hadn't altogether wiped away his arrogance, but you could sense it in the decadence of the house. He was an architect, he told me. I could call him *tú*, he said. But I continued using the formal *usted*.

They came by here, too, he told me. They turned everything upside down. They took off with some china and left the modern art.

And your wife? I asked.

Inés is shut in, he replied. In Esteban's room. She spends hours in there, going through his things.

He invited me into the living room. A picture window faced a garden, misty in the rain. In that room there was no shortage of Bernis or Gambettas. Or Kosices, either. There were tapestries, carvings, little modern sculptures. Brancusi, Echagüe the architect said at one point. Well-traveled people, I thought. Whiskey, he asked. No, thanks, I said. He brought over a bottle of Robert Browns.

I saw a photo of the couple with Esteban. A tent on the beach. A happily married, upper-middle-class couple. He wore a softened, fatuous smile. She was a tall, attractive woman in a one-piece swimsuit. Both of them were sitting on the sand. And Esteban, the only child, the couple's pride and joy, around ten years old, held up a ball in one hand and a shovel in the other, about to bat it toward the camera.

Inés is on medication, Echagüe said. She sleeps all day. Some days she gets together with other mothers at church. On Thursdays they go to Plaza de Mayo and do their rounds. That keeps her busy. She's under the illusion that Esteban is still alive.

You think he's dead, I said.

Esteban was a hero, said his father.

Like Che, I said.

Like Che, he repeated.

A rich kid, I thought. But I didn't say it.

Esteban told me about his teachers, Gómez, said Echagüe. He respected you. Said you talked to the students like friends, he said. My son considered you a friend.

42

I looked at the garden through the picture window. More than a garden it looked like a moss-covered wall.

I'm going to tell you something, the architect went on. We gave Esteban the best education, everything included: rugby, rowing. From Mafalda to the Beatles. And he had a sense of justice. He read all of London. Like Che, yes. An idealist. We educated him. We're responsible for his education. His mother is in a deep depression. She doesn't understand because she's a woman. My son was a courageous man.

I wondered if the architect was proud that his son ended up in a military prison. There was a sense of lineage there. I wondered if being the father of a martyr was better than being the father of an office clerk. Echagüe played the stoic. Everyone handles their pain as best they can.

You're a Peronist, Gómez, the architect said. It was a question, and yet it wasn't.

I didn't want to argue with him.

You know why this country is the way it is, he asked me. Because of the Peronists. Chickenshits, all of them.

Esteban was a Peronist, I retorted.

Don't fuck with me. Esteban was an idealist, a revolutionary. Like me—at his age I was a civil commando, he said.

I remembered '55. I remembered '55 beneath the bombs. I remembered '55 and that captain, a Navy pilot, who launched the bombs over Plaza de Mayo, killing my two female friends. One of them was his wife, and she was pregnant. I remembered '55, and the past wrapped around me like a mouthful of fire that destroyed everything, like those bombs, the dark smoke clouds rising from the puddles of gasoline and blood. Stumbling among the bombs, I realized that I had unearthed a baby's leg and was trying to figure out which body it belonged to. My memory never left me alone.

I had the feeling that the sooner I left the Echagües' home, the sooner I would free myself from a black, oily, combustible tide.

6 Professor Gómez takes a break. He stands up, walks slowly. You can see him enter the kitchen. You don't need to look at the apartment too closely to confirm that for years, maybe for decades, the place has been crying out for a good dusting—the bookshelves and the tops of piles of papers, a thorough cleaning to brush away the spiderwebs, get rid of the mold and dampness. An airing, yes. And a coat of paint, too. Its deplorable condition, deterioration, and murkiness are overwhelming. A naked bulb hangs from the ceiling, and if you turn it on after spending a long time in the semi-darkness of the living room, the light will dazzle you. Dirty dishes and a greasy griddle wait in the kitchen sink. The books and papers here have also taken over, multiplying on the sideboard, the folding table, in the cupboards. Dark moisture-stains dapple the sky-blue paint.

The professor returns with his pitcher of tea.

My books and papers are alive, he says. A person wants to forget. Terror is an invisible brand. Cattle, once more. We're cattle. In the country of the Rural Society, we're all cows, marching toward the slaughterhouse.

I'm reminded of a story I heard in Patagonia. A story about a puma hunt. A horse-cart driver, a guy named Abeijón, told it to me at the Touring Club Hotel en Trelew. And the story he told relates to our own times. A drove of sheep was coming from an English ranch. A puma attacked some of them. The drovers tried to protect the herd, but not

44

even the dogs could help them. A few drovers went off to search for the big cat nearby. They found its den, provoked it to make it come out, and when it did, they fired at it. But the puma managed to escape. One night the drovers noticed that the herd was very skittish. The puma had hidden where none of them could have imagined: in the heart of the herd. As you see, the professor says, sometimes the thing we want to talk about hides from us like the puma. It hides among the sheep. All of us, to a greater or lesser degree, have a puma crouching among our memories. You've got to summon the courage to plunge into the herd and face the puma.

Maybe this story symbolizes what I'm telling, the professor muses. The puma that lurks in the depths of our history.

The queens of the Foreign Ministry building, Professor Gómez, recollects. More than one of them fell during a raid of the public bathrooms, but they got kicked out of the police station. Fucking dictatorship was so macho, but they hired all those queens anyway. It was at a public toilet, I remember, that I picked up Niqui. The kid was attending a series of talks on semiotics at the Escuela Panamericana de Arte. Brown hair, almond-shaped eyes, athletic build, but not in a bodyguard way: he was slender, a dancer type. He had a Citroën, a 3CV. One winter night, I remember, we went to a birthday party for one of the queens.

Niqui had gotten all dressed up, very natty: black jacket, tight white T-shirt, white pants, very snug, platform shoes. No sooner did we get there than he started flirting with a little fag who wrote reviews for *La Nación*. They huddled in a corner, chatting about Mujica Laínez. Manucho this, Manucho that. I tried to figure out how to drag Niqui away from him. But in the end I let it go. I wasn't about to give him the satisfaction of making a scene.

Later he flirted with someone else, a captain with Aerolíneas Argentinas. The queen invited him to go to Easter Island. And Niqui listened, enraptured. If he really thought I was that dumb, he was screwed.

Easter Island elevates you, the queen told him. It's a dream, I swear. When we left, I threw that little flirtation in his face. The Citroën was parked in front of a barrier in the Flores district, where the Sarmiento line passes. I had taken that train so many times from the west. Because Lía, my friend, was renting a place nearby. I'm talking about the little Jew, the one who died in the bombing. I used to take that train to visit her at the apartment she rented on Calle Yerbal. Twenty years had gone by since then. The last time I saw her was among the stampedes and bursts of machine gun fire, among clouds of fuel. Lía died before she knew what had happened, her brains scattered next to the wheels of a trolley. Right next to her lay Delia, on her back, twisted, in a pool of blood that kept spreading. Even now, I still like to remember them as they tried to embrace among the shards, the destruction, the massacre.

The barrier was still down, the Citroën's motor was grinding, and we remained silent.

Just because someone's on a diet doesn't mean he can't look at the menu, Gómez, said Niqui. Besides, nothing happened with that guy.

I smacked him. He hit me back. I smacked him with the back of my hand. We got into it. Another slap knocked my glasses off. I landed a punch. As we laid into each other, we heard the din of a train going by. Suddenly headlights blinded us. Niqui's nose was bleeding. There were two patrol cars, one on each side of us. Then a green Falcon screeched to a halt. The Ithacas were aimed at us.

They beat us with their fists. They kicked at our ankles, knocking us to the ground. While the cops deliberated, we lay face-down on the sidewalk, our cheeks pressed against the wet cobblestones. Niqui's frightened expression moved me. His nose was still bleeding, and he was on the verge of tears. I stared at him hard as if to say, don't lose courage. A cop landed a kidney punch; he stepped on the back of my neck with his shoe. I heard the hammer of a weapon click. Another cop did the same to Niqui. They searched the Citroën. We could see their legs coming and going next to our faces pressed against the cobblestones.

I don't know what they were looking for, but it clearly wasn't us. And that made them furious.

They examined our papers by the light of a flashlight. They talked on their walkie-talkies; they checked their data terminals. With their guns still pointing at us, they ordered us to stand and put our hands on the car. They were from the Federal Police. One of them—short hair, heavy black sweater, black leather jacket, black jeans and moccasins, checked my ID. He was a Criollo Bruce Lee. Then he looked me in the eye. A feline gaze. Like a puma in the shadows. Finally he turned to Niqui. A weakling, that Niqui. He never stopped sniveling. The half-breed looked him up and down. Niqui was moaning; he had hiccups. The half-breed stood to one side as he interrogated us. What we did for a living, what we were doing there, he wanted to know.

A cop shook me. The half-breed, smiling slyly, stood at a distance from the interrogation. He stared at me. But I didn't look down: I stared right back. I understood: he was one of us. I knew he'd let us go. And he did.

Niqui was still trembling when they finally released us. He had trouble starting the Citroën.

You broke my nose, he said.

I didn't feel like going to his apartment. In fact, I couldn't wait to be alone.

Drop me off at the corner, I ordered.

I started walking. Not a soul in the streets. The clicking of my heels, the damp cobblestones, the lighting, some sparkles on the pavement. As I passed under a street lamp, my shadow projected, like a ghost, on the sidewalk. Despite the hour, the danger of the night, I once more had a feeling of freedom. I wanted to be alone with my anxiety.

I couldn't stop thinking about the half-breed.

The building no longer smelled like burning hair. One night, as I passed by the super's place, I saw a string of garlic hanging on Ramón's door. Everyone took care of their own as best they could. Just the same, even though it didn't smell like burning hair anymore, I didn't feel safe. Because in the next few days my phone began to ring. I wanted to concentrate on my papers. I had decided to write about Wilde. The fact that the jail where he had been locked up was called Reading was worth a short essay, at least. As soon as classes ended for the day, I returned directly to my apartment. No sooner did I start hammering away on the Lexikon 80, the phone would ring. I heard loud music coming from the other end. Palito Ortega, voices, and some shouting. An auto repair shop, maybe, I thought. Suddenly I started to fixate on the telephone. When I picked up the receiver, silence: the silence of someone who was there, testing my patience. Niqui, I thought at first. But Niqui wouldn't have called me from an auto repair shop. During one of those calls I thought I heard rapid breathing, panting.

From the other end came laughter. Someone knew my schedule, every one of my movements: the phone would ring in the morning, right after my alarm went off, when I awoke to go to class. And it rang again at night, just as I returned to my essay on Wilde. It was obvious that someone was spying on me. From the beginning, I clearly understood that he was trying to intimidate me. Because if someone had wanted to get rid of me, he would've done it already. It was also likely that my phone was bugged. I took greater precautions. I refused invitations, outings, meetings. The calls continued.

I was stuck on the essay. I became fixated on the telephone. In the morning I woke up before the alarm sounded, waiting for the phone to ring. Same thing when I got home at night.

7 One drizzly evening, as I left school, through the stampede of students, almost at the corner, I saw him. The black jacket. I never would have expected it. My legs buckled. I crossed the avenue, braving the traffic, half-blinded by the headlights. The half-breed cop turned his back on me. I picked up my pace. Now I was the one pursuing my pursuer. I could hardly breathe. The guy got ahead of me. I lost sight of him.

That night, when I returned to my apartment, I waited for the phone to ring. But nothing happened. I started revising what I had written. Every so often I glanced at the phone. Twice I stood up, went over to it, and picked up the receiver to make sure there was a dial tone. I had to be patient, I told myself. But patience never was my forte.

I tried a relaxation exercise. I had to lie face-up on the carpet, close my eyes, and place my arms alongside my body with palms open toward the ceiling, connecting myself to the earth. I had to breathe deeply. I had to pay attention to my heartbeat. I had to think about a setting I liked: the country, the mountains, the sea. But when I closed my eyes, I saw the half-breed that night at the barricade, while the cops and the guys in the Falcon thrashed us. I saw his sly smile again. And my heart started to pound. Nonetheless, I kept going with the exercise. Till the phone rang.

It was Niqui:

We have to talk, he begged. We can't stay angry like this.

What annoyed me most about his call wasn't his prudery. It was that he was tying up the line and making me miss the call I was waiting for.

Several days must have passed before the phone rang again and, as I picked up, I heard silence on the other end. It was a night when I came straight home from school. Hello, hello, hello, I said. And on the other end, silence. I had an idea. Maybe it would work, I said to myself:

What? I asked. You're afraid of me?

Nothing from the other end.

I know who you are, I ventured. You're afraid of what you feel.

Again, nothing. I challenged him:

I'll wait for you at the Pink Gin. Riobamba, close to Arenales.

Nothing.

I'll be waiting for you, I said.

And I hung up.

I arrived at the bar first, of course, says Professor Gómez.

The Pink Gin, he recalls. A dump filled with useless has-beens, a shadowy redoubt ideal for hammered, would-be players. By nightfall a considerable throng had gathered at the Pink Gin, but you could smell a discreet ambiance, the clandestine elegance of those who hide from disapproving looks so they can hit the bottle without entirely losing their cool. I settled in at one corner of the bar, against the wall. I ordered a whiskey.

An old broad with a salon tan came up to me. She looked like a former model and talked like a rancher.

May I, she asked, referring to the barstool next to mine. I need a drink too.

When you spend your whole life pretending to be what you're not, there comes a time when the pretense stops being pretense, when you end up resembling the person you pretend to be. Out of the corner of my eye, I saw myself reflected in the mirror behind the bar. I played the ladies' man in order to hide my penchant for the love that dares not speak its name. The difference between a ladies' man and an old fag is minuscule. No doubt the woman thought I fit into the first category.

Sorry, I said. I'm waiting for someone.

No sooner had I said it, as if saying it had been an invocation, I spotted him at the door. Freshly shaved, the collar of his black jacket raised, the black jeans, the black moccasins.

There was a rural lilt to his speech.

Follow me, he said.

I obeyed.

We left. And started walking in the night. He ahead and I behind. I wondered where we were going. We turned on Arenales and got to Montevideo Plaza. I sensed danger, but I didn't care. It had its attraction. He stopped. The trees concealed the passageway. The plaza was deserted. I walked over to him. We looked at one another.

Then he slapped me across the face.

I give the orders here, he said.

I nodded.

Let's go to your place, he said. Follow me to the car.

He had a blue Torino coupé.

In his own way the half-breed knew it: it's always a question of who gives the orders and who obeys. There was no need to state the obvious: I was the one who obeyed. He could have attached a leash to my neck and taken me out for a walk on all fours, and I wouldn't have said boo. The burning question is how I, who earlier had been stirred up by looking at that little Montonero, Esteban, was now turned on by this Indio.

Walter was his name. He had a country accent. Married, with three kids: two girls and a boy. He softened up when he talked about them. He showed me their pictures. One of the girls, the younger one, had a heart condition. It wasn't just a murmur. They were always taking her to Churruca Police Hospital. And his wife went to San Pantaleón church. The patron saint of the sick, he explained. Tell me Evangelina doesn't look like a little saint, I remember him saying to me. His wife had been a police officer, too. They met at Central Headquarters. He was in Robberies and Thefts. She was an office worker in Documentation. But after they married, she devoted herself to raising the kids. They lived in Ciudad Evita. They had bought a lot and were building. Walter grew animated as he described how the construction was coming along, the swimming pool they were building in back, near the barbecue area. They were going to fix up the barbecue area, as well. When the little one was better, they were going to throw a huge barbecue. An entire lamb.

All our meetings were in this apartment. He'd show up, remove all his gear, his .45, sit over there in the armchair, and I had to wait on him. Play some Tchaikovsky, he would say. Serve him a glass of whiskey. Imported. He would ask me to cut his toenails. He really loved that. And you should've seen the dedication and care I took in wielding the nippers and the little scissors. We listened to Tchaikovsky and I pampered him. Sometimes he showed up in a foul mood. Work, he would say. Nothing more than that. I tried not to look at the .45 on the end table. It was a temptation for me. And he knew it. He was nobody's fool. Sharp, quick, he was.

One night when he arrived looking like a wrung-out rag, he put the automatic on the end table and in a black mood, asked me:

Don't you want to pick it up. Go on, you could blow me away, he said. If you only knew the things I do.

I'd rather not find out, I said.

What a chickenshit, he said. Just like Beti.

Beti was his wife.

Another night, after making love, as we were smoking in bed and he was acting affectionate, I asked him:

I wonder if you'd do me a favor.

He cast a long, shrewd gaze in my direction.

52

You want to get a passport.

Why do you think that.

For someone like you, he said, it would be a good idea to leave. If I were you, I'd get the hell out.

Why would I need to, I said. I haven't got a record.

We're all hiding something, he said.

Like you're hiding these visits, I said.

These visits don't exist, he replied. You don't exist.

I picked up the bottle of whiskey on the night table. I poured some more. I took a swig to boost my courage and said:

I want to find out about someone.

Walter's expression changed. It was that crafty look of his again.

Who, he asked me.

I was about to lie, to say that it concerned a cousin. But I preferred the truth. It seemed to be the most sensible thing. It was best to be direct, rather than beat around the bush. If I made up a lie, sooner or later he would find me out.

A student, I said. He's been disappeared.

I thought you had something under your poncho, he said. All that love doesn't come free.

Walter's expression frightened me.

I've never asked you for anything, I said. If you can't, forget it.

The one you were with that night by the railroad tracks? He asked.

No, I said. A student.

A little macho.

I turned serious:

He was a student of mine.

Tell me what he was involved in.

Now Walter was somebody else. And the conversation had become an interrogation. I regretted having opened my mouth.

Walter grew fierce.

A Peronist or a Montonero, spit it out.

What does it matter, I said.

If he's a Perro, the Army's got him. At Campo de Mayo, you know. If he's a Monto, the Navy's got him at the ESMA. The Petty-Officers' School of Mechanics.

He got up to pee. From the bed, I called out:

He was a good kid.

I heard the stream hitting the toilet.

A lefty, he said.

A Peronist, I said.

A Peronist, he repeated. Don't fuck with me.

Walter came back to bed. There was no way I could like that half-breed so much, I said to myself. I felt ashamed.

My family is Peronist, he said. My old man and old lady are Peronists. My old man worked for Institec. He made the Graciela sedan. And my old lady, first she worked at Bernalesa Textiles, then at the Campomar factory. They met in Mar del Plata. We're Peronists. The real ones.

Esteban was just a boy, I said.

Then I realized something: Walter was just a boy, too.

8 I'm not even twenty yet and in a few days I'm going to travel to the capital. To the "cappy," as my mother says. You'll leave this place behind, she says. I forbid you to miss me, she says. You'll burn your ships, like Columbus. It makes me feel weird to correct her, so I don't. I'll be a hick, I think. You'll forget this place, she says. And what a great job of it you'll do! My mother is embroidering my initials on a white handkerchief and humming softly. "El Pañuelito," she sings. Those are her favorite verses. If they play that tango on the radio, she makes me stop talking so she can hear the words. I wonder how much it has to do with her story, with my unknown father, with me. I wonder about it. And I know I'll never ask her. *The white handkerchief.* She embroiders and sighs. *That I offered you,* she sings. *Embroidered with my hair.* Twilight is sad around here. Swirls of sand and dust. It's winter now, and every night it gets dark earlier. If the days are sad, the nights are even sadder. *It was for you,* she sings, in a near-whisper. *You've forgotten it.* The wind rattles the shutters. *Bathed in tears,* she sings. *I hold it before me.* Later, when she's finished embroidering it, she'll keep it in a little velvet-lined box. Pretty soon she'll hand me the box with the handkerchief when I take the bus that will bear me far away, far from this place, far from her. If you're homesick, don't cry. And if you cry, dry your tears with this handkerchief. It'll be just like I was drying them for you. But no matter how homesick you feel and how much you cry, keep on going. You don't have to come back here till you make good in the cappy, she tells me. Does my mother really talk that way, I wonder. Or is this what she's trying to tell me with her silence, with her gesture as she hands me the little box before I get on the bus.

It was drizzling steadily, as I was saying. The icy fog, the damp Buenos Aires winter, a winter that penetrates your bones. Only rarely did the gray storm clouds in that steely sky move aside, allowing a feeble, soft-boiled sun to peek through. It didn't last long, that sun. Then, lightning. And when it didn't rain, it drizzled.

It was sprinkling, as I said. In Plaza de Mayo the police cars and a line of cops stationed themselves between those women and the Casa Rosada. As I think I mentioned, the Seat of Government owed its pink color to the cow blood with which it had been painted during the Vice Regency. The fact that it still conserved its original shade was more than a metaphor for the slaughterhouse our country had always been. Now, this winter, according to Walter, there were officials and soldiers fucking beneath the dictator Videla's chair. Walter had had an affair with a grenadier who was hooked up with a captain. The recruit told Walter all about the fucking that went on right there, underneath the president's hall, in the Officers' Casino. Now the Casa Rosada was pinker than ever. That afternoon, while the mothers of the disappeared began their turns around the plaza, right across from them there must have been a bunch of upstanding little officers buggering recruits. I thought of San Martín's army.

The mothers had begun gathering by then. A dozen or so at first, they kept multiplying. They were identifiable by their white kerchiefs. On Thursday afternoons there was a march around the Pirámide de Mayo. I raised my raincoat lapels. A damp wind. There was also a truck carrying police from the Infantry Guard. At each side of the building, soldiers stationed in their Falcons. A few cops prevented anyone from getting too close to the marchers. Nevertheless, like one more curious observer, I approached those women. There were young ones and others not so young, but tragedy had aged them equally.

Once again, I can't seem to get away from literature. "The Monkey's Paw," that story by Jacobs. A fakir, a holy man, tries to prove that destiny controls men's lives and that no one can oppose it. The holy man has given special power to a mummified monkey's paw. If a person asks the monkey's paw for three wishes, the paw will grant them. The talisman usually fulfills one or two wishes, but the third is always fatal. A couple has lost their son in an industrial accident, torn apart by the machines at the factory where he worked. The corpse is practically unrecognizable. The cemetery where the dead son lies isn't far from their home. One windy, desolate night, the mother asks the monkey's paw to grant her third wish: that her son might return. During the night, the husband hears a banging on the door; he hears his wife open it and he also hears a shriek. Our reality is no less terrifying than that story. The dictatorship called its victims "the disappeared." The word implied that, in the event they were ever found, what those mothers would receive would be apparitions. No matter how many explanations and psychological theories might be offered to overcome that grief, they would always be ghosts, always, ghosts circling them, just as the mothers circled the Plaza demanding an appearance, an apparition, from that pink building. Perhaps terror was the most appropriate genre for recounting our national history.

I walked over to the circle of marchers. I recognized Esteban's mother from the beach photograph I had seen in her house in Belgrano.

I couldn't reach her.

Keep moving, a cop ordered me.

The city, like the country, had been divided into zones. Each one belonged to a division of the Army. The concentration camps were spread throughout the neighborhoods. "Detention centers" was the euphemism the repressors used. Esteban must have already ratted out his *compañeros*, just as they had done to him. What was I supposed to tell that woman: Look, señora, maybe at this very moment Esteban is in the muddy depths of the river, maybe he's floating toward the shore, maybe his corpse is one more of the many that the tide tosses on the beaches in the southern part of the province, maybe some local will find him in that area where the countryside turns into sea, a corpse nibbled first by fish, and then, on the sand, by vultures. What was I supposed to tell her.

The women didn't seem to feel the now denser drizzle in the cold wind coming off the river. Soaked and shivering, I turned my back to the circle and crossed over to the arcade for shelter. Then I heard a man's voice calling my name.

Gómez, it said. Professor.

The image I had retained of that boy from the English School was that of a child, stiff in his English School uniform. It wasn't easy to recognize that boy in this man. His seriousness was still there: he'd been such a poised child, too sensible for his age, I thought. His hair had turned dark brown, with a few premature strands of gray. He was pale, almost sallow. His mustache made him look like a cross between a military officer and a Mexican. He wore a sheepskin jacket. He was smoking: Particulares 30.

I'm Delia's son, he said by way of introduction.

His hand not only felt enormous and strong when he shook mine, but it was callused, too. His fingers were weathered by some form of hard labor. Those weren't the hands of someone whom destiny had assured a comfortable future as a Navy officer.

He looked toward the circle of mothers. Now they were beginning to disperse. Night was coming on. I asked him what he was doing there.

I've come to see, he said.

We crossed Bolívar. We passed close by the City Hotel. That night back in '55, the night before the 16th of June, had been a Thursday, just like today, the day of the Mothers' March. Delia and Lía had spent that last night in a hotel room. I remember the kid. I think it was at the Richmond. Delia brought him along one afternoon. Lía and I were waiting for her to show up to have *claritos*. Delia was secretly writing an erotic novel about a captive woman and an Indian while Lía worked as a journalist and wrote poetry for a literary magazine that barely made it to the second issue. By then the two women were lovers. For them it had been love at first sight.

Now, and now was that drizzly Thursday of the mothers in Plaza de Mayo, it seemed to me that the Puerto Rico would be a good place for a coffee, but Martín wanted to find somewhere else. Later, much later than that late afternoon on Avenida de Mayo, I would realize why Martín preferred somewhere else: a bar like the one on the corner of Chacabuco. It had two doors, two means of access, one facing the avenue, and the other facing the corner. That is, two exits. Martín chose a table and sat with his back to the street.

Later, but not much later, I would find out what had become of him: the naval academy forced on him by his father; insubordination with certain Peronist petty officers; desertion; his militancy in the left wing of the movement. For a while he had tried to study law. Then he was active in national labor syndicates. From cadet to one of Perón's soldiers. That Thursday, that late afternoon, like other Thursdays, Martín planted himself close to the mothers and watched to see who came near. They were being infiltrated, he said.

Tell me about my old lady, Professor, he asked me, never taking his eyes off the two entrances to the bar.

Martín wanted me to tell him about his mother. I explained how I had met Delia through Lía. I exaggerated his mother's merits and minimized her defects. I didn't mention her cowardice, the fear that for so long had prevented her from dumping that husband, the captain. I didn't mention her attempt to escape the country with Lía, crossing from Tigre into Uruguay, that morning of bombings in the Plaza. I didn't tell him that those two women loved one another. I spared him the fact that his mother was pregnant when the bombs fell. I didn't even mention that his father had been one of the Navy pilots. Or that one of the bombs he dropped that mid-afternoon could certainly have been the one that liquidated the two lovers. And another embryo of hers. Who was I, the eternally annoying witness, to stick my nose into other people's lives? Although my life was also other people's. Or rather: without others, I had no life. I spoke of literature. I made literature. His mother had been a talent, castrated by marriage, the atmosphere, conventionality. And when she decided to run away with her girlfriend, that thing had happened. And that thing was the bombing.

I told him what I, in his place, would have liked to hear: about Delia, about how she patiently waited since childhood on a ranch in Patagonia, readying herself to make the leap to the capital. Then her "concerns," as they were called, literary ones, her thirst for life. His mother's thirst for life, that's what I said to Martín. But she had married a naval officer. The atmosphere held her back. A pity that when she finally worked up the courage to make the longest leap, to leave everything behind, while she was crossing over from the Delia she had been to the Delia who awaited her on the other bank, Montevideo and then Paris, was the moment when the bombs fell.

The old man doesn't matter to me, Martín cut me off.

At some point Martín stopped referring to her as my old lady and started calling her mama. Mama, he said. I think it bears repeating: it was at that mama moment when that stiff grimace, a slight downward curve of his lips, more his father's than his mother's, dissolved. He was a curious boy who asked questions. And all his questions were annoying. Because I couldn't give him all the answers. He wanted to know more about his mother; he also wanted to know my opinion of her work, and in this regard, I was truthful: what Delia had left, that folder with hand-written first drafts and typed originals, carbon copies, all the unpublished stuff, in short, was more interesting as a project than as an achievement. In the end, I thought, the same thing happened to Delia's work as to her desire: the plot that fed the imagination was more charming. At heart, Delia cared more for literature as a secret pleasure and an assault on morality and respectability than as a career, a demand that often requires a workmanlike constancy. For Delia, literature was a forbidden vacation. She was afraid of being discovered. The proof was in that little novel, *The Tongue of the Indian Raid*, which I treasured. Though that little novel, and I explained that I used the term "little" affectionately, had its merit: it wasn't so much a forbidden vacation that she had taken from herself as it was an exorcism.

I tried to change the subject:

Are you married, I asked.

I have a partner, he said. She's a teacher.

Where does she teach.

In a slum.

Do you have kids, I inquired.

One on the way, he said.

And he glanced at the clock.

I don't have much time, he said.

And your father, I asked.

He's the enemy, he replied.

Before pushing his chair back, before standing up and asking for the check, he took a napkin from the holder and asked me for my phone number. I hesitated. But I overcame my fear. I gave it to him.

Give me yours, I said.

I'll call you, Professor.

He left through the side door, walking away from the traffic.

9 Let me make this clear: If I take sick pleasure in occasionally reading the literary supplement of *La Nación*, it's to confirm how many hacks who mounted the back of literature from the left side ended up dismounting, as Jauretche said, on the right. But I also must admit it's because when I read that supplement, I imagine how I would've turned out if I'd been a contributor. A bogus term, contributor. Might as well be "collaborator," since it concerns that newspaper whose editorials support the Grim Reaper. Getting old isn't serious, I tell myself. Getting old *there* is what's serious. Like at la SADE. The Mitre dynasty's paper was the only one that paid attention to la SADE.

In a country like ours, there was no way writers could form a group with any name other than that of the author of *120 Days of Sodom*. In a sinister, but humorous way, the Argentine Society of Authors was known as la SADE, feminizing the Divine Marquis. In this concentration camp nation, la SADE was a gathering place for the mediocre thugs who backed military coups and the persecution of workers.

One year before, I remember, during the coup, Ratti, the president of la SADE, together with Borges, Ernesto Sabato, and the priest Castellani, accepted a luncheon invitation from the dictator Videla. At the meal, I recall, the only one who had the guts to mention Haroldo Conti among so many authors who had been disappeared, was the priest, Castellani. As they left the luncheon, the press was waiting for them. Borges and Sabato, I recall, fell all over themselves in praise of the dictator. A gentleman, they called him. One year later, a year in which the events I'm telling you about took place, Walsh and Oesterheld disappeared. Walsh, before exchanging fire with a task force, had a daughter in combat, and his granddaughter had been kidnapped by the Army. Even crueler was the case of Oesterheld: four daughters and their partners, assassinated; his grandchildren kidnapped. Meanwhile Victoria Ocampo was proudly admitted to the Argentine Academy of Letters with a so-called feminist speech that made no mention of the mothers who clamored for their children in front of the Casa Rosada. I remember, yes. And maybe I should lay off this digression because it twists me into resentment. It's inevitable: memory and rage cannot divorce. One always comes with the other. Who is blameless, I ask myself. Accomplices are to blame. Also witnesses and survivors. But accomplices believe in God. And God absolves them. If terror has an objective, it's to render us all equal through slavishness. Differences between one and the other grow subtle. But, remarkably, these small differences become tremendous. An accomplice is not the same as a witness. A witness is the victim of what he saw. He becomes an accomplice if he remains silent. But if he tells, the witness is different. I try not to judge: under a terrorist regime, everyone does what they can. But they also choose: I forget or I remember. And if I remember, what for? To survive, then. To survive to tell the tale. Even though telling doesn't cure the damage that was endured. And yet, telling helps. To understand, that's what I'm looking for. But, I ask, why should a victim have the moral obligation to understand? And also: who understands the victims?

If a person had something to say, la SADE was the place to keep it mum. Any old fossil who wrote haikus merited a sash. I'll refrain from making jokes about sash and trash. A right-wing geezer didn't have to have a hyphenated last name or the distinction of being a Basque dairy farmer to be honored with canapés. It was enough to bend your head and applaud the other members' eclogues with spastic, Parkinsonian zeal. There were talcumed old ladies with canes and shaky old men with white-blonde manes—every last one of them reeking of mothballs. The women, erstwhile noble, middle-class fillies; the men, social climbers with delusions of grandeur. It's also true that among the geriatric crowd there were a few sickly young men who spouted off spiritual verses, begging for the kind of reaction that would garner them a prize, publication, and enshrinement in the Sunday magazine.

The book of poetry was in the literary supplement of *La Nación*, Professor Gómez recalls. *Simple Customs* by Gabriel de Franco. It was being presented at la SADE. La SADE: De Franco couldn't have fallen any lower.

De Franco and I were faculty colleagues till the end of '55. We cultivated a friendship that, to be honest, didn't include a confession of my proclivities. In any case, sincerity was De Franco's thing. But, even more than sincerity, he was into a kind of emotional theatricality that sought admiration. De Franco was a few years my senior, and, with subtle condescension, demanded that I treat him as an elder. I always wondered how De Franco would have reacted if I had confided my natural inclinations to him. He was, as they say, a complete gentleman. A disciple of Fernández Moreno, he had been involved in a messy affair with a female student, Azucena, a clerk in the lingerie department at Harrod's. De Franco was divorced, had two kids that his wife had set against him, and was quite a few years older than Azucena. Until she pressured him, wanting to rise in status, to be his wife and have children. The man got cold feet. The daughter of a Galician shopkeeper and a Tyrolean pastry chef, Azucena thought that her moment to start a family had arrived. And so Azucena got pregnant by a guy named Pedro, a sales manager at Harrod's who, according to her, was no less an artist than the poet De Franco. Later on, Pedro would set up a hardware store in Villa Ballester and play the accordion at Deutsche community parties on weekends. The two of them, De Franco and Pedro, had something else in common besides Azucena: they were Sunday artists. Sometime later, Azucena, pregnant, started working at Casa Peuser. The fact that the girl had dumped him brought the bard closer than ever to his muse. *What a Girl* was a collection of verses, inspired by Azucena, which De Franco ended up sending to a publisher. Nobody bothered to review De Franco's poetry. Then, defeated, De Franco decided to run away to the jungle in Misiones, shacked up with an indigenous Toba girl, and blended into nature, which, according to him, was amoral.

In the late '60s I received a letter with a Puerto Iguazú postmark. The envelope contained a photo of him with some naked Toba women. I compared their sagging, ample breasts with what had once been Azucena's small, perky ones. On the back of the photo, De Franco had written: The horror, Gómez. You had to admit that the simple, unaffected poet had become fearless. For a while I kept the photo on a shelf in the library. It had its anthropological features, that whole business.

In spite of everything, I went. Overcoming my allergy to that environment and remembering De Franco, I put aside my scruples and went. Besides, curiosity had gotten the better of me.

For De Franco, agreeing to this meeting represented a gesture of friendship on my part. Between triple secs and the cheap white wine that was passed around on a tray, he inscribed a copy of *Simple Customs*: For You, Gómez. Simply.

Several nights later, after the book presentation, De Franco called me. In a faltering voice, he called me. He urgently needed to see me. What had happened, he said. He couldn't tell me over the phone what had happened to him. He didn't want to abuse my confidence, he apologized, but it was essential that we meet. Right away. We agreed to meet for coffee.

It was nighttime. Raining, as I said. And when it wasn't raining, it drizzled. We were at Los 36 Billares. We formed a matched set, with our threadbare overcoats and our gins. Once again, after twenty years, I was to be his confidant. He had looked me up because, as he said, he needed an interlocutor. An exotic term, interlocutor, for someone who claimed to practice simplicity.

In the jungle, among the savages, I learned about mystery, he said. About spells, Gómez. Weeds have their powers. Evil spirits, *gualichos*, exist.

I thought De Franco was about to tell me about his experiences in the jungle. I prepared myself to listen. But no. He surprised me:

I saw her again, he whispered. She's a little chubbier, he said. But she's kept herself up. More Courbet-ish, of course. She came to my book launch at la SADE. Of course, you didn't recognize her, but I did. I'd recognize her if I was blind.

No, I didn't see her.

She's lonely, he said.

I put on an appropriate face. My curiosity was shameless. I imagined what was coming. I could have said goodnight to De Franco, interrupted the confession he was chanting, stood up and vanished along Avenida de Mayo. But De Franco wouldn't let me go that easily:

She's very lonely, he went on.

We ordered more gin.

Now it was windier along the avenue. The wind carried papers, leaves. The asphalt was shiny. And fewer and fewer cars went by. The atmosphere in the bar smelled of tobacco. Even though we were sitting next to the window, the sound of cues and billiard balls still reached us from downstairs and from the back. A few tables away, a group of Gypsies was arguing over cards. And some old guys were playing dominoes.

I wonder what attracts me about Azucena, De Franco said. The key must be in the past: in the fact that I was her first. It's like coming back to life again, Gómez. Tell me what you think.

This remembrance of old times was starting to bore me. I figured out how old De Franco must have been: in his seventies, for sure. He resisted the ravages and defeats of age. But I, a fifty-something who was once again assuming the naïve role of confidant I'd had twenty years before, also resisted. It wasn't just how this meeting impacted me, proving that I would never be the same. It was that the coldness of the night had infiltrated the bar and was chilling my feet. Why had I agreed to this meeting, I chided myself, when it would've been better to be in bed with my volume of Wilde and warm feet. But loneliness, I had to admit, seemed intolerable.

A couple walked into the bar. Along with the lovebirds, an icy gust of wind. I felt frozen.

Azucena and Pedro had a kid, De Franco told me. The kid was studying at the industrial school. It was his father's dream to send him to the Otto Krause Technical School. But the boy got involved in politics. First at the Concentración Nacional Universitaria, the Peronist right-wing group. Then he switched to the left wing of the movement. When the coup came along, Gabrielito was serving with the Northern Column. They kidnapped him from a house in Munro. His father, the railway worker, got a letter of recommendation to see a priest at the archbishopric. Azucena and her husband went together. The priest had a list of names. Gabrielito wasn't on it. As they said goodbye to the priest, he comforted them with a hug. They shouldn't lose faith, he told them. Gabrielito's destiny was in the hands of the Lord. When they hugged him, the couple noticed that the priest was armed.

De Franco was as remorseful as if the kid had been his own flesh and blood.

She named him for me, he said. He had the same name as me, he said. That means something.

I nodded.

After that meeting with the prelate, the husband signed some papers so that all his properties, the hardware store, a country place in Carapachay, some land in San Clemente, the car, the van, and other possessions would be in Azucena's name. Everything signed and sealed. Then he tried to shoot himself. He couldn't bring himself to pull the trigger.

Before he could try again, he had a stroke. Now he's an invalid in a wheelchair. However, even though he's half paralyzed, he manages to gesture, shake hands, and hold a copy of *Reader's Digest* when he wants to read. But who knows if he's really reading, or if he just sits there looking at a picture, his pulse trembling. There are times when, due to his illness or maybe just a whim, Pedrito digs his heels in and makes "no" motions, and Azucena has to feed him with a spoon. I think she does it to spoil him. Pedrito's had a few mini-strokes that prevent him from speaking, but not from scooting around the house in diapers, in his wheelchair.

De Franco paused. He studied me, as if calculating the effect of his story. Now not only my feet, but my spirit, was frozen.

And what do they live on, I asked.

Azucena rented out the properties, De Franco explained. So they manage to get by. Azucena is trying not to sell off everything, and she makes ends meet by baking pies. She inherited her baking talent from her mother.

De Franco continued:

Ever since the kid was kidnapped, Azucena keeps his room closed off. She spends her time collecting newspapers and magazines and cutting out Videla's picture. Every so often she grabs one of them, sticks pins in the eyes, and slips it underneath the door to the locked room. She never lets up with that voodoo. She's convinced that Videla will pay for the harm he's done to her. Videla will pay. Sooner or later, she says. One of his children. You'll see, she promises me. His turn will come. And I can't blame her. If the pins help her bear the tragedy, let her keep sticking them in.

I didn't know what to say. Maybe there was nothing to say. All I could do for De Franco was to listen.

At the beginning I would take the Mitre line to Villa Ballester and arrive at their house at siesta time. On those afternoons, Azucena forced her husband to take his dose of medication; she'd dope him up, and once he was knocked out, she'd let me in. Till one day, after we made love, I went into the bathroom and found the guy in the hallway, outside the bedroom door. He was drooling. The blanket that covered his legs had slipped off. I covered him. He dug around for something in his shirt pocket and tried to give it to me. It was a hundred mark bill.

De Franco fell silent, deep in thought. After an exaggerated pause, he coughed.

I understood, Gómez, De Franco said. He loved her. He didn't want her to lack for anything. And he was prepared to pay as long as she stayed by his side. One hundred marks. I looked at the bill. From a million years ago. The Weimar Republic, something like that. I'll never forget the husband's slobbery smile. From the bedroom she yelled to me: Grab him. Don't be afraid of him. He's very gentle. Listen to me, grab the wallet. No sooner had I taken it from him, he smiled, turned the wheelchair around, and went off down the hall, happy as a clam. He was paying me for the favor I'd done his wife. What do you have to say to that, Gómez.

Nothing, I said. I have nothing to say. I can't.

I advised her to join the other mothers, De Franco went on. The ones who go to Plaza de Mayo on Thursdays. Leave me alone, she told me. She was no Trojan woman. Everything that had happened to her was because it had to, she thought. It was destiny. And, in spite of everything that had happened to her, she still loves me, Gómez. She says it's not the same as before, but it's all right, it's only fair.

We ordered another round of gin. De Franco swallowed his in a single gulp.

You must think I called you to talk about Azucena, like in the old days. This time it's different, Gómez. I spent twenty years far from the city, far from the world. Buried in the jungle. And now I come back, with silver in my temples from the snows of time, and I find myself involved in all this tragedy. Compared to this, the jungle is paradise.

De Franco remained quiet for a few minutes. I didn't have much to say, either. My pity was turning into misery.

When I ask around if anybody knows someone with influence, they all look the other way, De Franco said. Because I'm looking for some contact who can put us on the right track to find the kid. That's why I called you, my esteemed friend.

De Franco lowered his chin a fraction of an inch. From that angle, he looked at me.

You don't have any contacts, he asked.

De Franco kept staring at me:

Do I have any contacts, I repeated.

You understand what that boy means to me, Gómez. Azucena gave him my name. What do you think?

And you, I asked. What do *you* think.

De Franco answered me with another question.

Why are we alive.

I didn't have the answer.

We're near the Pippo, he said. How about some vermicelli with fresh tomato and pesto.

Maybe De Franco was on to something: you had to go on living.

10 Martín kept calling me. He always arranged to meet me on a corner. Downtown, usually. Then we'd go into a bar. Martín was always the one to decide which corner and which bar.

Tell me about my old lady, he asked. Half-demanding, he would ask me. When Martín took on that sort of military tone, it confirmed that just as he had inherited his mother's gruff seductiveness, his father had given him the ability to issue orders. A couple of times I nearly asked him if he had ever killed anyone. But I didn't do it. It wasn't my business. I should have asked myself some questions, too. I didn't want to know. It wasn't my business to know. So I kept quiet. And he was the one who asked.

He was interested in knowing if his mother was a good writer. Better than whom, he asked me. He was never satisfied with my opinion. He suspected that when I commented on *The Tongue of the Indian Raid*, I attributed her with undeserved genius just to satisfy him. He thought that my enthusiasm for the work was an orphan's consolation. That I was exaggerating with my praise. Until he wore me out.

Stop bugging me, boy. If you want, I'll bring you the novel.

That way he could see for himself how much truth there was to my opinion. He could keep it, too. After all, he was its real heir.

The novel is safer with you, Professor, he said.

Your wife can take care of it, I said.

She's got enough to do just taking care of her pregnancy, he said. They're liquidating us.

I tried to talk about something else. I asked him what they were going to name the baby.

If it's a boy, Ernesto, he said.

And if it's a chick, Victoria. Like Ocampo.

Not exactly.

Predictable, I thought. So predictable.

I have to go, he said. I'll call you in a week, Professor.

If I asked him when, he always replied:

Don't worry. I'll call you.

How was I supposed to not worry, I thought.

One time he said to me:

I'm not my old man, Professor. I don't throw a bomb and split.

That's what he said to me. As if he'd always known what I didn't have the guts to ask him.

I started to fear his phone calls. Of course, just by meeting with him I was getting myself into a mess. But I was ashamed to tell him that he was jeopardizing me. Since I had made frequent trips to Rosario the previous spring, I had the idea of making up a story that I'd be going away, that we wouldn't see one another for a while because I had to teach some classes there. The lie worked out perfectly for me. But when the next call came, I couldn't refuse. My conscience pulled me in one direction, but my heart took me back to the past. Maybe what I thought of as conscience was terror and what I called heart was yesterday.

When Martín phoned me again he wanted to find out when I was leaving for Rosario. I made up a date, as soon as possible. With that subterfuge, I figured I'd be free of him. But I was wrong:

Then we have to meet, he said.

As usual, I have a book in one pocket. Wilde. But while I'm waiting it's impossible for me to concentrate on reading. Till I see him coming. I can still see Martín coming along a path in Plaza Irlanda. He looks to both sides, making sure there's nothing threatening around. He seems skinnier, haggard. He's carrying a newspaper under his arm. Both of us are sitting on a bench in the plaza in front of Policlínico Bancario. Rolled up in the paper is an envelope. I'm supposed to take it to Rosario.

You can refuse, Professor, he tells me.

I remember, the professor says. I asked myself how I would react in a torture session. Whom I'd denounce. I knew nothing about Martín. To escape, I would name anyone. I told myself that nobody knows who they are till they face torture. For what convictions would I risk my life? That boy, despite his hardnosed appearance and his choice of armed struggle, seemed to be begging for someone to relieve him of a burden that weighed more heavily on him than the automatic pistol I glimpsed in his waistband. Because when I thought about his mother, I couldn't help letting his contained despair awaken unexpected paternal feelings inside me. The memory of my massacred friends, the memory of his mother, the memory of that boy who no longer was one, but who seemed to need me to care for him just the same. That boy, now a guerrilla fighter, had arranged to meet me in this plaza in the name of . . . what convictions? He hadn't even asked me if I sympathized with his cause. And here he was. Implicating me, as people said in those days. Such a seventies expression. A person became implicated in a cause. But what Martín was doing was putting someone else in danger. And that someone else was me.

I plucked up my courage:

Tell me, kid.

Martín explained that a *compañera* of his would come by for the envelope.

Give me a password, I said. Or should I wear a red carnation in my lapel.

73

Not a bad idea, he said. But a book would be better.

Martín looked at my book. As a password, it wasn't bad: Oscar Wilde's poem in English. But the plan required a few additional details. A pack of Jockey cigarettes and some Ranchera matches. The first meeting would be at a bar. The *compañera* would be identifiable by a mole on her left cheek. The first meeting would be on Saturday morning at the Odeon, he said. If the *compañera* didn't show up at the bar, he said, the second meeting would be on Sunday morning in the plaza in front of the Cathedral. If the *compañera* didn't appear at the second meeting either, I was to destroy the envelope. And take off.

I should have asked him what was in the envelope. But I didn't. Better not to know, I repeated to myself.

Thanks, Professor.

I played the smartass:

Never send to know for whom the bell tolls, I said as I turned to leave.

I looked at my mother's hands peeling an apple, I looked at her leathery hands, I looked at the serrated knife blade paring the shiny skin. My mother's hands were the rough hands of a long-suffering woman, which didn't match her sweet expression, that Criollita smile that was so charming till she parted her lips, and then you could see that some of her teeth were missing. They say that whoever peels an apple in a single, long strip will get married.

You're going to get married, my mother used to say.

No, I would reply. *You're* going to get married.

No, you.

And we would laugh and laugh.

We both liked that game, But after eating, my mother's expression changed. When she cleared the dishes and threw the remains of the meal and of the apple into the garbage can, she grew sad.

My mother was single. The man who knocked her up without giving me his name would never return to that desolate cabin on the coast. And she would never be accepted by another man, accepted as she was, a single mother with a timid, whimsical child. Sly, she would call me. You're a sly one.

I watched my mother peel the apple and thought about how carefully she did it, while outside the sea wind bent the cardoons in half and blew the sand up to the metal screen door of the shed; the screen door was down at that time of day, past midday, siesta time.

Before going to sleep, my mother always took a Rosary out of the nightstand drawer, knelt beside the bed, and prayed. Every afternoon, before her siesta. Every night, too, before going to bed. She prayed a little longer at night. Maybe because she had frightening dreams. Maybe because the hours she was supposed to stay in bed and the darkness were, in her mind, sins.

I was awakened from this daydream by the rattling of the train. Night was coming on. Slowing down, the cars entered Rosario. In my dream, the little Wilde volume that I was taking notes in had slipped off my lap, along with the Parker pen. I reacted with a start, touching one of my overcoat pockets. The envelope was still there. I calmed down again. But not too much.

I scolded myself for my fatigue, for nodding off in a dream. Once more I wondered about the contents of the envelope. Maybe the best thing would be to tear it up, throw the bits of paper out the window, let them scatter into the wind. And make myself vanish.

The sadness of evening, damp winter. The train pulled into Rosario. Opening and closing my eyes, when I returned to reality, I didn't know if those images of my mother, such vivid bits of memory, had been part of a dream or a hypnotic state.

The gray sky pressed down on the poor dwellings on the outskirts of the city. A few lights blinked on. Soon the dwellings became a slum.

Then paved roads, taller houses, more respectable neighborhoods. The train was already in the city. Like everywhere else, you could see police cars and green Falcons on the streets. Also carriers and Army trucks. I felt cold. One of my legs had fallen asleep. My heart was pounding.

11 The previous spring, when I traveled to Rosario, it hadn't been for a teaching-related activity, as I had lied to Martín, but for a love affair. Although months had gone by since then, this time the first thing I did when I got off the train was to phone Sergio from the station. A fuck would calm my anxiety, I thought. But after so much time without seeing one another, it was rash to call on the spur of the moment. No matter. I phoned anyway:

Papa is very sick, Sergio cried to me over the phone. Very.

Calm down, I said. I'll be at the hotel.

I can't, he said.

Release will do you good, I said. You always could, with me.

I don't want to.

Is there someone else, I asked.

What does that change, he replied.

Let's meet, I said. For old time's sake.

Sergio hung up. The only thing I needed now was to lose control. Sergio's refusal pissed me off. So much sacrifice on my part during what had been our romance. Taking the train all those Fridays, traveling to Rosario, staying in a fleabag hotel, spending money I didn't have and all of it so that now the faggot could cut me off like this. What bothered me most was feeling jilted. The humiliation I was starting to feel. But I pulled myself together right away. I had a mission. And that gave me strength. Suddenly I understood the meaning of militancy: It helped you forget your loneliness. Because if you have a mission to fulfill, you can't just pansy around in some soap opera scene.

I took a bus heading downtown. I went to the same hotel as usual. I asked for the same room where Sergio and I had rolled around. I looked at myself in the mirror. I didn't recognize what I saw. I stared at the ceiling fan, its blades wrapped in spiderwebs. The place was a meat locker; it smelled of humidity. When I opened the closet, a stench of insecticide and confinement rushed out.

I had to control my fear. I swallowed a Valium and went to bed. I awoke on Saturday morning for the first meeting. The Odeon wasn't far. As I walked, practically measuring every step, I thought about the risk. Maybe these steps were the last ones I'd take in freedom. I turned on Mitre toward Santa Fe. I bought some Jockeys and a box of Ranchera matches.

There weren't too many people in the bar. I studied the scene before choosing a table. I took off my raincoat. I imitated the precautions I had seen Martín take: I sat between the two doors to the bar. If I had to dash out, I would head away from the traffic.

I opened the book, placed the cigarettes and matches on the table. I ordered coffee. I looked around. There were two or three couples who barely looked my way. Some boys arguing about soccer. A solitary customer hovering over his gin; judging from his looks, he might have been a plainclothes cop. After I had ordered my coffee, he ordered one. I could hear him ask for milk. The guy noticed me and then went back to his paper. He was pretending to read, I thought, and he checked the time, an annoyed expression on his face. He checked it on his watch and on the greasy, yellow wall clock. Drops of cold sweat trickled down my armpit. The bathroom was to one side of the counter, near the coffee machine. I needed to pee. But I couldn't chance it. The guy started watching again. The safest thing would be to pay for the coffee and take off. But what would happen if the guy followed me. I had to get rid of the envelope first.

Now the boys were arguing over a match between Newell's and Central. They were hardly more than teenagers, but that didn't mean much. They could've been young officers, and the others, their superiors. One of them nailed his eyes on me. He said something to the others. They, too, scoped me out. I pretended not to notice. They were sizing me up, I thought. Shamelessly, they laughed. They were laughing at me.

I imagined that the guy next to the window was the group leader. The boys were awaiting an order from the guy to jump me. There were six of them in the bunch. I was lost.

Then a girl walked in: jacket, tight jeans. The boys stopped talking so they could give her the eye. I figured that as soon as the girl came near me, they would leap on us. But the girl had no mole. She went over to the public phone and there she stayed.

The couples were looking at me, too. I had become everybody's center of attention. Even the waiter and the owner behind the bar were staring at me. They were looking at me out of the corner of their eyes. After scrutinizing me, they pretended to resume their conversation, a buzzing that was, I have no doubt, about me. No question about it: those couples were part of the operation, too. I had no escape route, I thought.

I arose slowly from the chair, calculating what my swiftest, most skillful movements should be if they were to jump me. That is, I got into a sort of crouch. I had the feeling that time had ground to a halt, and the smallest actions were unfolding very slowly. Also voices, sounds, stretching out, liquefying.

But no: nobody in the room moved. The guy next to the window was now chatting with a heavily made-up old timer; the boys were still carrying on their soccer argument, and the couples their romances. All of them doing their own thing, not paying me the slightest attention.

A prudent waiting period had passed.

I paid for the coffee, put away the book, the cigarettes, the matches. I went out into the street, threw on my raincoat. The city trembled in the drizzle.

I found a phone and called Sergio. I hope his sister doesn't answer, I said to myself. Gina never left her father, a fascist engineer who had amassed a fortune in real estate speculation. According to Sergio, the self-sacrifice his sister demonstrated for their father had a purpose: to make him sign a power of attorney, allowing her to be the executor of the fortune. Meanwhile, she went around keeping track of her brother's expenses. And his adventures. Refusing to accept Sergio's proclivities, she preferred to believe that his adventures were of a Mastroianni type. The phone rang and rang. Bad luck: the sister answered. Despite all the years she had spent in this country, Gina still retained her Italian accent.

Sergio isn't here, she said. Who's calling.

I hung up.

I went back to the hotel. There was no message from Sergio. I went upstairs to my room and took a Plidán. I lay down in bed without taking off my glasses or my coat.

When I woke up, my eyes were blindfolded. Someone had tied me up with wire and blindfolded me. My eyes felt wet: it wasn't tears. It was blood, And the blood was soaking through the blindfold and running down my cheeks. I tried to scream. But a wire constricted my throat. My voice couldn't get to my mouth. I moved my head from side to side. When I tried to stand, I fell out of bed.

I went downstairs to the lobby. No message, the concierge told me. I went out into the night, the drizzle. I found a restaurant, ordered a bottle of wine, a steak with mashed potatoes. I was more thirsty than hungry. I chugged down the wine. Now I felt warmer.

I passed by a kiosk and bought a flask of gin. Back in the hotel, I drank it till exhaustion and drunkenness overcame me. I lost my balance and fell down an elevator shaft. Hitting the street jolted me awake. A siren, running, shouting. The shouts came from some young people. Gunshots. Without turning on the light, I looked out the window. Some Falcons were loading up two boys and a girl. A boy with a bloody belly, more dead than alive, dragged himself against the metal curtain of a bakery. Blast him, a guy ordered. And another guy, at very close range, finished him off. The cars sped away. The boy lay there on the ground. Then, silence.

There's a loneliness that prevails in hotels. It doesn't matter how many stars they have. Or if they're luxury or fleabag establishments. That loneliness reigns in its rooms, even if they allow for an occasional pickup. That loneliness suspends you in a passageway where it's no longer your past or your tomorrow. You're far from the past. And your tomorrow is still centuries away. The present unfolds, but it's happening to someone else. Sometimes you can fool yourself and believe that the fantasy of fantasies has come true: to change your life, to be a different person. Like when we dream and realize that we're dreaming, but we can't quite get back to reality, at once so near and so distant, like a shore toward which we're swimming, and with each arm stroke, the shore recedes a little, we stroke, the shore retreats again, and so on. Now I was back in a hotel once more. Who is this *I*, I wondered. The loneliness was frightening. Anxiety is dangerous for weaklings like me. The dead boy was still lying in the street. I went to bed, covering myself with the threadbare blankets. My nose was cold. I was catching the flu, I thought.

When I dived into the river, I didn't imagine that the current would be so strong. I hadn't considered the risk adequately as I ripped off my clothes. Ripped, I said. And that was the right word. Because it wasn't that I was undressing: I tore off my garments. At some point I considered carefully removing my overcoat, my jacket, my pants, my shirt, my socks, my underwear, but that slowness would have been the jerk-off spectacle of a striptease, which, without a single spectator, would have made no sense. What I was doing, I told myself, was undressing decisively and running toward the water, in spite of the cold, the drizzle, and a trembling that ached throughout my entire body. And yet I kept going. At first with my feet sinking into the muddy riverbed, then stroking with difficulty. It wasn't just the cold that cramped my muscles and sapped my strength. It was also the power of the current, now beginning to surround me. I should have realized that my physical condition wasn't up to such a feat. Too late to turn back. I could no longer touch bottom, and the current was pulling me deeper into the river. It would be best, I thought, to save my breath for when I found myself floating along with the current, and then, yes, I could take advantage of the momentum to reach the opposite shore. The current was growing stronger. I plunged in. When I opened my eyes, it was impossible to see through that brackish water. With a final effort, I rose to the surface. I shouted, but it was more like the impression of shouting. Since my ears were plugged, the waves and my frantic splashing produced a stormy echo. I swallowed water, choked, and felt like throwing up. The river gushed into my mouth. As long as I could rise to the surface every so often, I told myself, I would survive. If I was lucky and didn't get caught up in a whirlpool, by keeping myself afloat I might have a chance. That was overly optimistic on my part: a delusional hope from someone condemned to death. A whirlpool, with its centrifugal force, spun me around. A lethal funnel. The river was swallowing me up.

When I awoke, I wondered if there really was another riverbank. I went over to the window. The boy's body was no longer there. There was no blood, either. The bakery was open now. People were coming out with boxes of pastries. It was Sunday. Sundays depress me. And that morning I still had the second meeting to attend. An echo of bells and a quiet military march resounded from not very far away. I looked out the window. It was drizzling. I put on my raincoat and went down to the street.

I walked toward the Cathedral, and turned onto the pedestrian street, crossing back and forth as I went along. When I reached a corner, I turned. When I reached another corner, I turned again. All the streets were as one. Until I arrived at Plaza 25 de Mayo. In front of City Hall, a police car. In front of the Cathedral, two carriers and soldiers. There were also several green Falcons. They were keeping watch over the parishioners as they left Mass. I could see the Army officers' brown dress uniforms interspersed among the faithful. They shook hands with civilian big shots. The women wore light makeup or had freshly scrubbed faces. The kids, almost all little blondes. To either side of the great military-civilian family, dodging them, passed other, poorer believers.

I found a bench and sat down.

I opened the book, putting the cigarettes and matches down beside me. I decided to wait. Smoking one cigarette after another, I was a wreck, scared shitless.

I had to wait.

The group of candle-suckers at the church had grown smaller. Some officers climbed into their green Falcons. The carriers stationed themselves, one in front and one behind the caravan of cars. Only the police car and a few families remained in front of the church.

Enough time had gone by. I didn't want to think about what might have happened to the girl who was supposed to come and pick up the envelope. I put the cigarettes away. Better to beat it the hell out of there. Get rid of the envelope, Martín had told me. Vanish. But I didn't.

I found a public phone and called Sergio.

His sister answered. She wanted to know who I was. A friend, I told her. And she replied that she didn't know if her brother was in. There was an argument on the other end. I recognized Sergio's voice. There was a third voice, a man's, terribly hoarse. And then Sergio picked up:

Don't you understand—I can't see you.

You don't want to, I said.

I need to hang up.

I thought I heard a whistling on the line, cables in the wind.

Are you still there, Sergio asked.

Yes, I said.

You're impossible, he said.

Sergio, I begged. Even if it's the last time.

The last.

Same place as always, I said.

Give me half an hour.

I found a kiosk, bought another pack of cigs, and went down toward the river. The drizzle wouldn't let up. I didn't want to get there first, but my anxiety got the better of me. At Rosario Central Station, I took shelter underneath an overhang, checked the time, and took out the pack. Right there, a stone's throw away, was the Paraná River. I remembered summer. One afternoon with Sergio, on the riverbank, drinking beer. If that wasn't an image of crazy, wild love, at least it was a good facsimile. My reveries of summer distracted me while I was waiting in the ever more insistent drizzle. I was soaked to the bones, as I said. I cut a pathetic figure, I admit it. I checked the time every minute.

The white 1500 came out of a side street. Sergio made an abrupt maneuver; the car skidded on the wet asphalt, raising water like a launch. Sergio was very pale, unshaven.

Get in, he said.

Let's go to the hotel, I said.

What for.

I laid my hand on his thigh, close to the gearshift. He pushed it away.

Don't be a pain in the ass, he said.

You can't refuse, baby, I said.

Don't call me baby, Gómez. You know I hate that.

I touched him again. This time he didn't say anything. He clenched his teeth, hit the gas, and turned again.

What are friends for, I said.

You're not my friend. You're a trap.

Don't tell me you got married.

I met someone.

I swallowed the blow. But I didn't show it.

Gina and I are fed up with the chemo, he said. With what the treatment costs. Prostate, he said. What a vulgar word: prostate. With what we're spending on treatment, my sister could go back to Italy and live like a countess. And me, what can I say. Morocco forever, Gómez. But Papa refuses to sign a power of attorney. You have no idea of the inheritance.

Who is it, I asked him.

Why do you need to know.

Curiosity.

Papa's radiologist, Sergio said. He's helping Gina and me a lot. We never discuss fees. I'd give my life if Rodolfo could take this Calvary off our backs. You don't know what it's like to spend and spend on death. Because there's no way out for Papa. We're paying to prolong his agony. If only he would die once and for all, but no way. Gina handles the Calvary better than I do. Of course, she deals with everything with candles and religious stamps.

So you have a partner, kiddo.

Don't call me kiddo again, he said.

You're getting hard.

Get out, Gómez. Don't be a jerk.

But you do like it.

Our story is a trap.

The last time, I said. And then we'll say goodbye.

It sounds like an Argentine movie, Sergio mocked me.

I pressed on with my exploration. He'd gotten very hard. While I was touching him, a green Falcon passed by. Three guys were watching us from inside the car. I didn't let go of Sergio. The Falcon slowed down. They were watching us carefully. I squeezed harder. The Falcon picked up speed and disappeared.

Sergio accompanied me to the hotel. His hesitation had vanished, at least for a while. When he walked into the room, he made a disgusted face.

How can you stay in such a filthy place, he asked.

Not so long ago you didn't find it so filthy.

It's the last time, he said.

I still have a few hours before the train leaves. The only thing I wanted was a dose of raging sex. We started to lick one another. I didn't want Sergio to go cold on me. It had been a real job just to get him up to the room. And I wasn't about to let him escape now. I started fondling him.

When Sergio left, I felt a chill. I was getting the flu, I guess. I took a couple of aspirins and a very hot shower.

I couldn't stop thinking about what could have happened to the girl who was supposed to pick up the envelope. Why didn't I get rid of that envelope, I asked myself.

I left the hotel and hailed a taxi. I told the driver to take me to the train station. All I wanted was to go back home. I was shivering. I had gotten sick, for sure. The drizzle was steadier now.

I was alone in the car. Half-asleep, I bumped my head against the window. It was growing dark over the soggy countryside. I had a fever. And the fever was overcoming me.

With a clatter of the train, I awoke. It was slowing down. Again, terror. Maybe the train was stopping for an Army checkpoint at the next station. I peered out the window. False alarm. My nerves were on edge. The train started up again.

I couldn't take it anymore. I opened the envelope. It was a letter from Martín to someone named Mara. A love letter. The letter began with a quote from a Benedetti poem, "Armored Heart." The fact that Martín was cheating on his pregnant girlfriend, who was in hiding, just like him, disappointed me. Besides, he had the nerve to criticize Mara for having her own history. Because for a while now he'd been suspecting that her heart belonged to someone else. If those little lambs were going to create the New Man with that double standard, at least they should have the decency to use a condom.

But what worried me most, as I said, was what might have happened to the girl.

And what if the love letter was a message in code, I wondered.

Why not.

The train advanced, burrowing into the night. There was lightning.

I tore up the envelope and tossed the bits of paper out the window, into the wind.

12 Burning with fever, buried under a pile of blankets, in a cold sweat, I wanted to sleep, but the pills had no effect. The movement of the elevator, an echo of footsteps, and a door opening were enough to electrify my reflexes, and I sat up again in bed: I swiped at my pants, put on my shoes, and dressing hurriedly; I went over to the door, looking through the peephole to see if the elevator would stop on my floor. If they came after me, I would jump off the balcony. Nothing. I undressed again, went to bed, dozed off, woke up again, got dressed, peered out into the hallway, calculated the distance between me and the balcony, till, in a frenzy, I pulled the mattress pad off the bed and placed it near the door to the balcony. Then I wedged the back of a chair underneath the handle of the front door, blocking it. I went back to bed. I didn't even have the strength to stick the thermometer under my arm. Between my exhaustion and my torpor, I dreamed I was sinking into a swamp.

When I pulled myself together, I glanced at the phone. I arose and walked over to the device to make sure it had a dial tone. I went back to bed. And got up again. Every time I got out of bed, I went over to the phone to check the dial tone. Always. It had a dial tone. But it didn't ring. Martín was supposed to call me. He had to. But Martín didn't call. And if he didn't call, I said to myself, it was because he may have met the same fate as that girl who was supposed to pick up the letter.

The fact that Martín had used me, the whole trip, the fear I'd had to swallow, no longer bothered me. I felt a chill coming on, and yet I was burning. The thermometer read 104.

I took a Zen koan and turned it into good old Criollo: If thunder freaks you out, just let yourself freak out. This feeling of terror, I reflected, was what the machinery of repression had injected throughout the country, even in those like me who always skirted the edges of a border without having the nerve to cross over. The imminence of punishment. First, a sleepless night. Then, another night spent goggle-eyed. I popped the Plidán as if it were aspirin. For sleeping, a Valium. But no use. If insomnia in general tends to unhinge a person, combined with terror its effect is an infinite round of tossing in bed every night, each time increasingly wide-awake. Terror attacks suddenly and paralyzes you. Then, slowly, thoroughly, it undermines you. Meanwhile, you cling to the mantra it won't happen to me. We all thought the same thing. Till it was our turn. Terror took over, first in small matters, until it invaded even basic language functions, the language of thought, the language of speech, written language, body language, each and every gesture. And here's another verb: to appropriate. Just look at this other example: It killed me, my students would say. It literally killed me.

Besides, daybreak was still so far away. Daybreak, I thought. And I clutched onto hope, the morning that was about to arrive. But even with the brightness of morning inching up the windowpanes, day didn't show more promise than night. Even though operations usually took place at night, there were also some carried out in broad daylight. Morning. So far away. Some fucking consolation, morning. Because, in the morning, the terror was still there, like the drizzle.

When dawn broke on Monday, I couldn't stand being shut in anymore. So I decided to leave, to teach my class. If death comes, I said to myself, let it find me fully alive. This Monday, this Monday morning, just like last night, like all the nights of these times, and like all their mornings. Like every morning, when you go into the city, the streets and the traffic sound like Piazzola's *bandoneón*. I take the bus. I buy my ticket. I hang on to the rail. Better to travel standing, I think. Because with all the tranks I've got in me, I might fall asleep and miss my stop if I sit down.

The iron gates, the caryatids, and the façade with its Latin inscription, the marble staircases, the wooden portico with bronze reliefs. Every time I walked into the school, I felt as frightened as a new student who doesn't know the rules and customs, the codes, the rituals. That fear of making a mistake and being reprimanded. Because the school was terror, too.

As I entered, I mingled with the throngs of kids. I smelled the odor of the crowd. I've said it before: that barely repressible scent of a herd in heat is unmistakable. Blending in with them, I felt like someone else. That morning, everything else was better than being me. Although possibly, I said to myself, they might be feeling the same thing: maybe they, too, would rather be someone other than themselves. But they weren't allowed to be. The boys: short hair, not even a trace of whiskers, the blue jackets and gray pants of their school uniforms, the polished shoes. The young ladies: also in blue and gray, with their hair gathered up and their skirts below the knee. The Process of National Reorganization had detailed not only their appearance, but also their heads. Ever since Esteban was kidnapped the class regarded me with sadness and pity.

One kid, with slicked-back hair and two surnames stuck together with a glue stick, came over to me in the schoolyard:

Echagüe had it coming, he said. He was involved in all that shit.

Who turned him in?

It wasn't me, Professor. It could've been anybody. Could've been a prisoner.

The kid was right. They could have made Esteban squeal under torture, but also here at school. The denouncement might have come from the faculty, the headmaster's office, the secretarial pool, the teachers' lounge. From the classroom.

And why are you here telling me this, I asked.

Because you're the only one who's still bitter about Echagüe. We all understand how you feel. I'm here to tell you, on behalf of all of us. It's not worth it.

Why not.

No one could stand Echagüe. He thought he was the smartest.

The teachers' lounge filled up during recess, but between classes, there were few of us there. Somebody was always drinking and chewing something. Brewed *mate*, usually. And cheap cookies. Anyone who had brought something more unappetizing ate it alone, secretly. I had a flask in my briefcase. But I abstained.

I started reviewing my notes on Wilde. I had begun to disagree with the philosophy of the jail poem. Up to what point, I wondered, did one kill what he loved. In general, I reflected, it was just the opposite. Especially these days. I was scared stiff. When I got here, I had a 102-degree fever. But I couldn't stand being locked up at home anymore, so I came to school. Better than that isolation was the stink of this pale gray room, the concentrated smell of tobacco and damp coats. A Vulcan stove with only three burners lit warmed one corner. A long table crying out for varnish, some broken-down chairs with mangy upholstery, and a wardrobe with scratched glass made up the furnishings. When the teachers weren't around, roaches and mice scampered around freely on the dull linoleum floor. Nobody stayed in this room very long unless they had a break between classes. Sometimes while I was reading or correcting quizzes, a mouse, which always looked to me like the same one, crossed the room and stopped right in front of my shoes, raising its head. It watched me closely and then, as though disappointed, went on its way, disappearing beneath one of the chairs. Then I, too, felt like a mouse.

At this early morning hour, killing time between one class and the next, there were only two colleagues. Each one doing his own thing. Silent. One of them was Iturbide, a diminutive doctor, very nattily dressed, with a little mustache. He liked to relate everything to the body, illness, and cures. A military sympathizer, Iturbide enjoyed applying medical terminology to politics. Cure society. Cut out the rot. Because now, at last, the country was going to have the thorough surgery it needed. The armed forces were excising the cancer of subversion. And according to his diagnosis, society was already showing symptoms of metabolizing the change. Iturbide was a physician, but he didn't practice. Evil tongues spread the rumor that he had operated on the wrong baby at the Sardá Maternity Hospital. The baby who was supposed to have the operation died. And the one he operated on, too. There was an investigation, a report. It was the end of his career. Iturbide ended up in teaching. But he insisted on being called Doctor, nonetheless.

The other colleague was Raimundi. Bald, scrawny, a Logic and Philosophy teacher who claimed to be a disciple of Carlos Astrada, Raimundi was marking a horse racing sheet with a red pen. An inveterate gambler, he once told me of an infallible plan he had worked out to beat the roulette wheel in Mar del Plata. Then I'll take off for the Black Forest, he confided. Where Heidegger's house is, the House of Being, Gómez.

I've got to admit it: there were times I really enjoyed listening to Raimundi.

I missed Wainer, a guy with salt-and-pepper hair, a beard, and thick glasses. Wainer boasted about his collection of literary journals. He owned entire collections. In addition to History, he also taught a subject that had been imposed with Peronism and whose acronym sounded like a pistol: ERSA, the Study of Argentine Social Reality. Shortly before the military coup, Wainer burned all his collections, his entire library, in anticipation, resigned his post, and went to Patagonia. It wasn't worth the trouble to wonder about his motives. Just before he left, playing the mystery man, as if it were necessary to explain himself, he invited me for coffee. There had always been a kind of good vibe between us, on account of the literary journals. Seeing what was coming, he told me, he was going into exile in Patagonia. According to Wainer, Patagonia was a refuge in the clouds:

Pure sky, he said. Hiding in the sky has its charms. A heavenly exile. The Andean foothills, south of Esquel. I'll send you my address as soon as I settle in, my friend.

Then he whispered with alarm:

You'll be left alone, he said. Do me a favor: take care of yourself, he whispered. Today even readers like us are dangerous. My grandparents died in a pogrom. If there's a part of my heritage that saves me, it's persecution, Gómez.

No sooner had Wainer left, Ortegosa, his replacement in the History department, arrived. A hefty platinum blonde with varicose veins who boasted about her knowledge of Rosacrucianism. She had gotten a substitute's position after the coup. A month later she was promoted to full-time status with tenure. And nobody had the nerve to ask her about her connections.

It looks to me like you need a healing, Gómez, she attacked me.

She laid a hand on my forehead.

You're burning up, my dear, she said. You should've stayed in bed.

She looked at me worriedly. Her occult knowledge came to the fore:

But not only that—you've got a spell on you. That thing they call the evil eye is negative energy that has invaded you. I know about all that. What you've got isn't just the flu. You have to say to yourself: "I am, I can, I want to." Of course, in your condition it's impossible to see the light. What's your sign, Gómez. Maybe I can help you.

I can manage, I said.

Do you have someone to take care of you, she hinted. Men who live alone don't know how to care for themselves. I can visit you, teach you meditation.

From his chair, Iturbide, legs crossed, raised his eyes from the newspaper.

A virus, Gómez. Lots of viruses going around.

Iturbide pushed Ortegosa aside.

Allow me, Gómez. I'm going to take your pulse.

From a distance, Raimundi observed sardonically. Philosophy's his thing.

The seriousness that Iturbide invested in studying me was impressive. He made me take off my jacket, my shirt. I resisted removing the thermal undershirt. Iturbide had me take a deep breath. Then, using a Bic pen, he made me open my mouth, stick out my tongue, say "Aah."

Penicillin, Gómez, he said. Go to a drugstore. And get yourself penicillin.

Raimundi was amused by the situation. While I bundled up again, he looked up from his magazine:

It's crazy to show up at the salt mines in your condition, he observed. You look like death. Sign out sick and beat it. Missing an hour of Literature won't change those slackers' lives. Their fate is sealed. Listen to me: beat it. But first play the soccer pool. Put a few pesos on forty-eight. That number exorcises the Grim Reaper. Listen to your colleagues: hit the hay, but first play the number. *Il morto chi parla.*

The bell rang. The swell of voices from recess. I grabbed my briefcase, and, like a sleepwalker, went to the secretaries' office, signed out sick, and left.

The clouds were dark, and the sun filtered through intermittently. The streets were damp. From time to time, an icy gust shook the bald tree branches. What I needed was to breathe pure air. But my stuffy nose fucked up my breathing. I walked aimlessly, not noticing which streets I was turning on. It took me a while to realize that I was heading west. Now the morning had a more luminous sheen, and the sky oscillated between silver and blue.

I walked quickly, with desperate urgency. I was hurrying to get nowhere. Every so often I turned around to see if I was being followed. Sometimes I stopped at a window to check out my surroundings in the reflection. Then I kept on walking, always adrift.

Around me, the city. There were markets, kiosks, banks, drugstores, rotisseries, auto repair shops, general stores, shoe stores, public offices, hardware stores, veterinary clinics, barber shops, variety stores, law offices, bakeries, fruit and vegetable stands, small appliance stores, doctors' offices, jewelry stores, bars, restaurants. There were old folks, men, women, young folks, girls, boys. They came and went, had their professions, did their usual thing, and always seemed to have meaning for everyone. The military operations, the kidnappings, the green Falcons had become invisible. Even if you were snatched and taken away, the others didn't change their normal routines: they worked, went through red tape, paid their taxes, fell in love, married, and then hated one another, came and went, talked about the game, reproduced, had kids, educated them, sent them to school, and went on with their lives, their usual lives, which that morning were their usual lives: eating, belching, digesting, defecating, copulating, reproducing, and sleeping. The next day, Tuesday, Wednesday, Thursday, Friday, Saturday, Sunday, and Monday again, which would be like this Monday: they would repeat the same gestures, acts, scenarios. Always. I would have liked to be just one more like them. But I wasn't like them. I was different. I could blend in with them, but I wasn't like them. How I would have loved to be the same. But who the fuck did I think I was. I was, prejudging. Because one of them might be like me. And that other person, like me, would be pretending in order to keep going. It is what it is, I said to myself. An expression, a cliché. Life goes on, I said to myself. And the world keeps on turning. But I didn't have the strength to keep on turning.

Exhaustion overcame me. When a cramp paralyzed my leg, I stopped in a plaza, chose a bench in the sun, and sat down. I looked around. There was playground equipment and there were kids. The swings, the slide, the seesaw. Young mothers and nannies chatting while they watched the little girls and boys. The children's shouts and laughter plunged me into sorrow. Any of those women, any of those kids could also be swallowed up at any moment.

13 De Franco and I met again at 36 Billares. He read me his latest poems, even though I didn't pay much attention. My most recent creations, he called them. Everyone knows that when an author shows you an original, he expects praise, not criticism. De Franco was easily satisfied. All I had to do was nod after his reading to make him smile with contentment. His poems were anachronistic: they spoke of girls who were always the same girl. They spoke of patios and balconies. Of sparrows and neighborhood streets. Of course, in his verses there were always daisies, jasmine, carnations, callas, hydrangeas, roses, a vast floral variety among which, noblesse oblige, white lilies—azucenas—predominated. His poetry evoked spring, but from winter's perspective. I recalled a popular saying: winter carries off the old folks. Maybe this winter it would carry off De Franco. And—why not?—me, too.

I paid more attention to De Franco when he explicitly recited his erotic feats with Azucena, honest-to-God geriatric acrobatics. While Pedro, the husband, rolled around the house in his wheelchair. While Azucena, at siesta time, mounted De Franco like an Amazon, in a frenzy that revealed more madness than desire, her husband, in the wheelchair, rolled from one corner of the house to another without stopping. De Franco described the noise the chair made as it rolled back and forth outside the bedroom door while Azucena bellowed out a Wagnerian orgasm.

When she's overcome by sadness, it's hard to pull her out of it, De Franco told me. I've invited her to the movies, to the theater. But she doesn't want to go. She says she can't distract her mind. That she always thinks about the same thing. Her little one. Then she starts rummaging in that pile of newspapers and magazines, cuts out pictures of Videla, sticks pins in them, and slips them underneath the door to the sealed room. That calms her down.

Doesn't making love give you some relief, De Franco asked her.

What we do isn't love, Azucena replied.

What is it, then, he asked her.

Something else, she said.

De Franco wasn't satisfied with that answer.

Don't be a pain, Azucena said to him.

As he told me this, De Franco, desperate to know, was hoping I would offer a convincing explanation of what was going on with Azucena.

Maybe the answer lay in what was going on with me, too, when I hit the streets at night. I wandered endlessly. What I was looking for wasn't "lovemaking." Beneath the icy drizzle, what I was looking for was something else. That thing Azucena called "something else." When I remember those nights, I see myself reflected in the store windows on Avenida Santa Fe, waiting for someone else's reflection to appear at my side.

After a silence, De Franco mused:

What damage absence can do, he said. God knows what's become of my kid, he said.

That "my kid" business struck me as a bit over the top. Because, more than twenty years before, when De Franco divorced his first and only wife, sometime in the fifties, he had left two children with her. It was true that his wife's hatred, a hatred she instilled in the children, made them reject him, and they never saw him again. De Franco wasn't replacing his kids with Azucena's son. He was replacing one absence with another. Maybe the absence of an imaginary son seemed more tolerable to him than that of his real children.

Let me see, De Franco, I said. I have an acquaintance who's a cop.

14 I was startled when I saw the creature. I say creature because in the darkness it was hard for me to tell if it was a boy or a girl. The creature, at the foot of my bed, barely stood out against the background, a landscape of jungle shadows. Then I recalled the children's books I read when I was a boy, those books in which brightly colored, flat figures made their appearance as you turned the pages, whether they were human beings or animals. The creature, rising from that background, was like a cut-out illustration that came toward me and then retreated, moved closer, and withdrew. I sat up in bed. That creature, I thought, had been there for a while, silently contemplating me, waiting for me to wake up, and now, blinking in surprise, I didn't know exactly what to say. Nonetheless, I managed to babble a question: How had it appeared there, I think I asked. It didn't reply. Where had it come from, I inquired. There was a spark of mischief in its gray-blue eyes, like aquamarines, although if you stared at it long enough, that naughty gleam in its eyes became evil.

Who are you looking for? I asked it.

The creature didn't answer.

It remained silent, watching me, but waiting, too.

The creature reached out its hand, inviting me to accompany it. Its tiny fingers looked metallic.

Since it was winter, I was sleeping in socks, underwear, and an old sweater. I was embarrassed by the situation and asked the creature to turn around while I threw on pants and shoes. But it didn't let me. Grabbing me by the hand, it tugged on me, urging me to come along with it. The jungle that had seemed unreal to me before was true. As happened more and more frequently in my nightmares, I realized I was in one. I tried to awaken. But I couldn't. I tried to free myself from the creature's tugging. Impossible. Its tiny metallic fingers were hurting me. And so, in my underwear, without taking time for anything, I followed it.

The creature issued a shriek. I thought I could detect the word mama in that sound. I must confess: it embarrassed me to go after a truth in my underwear.

15 I had returned from Rosario and was expecting Martín to phone me. But nothing happened. Maybe he had met the same fate as that Mara woman. The phone line was dead, as they themselves might have been.

One night it finally rang.

But it wasn't Martín. It was Walter.

Things with the half-breed had gotten out of hand. Walter wasn't just fatter. He was swollen. He drank a lot, more and more. In a few years, I figured, his exotic charm would evaporate. When I told him to ease up on the booze, he got angry. I reminded him of Beti, he said.

Just like my wife, he said.

Walter looked at me differently ever since I had inquired about Esteban. One night he nearly beat me up. Forewarned, I tried unsuccessfully to put some distance between us. With our passion in ruins, what remained was mutual suspicion.

Let's just end this, I said.

We both looked simultaneously at the .45 on the coffee table. We stared hard into each other's eyes. For one second, instead of my fearing him, he was afraid of me. But I can never hold on to anger.

After that night we didn't see one another for a few weeks. I thought the two of us had touched bottom. That there was nothing left of our story. It had lasted as long as any horniness lasts. Besides, I had a good excuse to calm my soul: to find out what had become of Esteban. The more I thought of Esteban as a pretext, the less embarrassed I was at having offered my asshole to a cop.

But the thing wasn't over yet. And one night the phone rang again.

Tomorrow at ten on the corner of Cevallos, Walter said. The bar diagonally across from the Police Department.

On the phone Walter was drier and more authoritative than in our intimate encounters. He gave the orders. He would always give the orders. Because that's how passion is, I said to myself: the one who gives the orders on the first night keeps giving them till the end.

Carriers and assault trucks were stationed all around the Central Department. An armored car circled the surrounding area. Even though it was noon and a constant swarm of people went back and forth going about their business, the area seemed to be plunged into silence, the kind of silence that attacks when your ears are stopped up.

I found a table and ordered coffee. After a while, I felt a tap on my shoulder from behind.

I shivered, but managed to hide it.

I didn't like Walter's smile.

Do you really want to know, he asked.

I nodded.

Your little student is being held by the Navy, he said, lighting a Benson. Why don't you get the hell out of here.

Walter stared at me, hard:

You've still got time. Listen to me, get the hell out.

I didn't know if it was a piece of advice or a warning. But I did know I wouldn't ask him anything about Azucena's kid.

16 The little boy in the photo wears his hair slicked back and is dressed in a suit: it's his First Communion. I like to call him the little boy. Not the kid, the little boy. He's wearing a dark jacket, a white shirt with an Eton collar, a tie, an armband. His hands are folded as if in prayer, a little prayer book with a white, mother-of-pearl cover, a Rosary with a crucifix. The little boy must be around eight. He lowers his eyes toward his folded hands in supplication. He has Criollo features. And he's slightly chubby. His eyes aren't quite slanted, but there's something Asian about him. More than devout, his expression is enigmatic. A detail: his short pants. If it weren't for the short pants, he would look older, maybe twelve. Without a doubt he would have preferred to wear long pants on this occasion, the occasion of the photo: his Communion matters less to him than the photo, because we forget ceremonies, no matter how sacred they may be, whereas when we have our picture taken, the occasion becomes transcendent: it survives over time beyond any oath, declaration of principles, affirmation of love. If the little boy would have preferred to wear long pants, it wouldn't have been so much for the sake of playing grown-up as to conceal his squeezed-together thighs and his plump knees.

His mother never speaks to him of his father. Never. Not even when she discovers him rummaging in the dresser, the *secretaire* with its documents, or when the little boy besieges her with questions does she let her tongue slip. The little boy suspects: his father might have been one of the travelers she used to put up in those two rooms. He might have been a traveling salesman, a trucker. But, infected with his mother's romantic imagination, he likes to think that his father was a fugitive from justice, an innocent man condemned for a crime he didn't commit. The fugitive escapes into the open country, toward the horizon. The little boy imagines him fading into the distance, profiled against a background of sudden clouds. He tells his mother about this dream once; she smiles at him. If his mother smiles and remains silent, the little boy believes, it's to hide from him any clue to the whereabouts of the fugitive, who, once his innocence is proved, will return for his beloved and the son whom he has unwittingly sired. A son who, no doubt, resembles him. When the little boy asks his mother if he looks like his father, she smiles again. Silence means consent.

The little boy is no longer so little. He also stops asking. Rumors of his origin circulate in the village. When his classmates tease him at school, instead of replying with his fists, he retreats. He will never forgive himself for this cowardice, or for the shame and humiliation. Because it's not about his honor. It's about his mother. Son of a whore is more than an insult, he thinks. It's the truth. He wonders if it's possible to fight against the truth. If this is, indeed, the truth.

When the little boy becomes a young man and the young man finally leaves that place to study in the capital, before he boards the bus, his mother hands him that velvet box with the handkerchief. As the bus advances along the dirt road, the boy wonders if his mother knows what he, for his part, is hiding, just as she has always hidden his father's identity.

If I were telling this as a movie, this part would be in black and white; it would have the rough, grainy appearance of a late-seventies newsreel. Here we see the borders of our homeland, the narrator would say. A melancholy guitar would accompany the projection with a southern-style *milonga*, and we would see a bus stopping at a desolate service station to fill up with gas. We would see the Automobile Club, a hotel-pastry shop-restaurant, some trees gnarled by the wind, its branches stripped bare. There's a flagpole, a flag flapping in the wind. All around, desert. The passengers get off the bus. Rushing into the wind, they walk toward the pastry shop. A girl with a kerchief on her head waves to the camera. Among the passengers is a dark-skinned guy with a mustache: I turn for a second to look at the camera. My smile is a brief rictus. Raising my lapels, I turn my back to the camera and follow the other passengers into the pastry shop. It's winter, the journey is long, and the temperature is below zero. My back hurts. My seat on the bus has a hard back and I barely slept the night before. I'm numb. I'm in a foul mood. But not only because of the trip. It's just that I'm returning to my home turf. A week ago I received a letter from my mother. She's sick. And yet she started out her letter by writing: I'm in good health and hope you are too. *Espero que tú también.* I wonder why poor people idealize the written word and on these occasions resort to the starchy *tú* form, when *vos* would sound so much more normal. My ruminations are literary. My mother's, on the other hand, are the kind one talks over with the priest.

At that moment in my life, the letter coincided with an unrequited love. As sometimes happens, we use one pain to cry over another. My mother's letter was perfect for distancing myself from an unreciprocated passion. Whenever I feel like crying over an ungrateful lover, I cry for my mother, and that way I feel less abandoned.

Whoever said that childhood is a man's homeland? asks the professor. And he hesitates: If that's true, we are all exiles. And if we manage to survive exile, if we figure out some way to keep going, it's better not to return to that lost land, that forgotten tongue. They say it's a bad idea to go back to the place where you were happy. But, I ask myself, was I really happy during my childhood? No, I don't believe all past times were better. And I agree it's not necessary to return to that place where you thought you were happy, that idealized, and therefore accursed, place. But with my temperament I couldn't handle it: the exile who came back, that's who I was. There should be a digression here, with reflections on motherhood and homeland, a reminder that the Russians call their country "little mother."

At the Automobile Club café, the mustachioed guy in the overcoat has a coffee and a beer. He seems lost, stupefied by sleep, even though he's hardly slept at all. On the wall is a national map. And again, as if it were a film, the camera zooms toward a point in the southern part of the province, an almost invisible location.

The last time I was there, the village had expanded only slightly, with a few construction projects, some small, half-whitewashed chalets, and one paved street connecting three or four shops, a district post office, a service station, a gendarmerie post, and a chapel. A few trucks and a long-distance bus passed along the pitted road twice a week. The houses had been built with their backs to the sea. But you could feel their nearness, their sound; a permanent, stormy breathing could be heard in the interstices of a conversation, in a silent meal, and in the calm of siestas and desolate nights. On that part of the coast, there were more cliffs than beaches, and the beaches were rocky and narrow. Southeasters were frequent. And sometimes, during a storm, it was unwise to get too close to the sea: the wind was so powerful that it could blow you off a cliff. In spite of the danger, I liked to escape to the coast, stand at the edge of the highest cliffs, and from there, like one of Byron's heroes, defy the unleashed forces of nature. Because ever since I was a little boy I've had a Byronian temperament. As the squall lashed me, as the waves struck their talons against the rock, as the hurricane enveloped me, I imagined that this would be how I'd fend off the blows of destiny.

The bus advanced along the route. Countryside on both sides of a gravel road. Somewhere there's a sun trying to worm its way into the silvery gray sky. The wind bends the cardoons in half. The bus stops and the mustachioed man gets off. As the man stands there, the bus pulls away. Before him lies a road that stretches toward some distant buildings. A few of them have TV antennas. The wind whips the man's overcoat.

Then we see a Geloso, a gigantic, black-and-white television set. I like to imagine these parts of my life in black and white: we note that a show is about to start. A Criolla, about seventy years old, is knitting and watching TV, lowering her head toward her knitting needles and raising it toward the set. Beside her, sitting at the table and drinking brewed *mate*, is the mustachioed man. I've said it before: I am that man. If they were showing a newsreel on this TV, it would be an obvious sign of the times, a redundancy. For example, Peronist guerrillas execute Fusilier General Aramburu; military government uneasy in the face of a strike by leftist workers in Córdoba; city transformed into battlefield; attack sends military officer flying through the air; guerrilla fighters shot on naval base in Trelew; political activism growing; more information about guerrillas in Tucumán mountains; insurgency taking over the entire country. Perón prepares to return.

Here, in this place, those news items come from the outside. On this TV there's a show. The mother and son are silent. They have nothing to say to one another, it seems. The image on TV turns ghostly. The screen, with its white flashes, blinds us. Then you can hear the wind.

The wind, says the old woman.

The antenna, says the son.

And he walks out into the night.

In the night, a street of dirt and sand. The wind forcefully kicks up swirls of dust. A streetlamp on the corner, rocking from side to side, barely illuminates the block: the light comes and goes. The block lights up and goes dark again. You can see a structure with its metallic blinds lowered. It might have been a store. A ridiculous sign reveals the word "fashion." There is a door on one side of the structure: we see the mustachioed man go outside with a ladder. He rests it against the front of the building. Then he walks against the wind on a tin roof and tries to straighten out a TV antenna. The wind is untamable; in addition to disheveling his hair, it twists the antenna. The man in the wind curses, looks at the black sky, shouts.

Now it's the old woman who walks out of the building. She responds to the man's shouting. But the man doesn't seem to hear her. Then she grabs the ladder and tries to climb up, but she can't manage it. The man looks down and yells at the old woman: he's terrified she won't listen to him, that she'll keep attempting to climb up.

The wind yanks out the antenna, drags it along, lifts it, and hurls it into the night, the blackness. While the son shouts at his mother, while the antenna flies away, while the mother holds on tightly to the ladder, the wind is a deafening whistle.

Let's focus on this scene for a moment, says Professor Gómez. Tell me what you see.

17 I got up, walked slowly toward the kitchen, swallowed a Valium with a glass of water, and went back to bed. As I anxiously waited for sleep to come, tossing and turning in bed, I started to remember and remember, and in each memory I thought I had found an interpretation for each dream. Soon I realized that this was an exercise in paranoia. The only thing for sure was that that dawn, like so many others, insomnia had besieged me, and in addition to a complex lucidity, what I felt was glacial fear. A fear that grew whenever I remembered Martín.

A siren, a screech of brakes, a scream, the elevator door opening on the ground floor, the movement of the metal cage, the creaking of the mechanism, and then, relief, expelling the retained air, because the elevator eventually stopped at another floor.

Since the trip to Rosario I hadn't heard a word from Martín. Every night, cornered by terror, I didn't stop thinking. Hopefully Martín had managed to swallow the cyanide pill. I also recalled what he had told me about his *compañera*, a pregnant girl, somewhere, alone in bed, shaken like me by street sounds, trying to sleep with a grenade on her nightstand. One hand resting on her belly, as if protecting it. In the other, an automatic pistol.

Part Two
NORMAL LIFE

1 I've always resisted attributing prophetic qualities to dreams. And yet, if I poked around in the latest dreams that had made me sweat on my pillow, I ended up finding a key. Let's put it this way: my dreams had preceded the events I'm telling about now. It's true that if I dug through my yesterdays, I would also find, on a more realistic level, keys that struck me and explained these facts. When I say yesterday, I'm referring to '55, but also the days when Esteban was kidnapped and what happened afterward. All of that is yesterday. And sometimes nothing is as remote as that yesterday.

I still hadn't shaken off the flu, and my cold was getting worse. I shut myself in my apartment. I was losing my strength and my desire for night wandering. Even though a blow job, the aftertaste of cum in my mouth, might not have been such a bad idea, fatigue and indolence had weakened me. I was planning to get into bed with my Valium and a cup of tea.

One night, when I was already in bed, the downstairs buzzer sounded. I felt my heart bursting, a kick in my chest. I looked at the clock. After one-thirty. My tongue stuck to my palate. Maybe that's what it was like to be tortured with an electric cattle prod. I put on my glasses and went out to the balcony. I could see two shadows on the sidewalk. One was Martín. The other, a girl. The fact that it was them, and not a police operation, brought me some relief, but only some. The street door required a key. I had to go downstairs to let them in. I pulled on

113

my pants and shoes without socks. I went down with my coat over my sweater.

Martín was with a freckled redhead who couldn't have been more than twenty. She was pregnant. Martín wore his sheepskin jacket and carried a bag, and she had on a trench coat. Her coat was open: impossible to button it over that baby bump. She held a hemp bag and a Pan Am duffel bag. They both smelled of the countryside.

This is Red, Professor. My *compañera.*

He didn't need to explain who she was. They didn't even give me time to greet them properly. Martín looked to both sides, making sure, as usual, that they hadn't been followed. Neither one asked permission to enter. They just did.

As the elevator rose, Martín switched off the light. We were three shadows: Martín, Red, and I. Three shadows rising in the elevator. The gears were noisier than ever. The elevator stopped two levels below the floor where my apartment was. Martín took out a 9 mm, opened the accordion door. Red took out a .22. Through the grating we watched Martín climb the stairs, step by step, gun in hand.

Who are you people? I whispered. Bonnie and Clyde?

Red ignored me. We hung on the silence. Martín had been swallowed up by darkness. Time stretched out. Red and I remained in the elevator, silently, staring upward. We heard a brief whistle.

Decisively, Red closed the elevator door and pressed the button for my floor. Again, the gears. Again, we rose.

Once we were back in the apartment, I noticed the floor. The linoleum and carpet bore traces of mud. They must have come from the provinces, from unpaved streets. From a place they could not return to.

I double-locked the Yale. Then I double-locked the Trabex. For good measure, I secured the chain. Martín and Red, standing motionless, looked around, studying the place. They both emitted the chill of the street.

Martín checked to see if the phone had a dial tone. Then he explored everything: the kitchen, the bathroom, the bedroom . . . He opened one of the balcony doors and stepped out into the night. A blast of cold, damp air stirred my papers. Martín closed the door again.

I couldn't let you know sooner, Professor, he said. Nothing will happen.

I looked at her. Her breathing seemed labored. I helped her take off her trench coat, invited her to sit in the armchair, and offered her tea.

You'll be okay here, Martín told her.

And to me he said:

Relax, Professor.

I nearly burned myself with the teakettle when I poured a cup for the girl. My pulse was racing. The tip of the china spout clinked against the edge of the cup.

She didn't look quite so pale now. Color had returned to her face, and her freckles were more noticeable. But her smile faded as soon as she began stirring the tea, deep in thought. I could see that around her wrist she wore a little red ribbon with three knots in it. Red to combat the evil eye. Each knot, a wish. When the little ribbon wore out and fell off, her three wishes would be granted. Just one look at her expression was enough to understand that birds of ill omen flew among her thoughts.

In the silence, even the tiniest sound was an alarm. Then the three of us would look at one another, Martín at Red and at me, Red at Martín and at me, and I at those two desperate creatures who were struggling to stay calm. A simple screeching of brakes in the street below sufficed to make us shrink back. There was one moment: Red and Martín looked at each other and at me. I had the feeling they didn't know what to do with me. I was an intellectual. And for the militants, intellectuals were wankers or chickenshits, incapable of taking action. Martín laid his automatic on top of the pages of my essay on Wilde. It seemed heavier and thicker than it was. A firearm. It seemed to be burning through the paper. No wonder people talked about packing heat. They were everywhere, even in poetry: a weapon loaded with future. Firearms as lyricism, those kids thought.

Martín embraced the girl.

How do you feel, he asked her.

She touched her belly.

It's not kicking anymore.

You'll be okay here, Martín repeated.

And Mara, she asked.

You ought to rest, Martín replied.

There's the bedroom, I said. You can use my bed.

Red brushed her hand across her face, rubbed her eyes like a sleepy child, and allowed Martín to lead her away.

From here, from this living room, through the half-open bedroom door, I saw how Martín untied her boot laces, saw her bare feet. I could hear the murmur of a nervous, staccato conversation, mostly Martín's voice, soothing her. Red was arguing in a quiet voice and Martín was soothing her. From the living room I could see Martín, from the back, sitting on the edge of the bed. I couldn't see any part of Red except her legs, one of Martín's hands gently touching her belly, as if taming an animal. Although I couldn't see her, I knew she was crying. When the voices quieted and the silence was complete, Martín returned to the living room.

I need a shower, he said.

Typical of Martin, who never asked for or requested anything: he ordered.

I pointed to the bathroom.

He didn't thank me, either. I went to the kitchen and made more tea. I heard the heater bellowing. It didn't take long. Martín showered and shaved in minutes. And when he emerged, shaved and showered, he was a new person. He seemed much younger without his mustache. He was, in fact, young. Only I hadn't realized exactly how young till that moment. The towel was around his waist, and he smelled of my cologne. But what really caught my attention, even more than the missing mustache, was the little chain with the crucifix.

I recalled a passage from his mother's novel. The Indian raid attacks the fort. A lance kills the heroine's military officer husband. An Indian grabs her and hoists her onto his horse. Kidnapped in the raid, having left civilization behind, and seduced by an escape that she had so often dreamed of, she isn't the typical, weepy captive. As she gallops along, clutched by the Indian, she yanks off the crucifix and tosses it away. A real symbol, that act. As she rids herself of the crucifix, the protagonist repudiates not only her origins, but also her class and her faith. Of course I had noticed Martín's crucifix. It surprised me even more than his *compañera's* little red bracelet.

I could really use something warm, he said.

And I served him a cup of tea.

Something strong, too, he said.

I took down the bottle of whiskey from the shelf, removed two glasses from the cupboard.

By way of thanks, Martín said:

I needed that.

I didn't say anything.

It'll be only for three or four days, Martín said. It's just that we've got no place to go, Professor. They ransacked the whole house. Luckily we weren't there when the military showed up. There were documents there. Our *compañeros* are going to fall.

Do you believe in God? I asked him.

No, he said.

And that crucifix, boy? I asked.

It was my mother's. What about it.

I felt like exploding with rage, but I contained myself. Martín realized I was pissed off. He went back to the bathroom, picked up his clothing, and got dressed.

I really apologize for coming, he said. It was the most convenient and safest thing.

Stop apologizing, I retorted. It's not about what might happen to me. It's about her, about the life she's carrying.

The baby is the future, he said. And Red is my *compañera*.

Compañera, my balls, I said. You're a manipulative piece of shit. You think I'm an idiot. Why didn't you call me after Rosario, I challenged him. What happened with that Mara girl, I asked.

Don't worry about her, Martín said. She's all right.

I'm no purist, I said, but if you want to change this world, start by admitting you're a scam artist, like everybody else. Don't play the big shot with me, boy. *Compañera* here, New Man there, but you've got the double standard of the typical Argentine macho. Her with her little red bracelet and you with your crucifix. You people have an explanation for everything. What do you take me for.

Martín downed his whiskey in one gulp.

You opened the letter, Martín said. You read it.

We were silent again. For a long time.

What happened to that girl, I insisted.

The way things are, Martín attempted to explain, I couldn't ask anyone from the organization to take that letter to Mara. Besides, if Red finds out about Mara and reports her to the organization, they'll demote me. Article 16. Mara is Red's best friend. I'm responsible for her. Mara couldn't make the appointment because she had to move out of a house. I can't tell you anything else.

Martín walked toward the living room. He grabbed the 9 mm, stowed it, and before heading for the door, said:

If it's me calling, I'll hang up after three rings. Three rings and I hang up.

And if you don't come back, I asked.

I'll come back.

And if they come, I said.

118

Red knows what she has to do.

The cyanide, I asked.

Martín stuck out his hand. I didn't respond to the gesture. Maybe I should've asked him for a pill for myself, too. It was more than likely I'd need one pretty soon. When he left, I turned both locks and fastened the chain. I heard the elevator descending, the front door opening, and, once more, silence.

In the living room, next to the armchair, lying on the carpet, was the hemp bag. I picked it up. It was heavy. It contained a grenade and a pistol. I grabbed the bag and went to the bedroom. The girl was sleeping. I laid the bag next to the bed.

Stealthily, taking care not to disturb her sleep, I pulled two blankets out of the wardrobe. I covered her with one of them. With the other, I returned to the living room, collapsed into the armchair, and curled up.

2 Red spent a few days in the apartment. She wouldn't go out, she promised me. Martín had forbidden her to poke her head out into the street. It was wise advice. We had our first exchange when I saw her examining my library. From one end to the other. She came and went.

Lots of English, she said.

What do you have against the English? I countered.

You're kind of a Sepoy.

I didn't answer.

Why don't you have a TV, she complained.

What's your name? I demanded.

Why?

I may be a Sepoy but I'm no snitch, I said.

Red studied me.

So you met Martín when he was a kid, she said.

She looked pensive. And then:

Diana, she said. Let's say my name is Diana.

The huntress.

More like the hunted, she corrected me.

Which one are you, then?

Both of them, she explained. The huntress and the hunted.

Diana, and from then on she would always be Diana, turned on the radio. She listened to the news stations. Rivadavia and Mitre: she went from one to the other. According to Muñoz, the entire country was getting ready for the 1978 World Cup, a huge deal. The World Cup captured everyone's attention. She was obsessed with the news.

Diana asked me for newspapers, too—all the newspapers. She read them intently, with anguished interest. I could imagine what she was expecting to read.

Subversion has been put down, said the papers. The military reported that the voting urns were well guarded. But the politicians, as if nothing was amiss, kept on massaging the military's back, hoping for a favor. Nobody paid too much attention to the internal struggle among the armed forces to see who would end up in control. According to the papers, the Junta was studying the possibility of the three branches of the armed forces handing over the presidency to a military officer chosen by mutual consent: the fourth man. A Human Rights functionary from North America had traveled through the country. The Yanquis, the driving force behind the coup and proponents of a swift extermination of the insurgency, as Kissinger had advised, now seemed annoyed by the Argentine military's sloppy butchery. This dictatorship had become an international scandal. Now the Yanquis threatened to withdraw their support. The Communist Party denounced this North American interest in human rights. They criticized it and rejected it as just another imperialist intervention. The Bolshis' betrayals were historical. At this point, they had good reason: the dictatorship was selling wheat to the Soviet Union. The only safe topic of conversation was soccer. All attention, as I said, was on the World Cup. We Argentines need this World Cup, said Muñoz. We were going to set an example for the world.

Diana didn't need to tell me what piece of news she was looking for in the papers. Luckily she didn't find it. She smoked and walked endlessly.

Don't you have any *mate*? she asked.

I drink tea, I said.

How British, she teased me.

I may be a half-breed, I replied, but I've got class.

Oh so British, your thing: Wilde and tea.

If you're granted political asylum at an embassy, you don't question the flag.

Touché.

In the morning, when I went off to school, I felt unburdened. But later, as the hours went by, whenever I thought of Red, my fear grew. I returned to the apartment with my heart in my throat.

Her swollen ankles covered by a pair of wool socks, Diana paced back and forth. Then she would sit down and clutch her belly. Now I was the one pacing back and forth. And she followed me with her eyes. After a while, I would try to concentrate, read and write for a bit, but it was impossible. Now she was the one walking from one end of the apartment to the other. She moved the .22 from the nightstand to my desk, from the desk to the armchair, from the armchair to a kitchen shelf. Wherever she went, that firearm went with her. Even to the bathroom. Every so often she took the grenade out of the hemp bag, placed it on the coffee table, and put it away again.

Without cigarettes, Diana became unbearable. She constantly asked me to go downstairs to a kiosk, to bring her cigarettes. She smoked dark tobacco. Particulares, like Martín. I obeyed. If I brought her two packs, she smoked them right up. She smoked endlessly. I chided her:

Tobacco is terrible for you in your state, girl.

What state? she asked. A state of siege.

I pointed to the little red ribbon she wore on her wrist.

And that red? I asked. Bolshevik or Ecclesiastical?

Red for danger, she said.

Put out that cigarette, I challenged her. Diana was skinny, angular, and thick-lipped. She was attractive in an Anouk Aimée sort of way. As with Martín, I especially noticed her broad, bruised hands. Why had she gotten involved in this violence, I wondered. What the fuck business was it of mine, I reproached myself. Who did I think I was to go around sticking my nose in these kids' lives? But, I asked myself, were they really kids? Why underestimate them? If there was one thing that couldn't be denied, it was that they had rejected all guarantees of a warm, shiny future and chosen to risk their lives for a better world. Even if they were more like missionaries than militants, I couldn't underestimate them. Who was I to question the girl's reasons for teaching reading in a slum. I, too, had my populist heart when I taught my students Sarmiento from Hernández Arregui's perspective. It made no sense to confront Diana with my weak, well-meaning, middle-class schoolteacher arguments. The fact was that these kids, by entering my life, had shaken my foundations. Maybe it was just that I, an immature old man, didn't recognize the passage of time, and no matter how much I might have denied it, I was grateful that the young folks had restored my lost intensity. Dawn was breaking again. Diana had fallen asleep in the armchair with the radio on. I turned it off.

She woke up.

Just go about your normal life, she said.

What about you, I asked. Do your parents know?

Turn on the radio, she said. My parents know what I chose.

Do you want me to call them?

Their phone is probably tapped.

I looked into her eyes.

Put yourself in their shoes.

And who's putting themselves in mine? she replied.

I shouldn't have added:

And in the baby's? Who?

But I said it.

I noticed her eyes were weepy. I found the handkerchief that my mother had given me, the one with my initials embroidered on it. Diana took it, dried her eyes, and returned it to me.

I know what I want, she said.

But she didn't seem very convinced. No matter how many tears she swallowed, she didn't seem convinced.

I'm going to buy you *yerba*, a *mate* and a *bombilla*.

I turned the radio back on. Even though I couldn't stand any more commercials, I turned it on.

Diana seemed to read my thoughts.

It's not a good idea for you to know a lot more about us, she cut me off. And it's not good for us, either.

She said the same thing as Martín: Do your thing, Gómez. When we leave, don't turn around. Look straight ahead and go about your normal life.

One morning I was coming back home with the newspapers and her cigarettes. I had stopped at a little market, too, and bought meat, vegetables, fruit. Also a package of Nobleza Gaucha *yerba mate*. Ramón intercepted me at the entrance to the building.

You're very domesticated, Professor, he said. Your visitor keeps you busy.

My niece, I said. Pregnant. She came to take some classes.

You never talk to me about your family.

She's from Patagonia.

And her husband? Ramón asked.

He had to stay in Comodoro, I said. He works for an oil company.

Patagonia, Ramón said. It must be another life there.

Ramón's vigilance forced me to stay alert, but there was an even greater risk. That Walter might return. All I needed, I thought, was for Walter to interrupt my normal life. I had to invent an explanation in case Walter took me by surprise. Not only would I have to justify Diana's presence to Walter. I would also have to justify my relationship with Walter to Diana. How could I say to her: Look, girl, the thing is—I fuck a cop. I had grown accustomed to wiggling out of messes as

124

they came along. But you didn't screw around with terror. What I was now hiding in my normal life was no joke. Now my normal life was different.

At night I bought food at the corner rotisserie, lots of food. Chicken on a spit, roasted flank steak, french fries and salad, flan and baked apples. From the beginning I thought Diana looked anemic. And I wasn't wrong. She also had cavities. Her teeth ached.

So much future, so much future, I prodded her. Do you want to tell me where you're going to get strength for the future.

You act like my mother, she teased.

I could be your grandmother, I corrected her.

Unlike Martín, Diana called me *vos*. I liked that confidence between us. In spite of everything, these days and these nights we spent together, she drinking her *mate* and I with my Wilde, could be lived naturally, which, however, didn't prevent us from being reminded, every so often, of the terror.

Another morning I took a walk along Calle Florida, walked into La Franco Inglesa, and bought her a lipstick, some makeup. Then I found a drugstore, I bought iron pills, Vitamin C.

All this, for what? she asked, bewildered.

Because you're a sorry mess, girl, I said. You're a fugitive, not a prisoner.

Diana smeared on some rouge.

How do I look?

Too provocative, I said. A lighter color would look more delicate on you.

I still hadn't taken off my coat.

I'll be back, I said.

Where are you going?

I've got things to do, I replied. And, giving her a wink: Normal life.

I needed a break, to take another walk, to pass by the Broadway on Lavalle, pick up a taxiboy. A fuck doesn't cure desperation, but it numbs it. I went down to the street and plunged into the fog. Instead of fucking, it would be better to think about the situation. I walked aimlessly, always against the traffic. I reached Plaza Once. The drizzle mingled with my sweat. I was nothing but a coward with my tail between my legs.

Even though they could swallow me up, those streets were a better guarantee of saving my ass than being locked up in the apartment, a real rat trap. I walked between the railway platforms at Once. I was toying with the idea of getting on a train, splitting, becoming someone else. I walked around and around the empty platforms. I wanted to get on a train, travel without a given destination, get off in an unknown town, take a room in a *pensión* under a different name, be someone else, and expect nothing, absolutely nothing, from tomorrow, not even the expectation of awakening. I bought a ticket. It was the last train of the night. A whistle blew. I ran. I ran against the drizzle, leaping over puddles. I ran, I skated, I nearly lost my balance. With my heart in my throat, I ran. I was close. The door of the train closed first.

If my eagerness to run away had been genuine, I wouldn't have missed the train. I have to admit it: if I didn't catch the train, it was because I never would have forgiven myself for abandoning Diana. It was for her sake that I didn't run fast enough to catch the train. But also for my own.

The incredible thing is that, despite the terror with which I watched over Diana in the apartment, sometimes I had the warm, comfortable feeling that we had lived there together forever. Maybe I was like a mangy dog, I said to myself. I was hungrier for affection than I had imagined. I, her protector, was now her charge. Like that night when I returned to the apartment and found that she had turned it upside down, dusting, sweeping, and cleaning it from top to bottom.

You're crazy, I said. You shouldn't overdo it.

What I can't do is be here all fucking day long, biting my nails, she replied. You had a phone call.

And then, guiltily:

It rang all morning, she explained. Sorry I said "fuck."

Martín's instructions? I said.

I thought I was going crazy, she said. As soon as you left, it started ringing. Till I couldn't stand it anymore and picked up the receiver. I was very quiet, listening. Till a man started to speak. An old man, I thought, judging by his voice. De Franco, he told me he was. Said you should get it touch with him—it's urgent.

A police siren rose from the avenue. We looked at one another for a few, unbearable seconds. Then the siren faded in the distance.

You're shivering, Gómez, Diana said. I made rice soup. It'll do you good.

3 You're not gonna believe me, Gómez. The fright.

At the table in 36 Billares, a troubled De Franco, in that gray over-coat dampened by the drizzle and smelling of mothballs. Dark circles under his eyes, his sickly appearance. He wasn't acting: he was scared. He drank the gin that had spilled over into the little tin saucer; he ordered another. He was exhausted, poor guy:

I shouldn't have fallen back into this affair, Gómez, he started out. But it's too late for me to disappear, you know. To be honest with you, and in plain Criollo, I'm in deep shit. And I can't get out of it.

He spoke falteringly. Tonight, for once, De Franco wasn't projecting his voice.

Unburden yourself, I urged him.

I had been begging my girlfriend for a whole night, Gómez, he said. I wasn't satisfied with a siesta, I nagged her. We should spend a night together, like when we were young. Finally she gave in. But not in some sleazy hotel, she said. You could catch God-knows-what, she said. And it wasn't just a matter of hygiene. It was financial, too. If we did it at my *pensión* and she was away from her house all night long, she'd have to call a neighborhood nurse to take care of Pedro. And it would cost her a bundle. Better to do it at home, she said. If Pedro didn't put up a fuss during our siestas, he wouldn't do it at night either. Saturday, she said. You'll come over this Saturday. Come early. I'll put something in the oven, the three of us will have dinner together, I'll slip Pedrito a Rohypnol, and we'll all go beddy-bye.

That drizzly Saturday afternoon, the Saturday when he was finally going to spend a whole night with Azucena, De Franco suddenly had a strange feeling as he walked beneath the arcades of Retiro Station. The strange sensation grew as he counted out the coins, bought his ticket for the Urquiza line, got on the train. He recalled all the afternoons when he had begged Azucena not to get dressed yet. To allow him a view of her charms for a moment longer. If I could only be lucky enough to spend a whole night with you, he would whine. But once satisfied, she would declare the siesta over, as she sat on the bed, fastening her bra:

What's wrong, she would ask. Don't tell me you're still in the mood. You won't be able to handle it.

I'm always in the mood, De Franco replied.

You're a dirty old man, she told him.

De Franco expanded: I'm in the mood for you, he said. Only for you.

You know I can't, Azucena said. I have to give Pedrito his milk. Don't be jealous. You saw what he's like. He's a wreck.

I love you, De Franco persisted. Please, one night, a whole night.

You think what we have is love? she asked him.

And he:

What else could it be.

Vice, Azucena replied.

In the swiftness of her response, De Franco realized that Azucena had been thinking deeply about her feelings.

Love is what young people feel, she said. At our age it's vice.

When De Franco told me about his siestas with Azucena, it seemed to me that he was telling them to himself, trying, in the slow recounting of the details, to relive the flirting, the conversations, the caresses.

My visit didn't last more than two or three hours, Gómez. For a while we used to think we were the same as before, the two of us in the splendor of our past. Once Azucena had given Pedrito his milk, we would say goodnight at twilight with a cup of tea and some anisette, before our romantic conversation degenerated into banality, because neither of us felt like getting into a recital of the day-to-day grind and its frustrations. As soon as night fell, I would take my leave, discreetly, just another neighborhood shadow. Deep down, without daring to recognize it, we had lost one another decades ago, and now that we'd run into each other again, we weren't just two lost souls, we were two losers. Not only had I lost her when she was a girl in bloom, I had lost myself, too, with my dreams of exile in the jungle, chasing after an illusion that was more poetry than real life. There's no denying it, Gómez: instead of infusing my poetry with savagery, I had infected it with nostalgia. It's true that I almost succeeded in adapting to a primitive existence among the foliage of the mission, to that soporific heat that I sweetened with the gentleness of a Toba woman. But balconies, patios, and lilies—those white *azucenas*, always those lilies—inevitably showed up in my verses, again and again. When I returned to the city, my children had buried their mother and refused to see me. They wouldn't even let me see my grandkids. Grandpa died, they told them. And so there I was, going along with no compass but my verses, when I ran into Azucena again. What can we do. For me to persist with my poetry is as useless as for Azucena to keep sticking those pins into Videla's photos. My verses won't bring back my golden years, and her pins won't bring her justice. I don't know if I'm making myself clear, Gómez.

Saturday, De Franco, I reminded him. You were telling me about Saturday.

I don't know if it would be indiscreet of me to tell you, Gómez. Besides, if I tell you, you won't believe me.

De Franco turned toward the window. It was raining again. It was always raining. Avenida de Mayo was deserted.

Then he asked me:

Do you believe in ghosts, Gómez?

From the back of the billiard hall came the echo of a cue stick striking a ball. And voices celebrating a carom shot.

I didn't believe in them either, De Franco went on.

That Saturday, the drizzle grew denser during his train ride to Villa Ballester. At last Azucena was going to grant him his whim: they would spend the night together. Although Saturday evening was still far away, before De Franco got off at the station, the sky had already grown black. During the train ride that afternoon, De Franco had noticed that, unlike on so many other occasions, the trip was starting to make him anxious, and he was ready to get off a few stations earlier, cross over to the opposite platform, and go right back to Retiro: he'd figure out some excuse on the phone, any old pretext. And yet, overcoming the temptation to return, a temptation that was growing ever stronger, he got off in Villa Ballester.

With every block I walked, my chance of escape diminished, De Franco told me. I found myself pushing open the screen door, walking up the little sandstone path to the chalet.

De Franco described the chalet to me. You walked directly into the dining room and right away you could see Azucena's obsession with decorating. Skillfully and neatly, she decorated every corner. Plates on the walls, decorative oil paintings: a stormy seascape, a garish clown, a bucolic forest with deer. There were also diplomas. Diplomas earned by her husband in accordion contests. And the diplomas garnered by her son in judo competitions. The semi-darkness was a spiderweb in which you could catch a glimpse of family photos: the wedding portrait, a picture of the baby, the boy, the young man. There were countless photos of their son. On shelves, inside a piece of furniture with a glass door, on top of a cabinet. Interspersed among the photos were little terracotta and porcelain figurines: an elephant, a Chinese man pulling a rickshaw, a shepherd with a pipe, a classical ballerina, a bullfighter, and a couple of Tyrolean peasants. All the furniture was covered with fabric mats or tablecloths, and the chairs were slipcovered. Throughout the house you could hear the tick-tock of a cuckoo clock. Every time the bird popped out, the cuckoo accentuated the silence of the house, a sadness as sticky as the layer of grease clinging to the porcelain and the crystal glasses, the figurines and the trophies.

The dining room connected to a short hallway. It was the necessary path to the bedrooms—the master bedroom and the one that had belonged to the son. At the back, another little room. Everything faced a side garden. The windows were barred. And the blinds, ever since the boy had disappeared, usually remained closed. The room that had been his was locked with a key, De Franco explained. That was where Azucena would always slip the pin-pricked photos of Videla under the door. All you had to do was to pass close by that door to feel the cold coming from the dark stillness on the other side. Then came that little room, with a single bed, where Azucena had confined her husband. Because she had chosen to confine Pedro in the house rather than in a nursing home.

That Saturday, as usual, when he arrived at the chalet, De Franco rang the bell. A short, almost secret, buzz. Then the porch door opening slowly and Pedrito in his wheelchair, drooling, gesticulating, inviting him to come in. They shook hands. As he took Pedrito's hand, De Franco felt as though he was clutching a hook. And he realized, in those few seconds as he prolonged the handshake, that he had made an unforgivable mistake by begging Azucena to spend a night with him. He could deal with the afternoon siestas, but not with a night, an entire night in bed with Azucena while Pedrito might take off and wander around the house in his wheelchair in the dark. As he gave his hand to the paralyzed man, De Franco understood that it was late. Too late to run away. He let go of Pedrito's grasp and rubbed his hand against his pants, as if to clean himself off.

132

But I had begged Azucena for a whole night together, De Franco sighed. And now I couldn't back down.

Then, what had to happen, happened.

That night De Franco was struck by the naturalness with which Azucena moved about during his visit, a spontaneity he didn't recognize in her, because this Azucena was a married, domestic Azucena and not his lover. Azucena laid the cutting board on the counter, on top of it a piece of round steak. She chopped the garlic, the parsley.

An Italian vedette sang on TV: *Qué fantástica la fiesta*, opening a large, lipsticked mouth, wiggling her hips, leaping acrobatically into the air and into the arms of some boys. De Franco couldn't concentrate. He was still disturbed by the fatalism that had assailed him that afternoon as he boarded the train:

A premonition, Gómez. The feeling wouldn't leave me alone. Instead of relaxing me, Azucena's ease, the sound of the knife chopping garlic and parsley on the cutting board, and Pedrito's familiarity—he winked at me every so often, tilting his head toward the Italian singer, whose legs were now spread wide—it all made me nervous. There was something threatening about that nice, homey setting.

Change the channel if you'd like. Maybe there's a movie on.

No, I said. This is fine.

The three of us remained in silence. The clatter of the knife chopping; Azucena, with her back to us, concentrating on preparing the meat; the lighting of the stove; and the two of us, the husband and I, watching TV: the invalid in his wheelchair and me, with my elbows on the table and a bottle of Gancia, some sparkling water, and a little cuartirolo cheese with a few slices of bread. Pedrito had become a sort of brother-in-law to me. Anyone seeing us would have thought it a family scene. They were showing a cigarette ad on TV: Claudia Sánchez and El Nono Pugliese reflected a lifestyle even more extravagant than that of ordinary snobs. El Nono with the unmistakable air of a Don Juan, the girl with a smile that fluctuated between seduction and disdain. The pretentious idiots were parading along the most sophisticated, glittering beaches. The sun had been created for their sake. The world was too small for them.

De Franco took a sip of Gancia and turned toward Azucena.

One of these days, he said. A little trip.

What, she taunted. To Taormina, maybe?

Córdoba, he said. The mountains.

Azucena didn't reply. She opened the oven door, shoved in the Pyrex dish with the meat. She sat down at the table and added more soda to her Gancia.

Should we take Pedro? she asked.

Pedrito looked at them. First at her. Then at him. Once more at her. Again at him. He was waiting for an answer. De Franco was supposed to provide it.

Of course, he said. All three of us will go, Pedrito.

Maybe he should have set his premonition aside. After all, that Saturday night the three of them were as close as anything could be to a family. De Franco should have been grateful to Azucena. Time had managed to figure out a way to tame passion. It made things easier. A flash of lightning lit up the kitchen window with a glow that was pink at first, and then blue. Then another, and yet another.

Maybe on that night of lightning and thunder, this family that the three of them had cobbled together was the best thing for De Franco. Better not to think about the one who was missing while the fat raindrops fell slowly, rhythmically. Better to watch TV and wait for the roast to be ready. Better to accept things as they were. Soon the rain grew heavy and thunderous. It was deafening.

The universal flood, said Azucena.

Maybe, said De Franco.

You know what day it is today, she asked him.

Our anniversary, De Franco ventured.

One year since they took him away, Azucena sighed. Exactly one year today.

Pedrito, staring at him, nodded a few times. He knitted his brow, bit his lips, and, agitated, turned his wheelchair around. He headed down the hall. They could see his shadow bumping into the shadows of the furniture and any other obstacles in his way. Like one possessed, he charged into the dining room furniture till he got back into the hallway, picked up speed, and crashed his head against the door to the closed room. Again and again the paralyzed man attacked the door with his forehead, and each one of his head blows sounded like it was striking the lid of a coffin. Azucena and De Franco pushed and shoved behind him. Nearly throwing himself from the wheelchair, Pedrito resisted being restrained and banged his head even harder against the door. They held him down. The invalid pouted and issued guttural grunts.

Don't let him go, Azucena ordered. I'll get the pills.

They were showing a government announcement on TV. A soldier winked at a little boy as he asked to see the father's documents. Thunderclaps seemed to move the house off its foundations. The rain riddled rooftops and windows. De Franco hung on to the invalid. For a moment he hesitated: maybe he, not Pedrito, was the one who needed embracing.

My hands felt wet. Blood. Pedrito's head was bleeding.

I shouldn't have stayed, De Franco thought.

But it was late.

And it was flooding.

Azucena put her arms around Pedrito. She stuck two pills in his mouth, calmed him down, and bandaged his head. When the meat was ready, we sat down at the kitchen table. The TV show had ended and they were showing a Charles Bronson movie. Azucena fed Pedrito mashed squash with a spoon. Open your mouth, sweetheart, she said to him.

The invalid opened it, never taking his eyes off the TV. Pedrito was very subdued, although every so often he would buck suddenly.

He gets this way whenever a storm is coming, Azucena explained. Can't do anything about it, just increase his sedatives.

The downpour was getting worse, Gómez. Water was starting to filter in through the kitchen window. Grumbling about the weather stripping, Azucena plugged up the leaks with newspapers. I kept quiet. I had nothing to say. Azucena had placed a bottle of Cruz del Sur on the table. And the level in the bottle kept going down. The two of us were making it go down. Me more than her, of course.

When the thunder started to crash again, I asked Azucena to turn up the TV. It was a good excuse to avoid hearing the invalid eat his mashed squash. Azucena peeked at the movie every once in a while. And during the commercial breaks she would get up and wash something in the sink. Another government announcement. A piece of barbecued beef in the shape of the country. Let's unite to keep from being swallowed up by subversion, the announcer exhorted.

Do you like the meat? she asked.

Exquisite, I said. A delicacy fit for a king.

You're a bullshit artist, as usual. Can't help it, Azucena joked as she peeled an apple for Pedrito. You're a romantic.

It's the rain, Azucena, I said. The rain.

After Azucena had fed Pedrito the squash, his eyelids began to droop. Azucena turned the wheelchair toward me, pushing it in my direction.

Say goodnight to our friend, dear.

Good night, Pedrito, I shook his hand. I also gave him a couple of pats on the back.

The invalid and I said goodnight. Azucena pushed the wheelchair with Pedrito in it, sleepily nodding off. As soon as they left the kitchen, I went to the sink and rinsed my hands with detergent. Pedrito disgusted me.

Azucena returned after a while. She gave me a quick kiss on the cheek. The kind of kiss you'd give to a friend, I thought. I had dreamed about Azucena for so many years. Nothing worse than a dream fulfilled, Gómez. May God, if He exists, free us of fulfilled dreams.

Azucena began clearing the table and then went to wash the dishes. Finish watching your movie, she said. I'll be there right away.

Azucena's "right away" was forever, Gómez. The movie, interrupted by commercials, grew longer. A government announcement called for time and effort, essential for any achievement. I had lost interest in the TV. I got up and turned it off.

I drank the last sip of wine and grabbed Azucena from behind. The rain was falling more slowly. I couldn't wait for us to get into bed. Because I could no longer withstand the urge to sleep and wake up in the morning, leave, and not come back for a long time.

Will you be much longer? I asked her in a whisper, lifting the hair at the back of her neck. I'm burning up, baby.

I bought you a toothbrush, she said. It's the dark blue one.

I can't take any more, I said to her. I'm beat, I said.

I still felt a sliver of desire. Just enough to do it and then, off to sleep. The rain was stimulating me.

I tied Pedro down, Azucena said. So he won't throw himself out of bed. Go to the bathroom and get into bed, and I'll follow you. Don't make that face. I didn't tie him so tight. Nice and loose. Just enough so he won't fall. Especially when there's a storm. What if he throws himself out of bed, hits his head, and kills himself.

It was pretty much a sure thing I'd have trouble summoning up even a tepid eroticism that night. Once more I thought of escaping. But there were no trains at that time of night.

I went to brush my teeth. Or rather my dentures. I wouldn't take them out to sleep with Azucena.

Then came the part that De Franco couldn't quite reconstruct clearly. The supernatural events of that night in Villa Ballester, De Franco called them. The events that confirmed his dark premonition. Now, at the 36 Billares bar, it was no longer a question of his describing the matador moves that awaited him in bed, says Professor Gómez.

The premonition, even though De Franco couldn't define it, warned him of the imminence of something evil. As if to confirm its fatalism, the signs came gradually and incrementally, one situation after another, proving that he shouldn't have spent that night at Azucena's house. First he had felt the hoof. Then, the thunderclaps and the paralyzed man's reaction, smashing his head against the door of the closed room. And now, no matter how much Azucena may have drugged Pedrito, De Franco was unnerved by the idea that the invalid might untie himself during the night. He was frightened.

Despite her attempts to arouse him, despite De Franco's painstaking efforts to respond to her caresses, their mouths and tongues were overcome by fatigue. The caresses became burdensome, their mouths grew dry, and their tongues grew sandy. Exhaustion and sadness were one and the same thing.

Your feet are cold, Azucena said. Azucena curled up beside him and tugged on the covers. The rain hammered against the roof. De Franco realized, and this was another sign, that it would be impossible for him to sleep a wink that night.

What are you thinking about? Azucena whispered into his ear.

You remember the bat? he asked her.

Azucena remembered. That was more than twenty years ago. When they were young. Well, when Azucena was, because he was already over forty at the time. It happened one summer night, at the apartment of the divorced professor De Franco. They were naked, after making love. There was a fluttering of wings in the darkness. De Franco grabbed a shoe and tried to knock the bat down. That night De Franco imagined that the bat, which had burst in, flying over their heads after lovemaking, was an omen. And the omen came true. Shortly thereafter, Azucena married Pedrito.

What reminded you of the bat? she asked him.

Every time I remember it, I laugh, De Franco lied. It was funny.

De Franco thought that sleep might come if they embraced like two good friends who were snuggling close in a tent for warmth.

What are you thinking about? she asked.

Nothing, De Franco said. I'm not thinking about anything.

I don't believe you. You're probably thinking about something strange, and you don't want to tell me.

About the music of the rain, adding the finishing touch to the miracle of this night, together at last, he said. All night long.

Liar, she said.

And she kissed him.

Azucena turned toward the nightstand, took out the Valium, and swallowed half a pill with a glass of water. Then she turned off the light and embraced De Franco again, resting her head on his chest.

Am I too heavy on you? she asked.

Not at all, he said.

Liar. You never stop lying. The incredible thing is that I love you anyway. Maybe because it's impossible to live without lies.

Now the rainstorm was lessening.

What a day, today, Azucena yawned.

I love you, De Franco whispered.

Azucena yawned again. And fell asleep. She seemed to be sleeping soundly. De Franco slipped her head to the side, moving it off his chest. She rolled over, and De Franco clung to her back.

Azucena had left the blinds half-open. De Franco was able to adjust his eyes gradually to the darkness. He could see the outlines of the skeletal branches, glistening with rain. Every so often a gust of wind shook the branches in the shadows, and the silvery drops flew into the darkness. A long period of calm followed. The drops fell rhythmically in a silence that weighed on their breathing, pulsing, muttering, creak-ing, and the croaking of some toads. A gutter discharged its contents.

A poet trying to fall asleep might well count raindrops instead of sheep jumping over a fence.

A flash of lightning shook him from his sleep. An explosion of pink and blue sparks lit up and extinguished the scene again and again. Then a thunderbolt shook the walls and the roof. Azucena, wriggling in her sleep, muttered something. De Franco thought he could make out what she was babbling. According to De Franco, Azucena was scolding the kid. She had warned him not to get involved in politics. That's what happens when you don't listen to Mommy, he thought he heard her chide him. She spoke in short bursts. Bits of phrases: I warned you what would happen to you. Don't say I didn't warn you.

She was distraught, crying. And you didn't have to be a poet to reconstruct what she was babbling in her nightmare: I hear you, son. De Franco tried to awaken her gently. There was no way. Tell me what they did to you, she muttered. And he couldn't bring her back to reality. Azucena was held prisoner somewhere else.

It'll pass, she muttered. It hurts a lot, it hurts, but it'll pass. Mama is with you, son.

Azucena muttered and muttered. De Franco held her. But she wriggled free from his embrace and continued that monologue, which was more of a prayer and a lullaby. A clap of thunder, then another, shook him. De Franco thought that, just as thunder follows lightning, one sign should follow another. He knew that the terrible part, the most terrible, hadn't happened yet, and that it might happen at any moment.

Azucena sat up in bed. De Franco didn't recognize her in this new personality. The sleepwalker was not her:

You want *The Eternaut*, I know, Azucena said. It's coming, son.

The thunderstorm lashed the house. Azucena got up. De Franco stretched out his hands, trying to restrain her. Azucena had always been strong. She pushed him aside. She was walking naked, illuminated by the lightning. The atmosphere had become electrified, and De Franco, naked too, hurrying, tripping, unable to stop her, followed behind. The floor and walls echoed with each thunderclap, and it took a while for the calm to return. A brief respite, another thunderbolt. And another. The volleys were about to bring down the house.

Azucena faced the hallway. Amid the clamor of the storm, another downpour. Between the thunderclaps, De Franco heard the invalid moaning. As he passed by the open door of his room, he saw that Pedrito had emerged from his stupor and was trying to untie himself. De Franco would have calmed him down, but his first duty was to Azucena. She was struggling with the door to the closed room, trying to open it.

I'm coming, Gabrielito, Azucena said, and De Franco couldn't tell if she was laughing or crying. I'm coming, sweetheart.

That's when it happened, De Franco recalled. Azucena was struggling to open the door to the closed room when the door handle began to move of its own accord. The lock also moved one way and the other; it jammed and unjammed with a series of dry clicks. De Franco grabbed Azucena. He wasn't about to let her go. His desperation now gave him the strength to restrain her. From underneath the closed door came an electrical glow, like from a short circuit. It might have been the reflection of the lightning. But no. Those bright, intermittent rays were not from lightning. Like a neon sign that flashed on and off under the door. There was a bolt of lightning. He kept holding Azucena from behind, as tightly as he could, by the breasts.

Let go of me, she screamed.

But De Franco didn't let her go.

When it was all over, Gómez, dawn was breaking. The cuckoo clock woke me up. It was raining lightly. Azucena and I were in the hall, side by side, naked, against the wall. She was seated, her mouth facing upward, more unconscious than asleep. She was breathing quietly. I had my arm around her waist, my head resting near her pubis. Both of us frozen. The cold that froze us, like the smoke from cold-storage rooms, came from beneath the door of the locked room.

4 The wind swept along Avenida de Mayo. A gust fluttered my raincoat and whipped De Franco's overcoat. As we said goodnight at the door of 36 Billiards, I felt like I was leaving him in the lurch. I placed a hand on his shoulder. An unusual gesture, as we never went beyond a handshake. A compassionate gesture on my part. I couldn't take any more. Diana would be waiting for me. I hailed a taxi.

The taxi smelled of room deodorizer. The dashboard was a little purple altar with a plastic statuette of the Virgin of Luján. Every so often the driver, a large guy with slicked back hair, pulled a aerosol can out of the glove compartment and squirted a few little bursts of spray.

Does it smell a lot? he asked.

The deodorant? I said.

The stink, the cabby explained.

What stink? I asked.

You have no idea what it was like, the cabby went on. A pregnant chick. About to give birth. Looked like she was about to pop. She stopped me at Jonte and Nazca. Wanted me to take her to Durand Hospital. If she was out alone at that hour of the night, there must've been a good reason. What about your hubby? I asked. Gone, she replied. I didn't ask her any more questions. I played dumb. These times, you know. Paranoia. She was doubled over in pain. She couldn't stand the contractions. Pray, I told her. That helps. I don't know how to pray, she told me. Are you from here? I asked her. Muslim, she said. Impossible that she would be putting me on. Muslim. Chicks know how to tough things out. Her water was about to break. And she didn't say boo. I hit the gas like Fangio, to try to get to the hospital. And those cobblestone streets, besides. We were approaching Donato Álvarez when the military stopped us. An Army truck, a green Falcon. Reflectors and weapons everywhere. They poked an Ithaca against the back of my head. The military squeezed the girl. I don't know what the hell they were thinking. Like maybe she was carrying explosives instead of a fetus. The chick didn't act scared. She got mad instead—she started to swear at them. They pulled her out of the cab by her hair. As she fell outside of the car, her water broke. They'd have to take her to a hospital, I said. They didn't take the Ithaca away from my head. You guys turn on your siren and we'll get there faster. Keep going, one of them shoved me. They stuffed her back in the car. So I stepped on the gas and took off like a whip. She kept swearing. She was crying, vomiting, she shit herself. All kinds of stuff was coming out of her body. A huge mess. Don't tell me it doesn't smell. She looked like the girl in *The Exorcist.* I pulled up to the hospital, honking all the way. I hit the horn and flew to the emergency room. I found a lady doctor and an orderly. When we got to the car, the chick was giving birth. She had it right up here.

What was it? I asked.

I didn't even notice, maestro. I ran to get a bucket and started cleaning up the mess. It's not like I've got no feelings. Up here I'm used to seeing everything. And yet I still haven't lost my good feelings. But the new upholstery with all that mess.

Then, with another burst of spray:

It really doesn't bother you? It's floral, the fragrance.

I asked him to let me out a few blocks before. Paranoia again. I started walking. A green Falcon slowed down.

There were three of them in the Falcon. I managed to see that the guy in the passenger seat had a shotgun sticking out the window. They looked at me. And continued on their way.

I raised my lapels, picked up my pace.

The drizzle was impenetrable.

Before taking out my keys, I looked toward the corners. Then I entered the building. Ever since I had Diana in my apartment, no precaution was too great. I rode the elevator distrustfully. And my distrust followed me with the keys in my hand. When I opened the door, I was startled by the darkness and a current of cold air. A gust of wind came from the balcony. In the blackness, through the half-open living room door, I saw a silhouette slip into the bedroom. Diana broke free from the shadows, and her profile stood out against the tenuous light that rose from the street. She was aiming at me steadily. She held the .22 in both hands. When she saw that it was me, she turned around, closed the balcony door, and came over.

Sorry, she said.

I turned on the light. It was hard for her to walk. She put one hand on her belly. And dangling from the other hand, the pistol, like a hair dryer.

Did he call? I asked.

Diana replied to my question with another question.

You didn't bring me a chocolate bar?

She settled slowly into the armchair. Her movements were wearier and wearier now. She left the automatic on a pile of magazines. Then, exhausted, she leaned back and put her feet up on the little table. Her ankles were horribly swollen.

The guerrilla girl who had just nearly liquidated me was once more a mother, worn out by her baby bump. It almost moved me. But I was still frightened. The question popped out of me like a spring. The question that kept hammering away at me. This was a good opportunity to

144

ask her. But the same thing happened to me as with Martín. I didn't have the nerve to look those kids in the eye. But they weren't kids. Or fools, either. That would be underestimating them. And less inquisitive on my part.

Have you used that before? I asked.

Diana regarded the .22 on the coffee table.

What's your problem, she shot back. I told you, Gómez. The less you know, the better.

The silence was dense. You couldn't even hear the echoes from the street.

I've got good aim, Diana said.

In love, too? I asked.

That's my business, she said.

She nervously grabbed the pack of Particulares. She pulled out the last one.

Oh, great. I have no more cigs.

She lit it tensely. And then:

Why didn't you bring me a chocolate bar?

Because you didn't ask me for one, I said.

Am I a big pain in the ass? she asked. It's just that I can't take any more.

Be patient, I said.

If Mara fell, Martín will fall, too, Diana said. She stayed in Rosario. Till our *compañeros* started to fall.

Diana puffed anxiously.

If only Martín can pull it off. The idea is that Mara will split with us. All three of us.

Then, quietly, thoughtfully, she began to make a ballerina out of the aluminum foil from the pack of cigarettes. When she finished, she looked at me.

Here, Gómez. A souvenir.

I held the souvenir silently, the professor recalls.

I can't take any more, Diana said. If he doesn't phone me tomorrow, I'm leaving.

You're crazy, I said.

I'll end up crazy if I stay here.

If you go, I said. And I didn't finish the sentence.

They won't catch me alive, she said.

I should have held my tongue.

If you take the pill, two people die, I said.

We assessed each other for a moment.

I stood up, went to the library and took out the Whitman book. There were some bills inside. Not even two thousand. I offered them to her.

You're crazy, she said.

Take them, girl.

You want to get rid of me? she asked mischievously.

I didn't answer.

Diana bent her head.

Forgive me, she said. I'm messed up.

She burst out crying like a baby. I went to the kitchen and brought her a glass of water. She curled up next to me, and I could smell her cheek, her ear, her neck, her hair. She had a warm scent. Now her crying had subsided.

Now I know what you're going to be to this little one, she said, slowly caressing her belly. I know.

I swear I was expecting what she was going to say.

Its uncle.

Its uncle, I repeated.

Diana smiled. She smiled with tears in her eyes. We remained silent.

I'm afraid, she said.

Me too, girl.

And we held hands.

5 I had grown quite accustomed to Diana's company. Sometimes, when we were having soup, the cold and danger seemed far away. Outside was far away. But later, in the morning, I had to go out to that country which was the outside, the cold, the drizzle, occupied territory.

One evening, as I was coming home from school, I had the feeling I was being followed. It wasn't just a simple feeling. The fear was physical. I felt it all over my body. I stopped in front of a store window and looked behind me, trying to act casual. Two guys who looked like cops were coming up behind me. I crossed the street. The guys continued on their way. I took a deep breath. But the paranoia took over. All of reality was cop-colored.

By now it was night. I went downstairs at the Pueyrredón station to catch the Palermo line. Since it's a double station, I could once again check to see if I was being followed, and at the last minute, like in detective films, hop on a train and hop right off again before the doors closed. I was too slow. I was stuck inside the car. Then I saw him.

The guy, well dressed, hadn't lost his foppish air. He had a black eye, a couple of bandages on his eyebrow, and his right arm was in a cast, suspended by a sling. Nonetheless, he managed to preserve a touch of pride. He was still the sort of guy who worked things out so as to wear his defeats like merit badges. Like me, like so many others. Echagüe was just another example. A relative of his, down on his luck.

His pride dissolved a little as we exchanged greetings. It was hard for both of us to speak.

I've just been to visit my wife, he said. Inés is in the hospital.

We got off at Plaza Italia and went upstairs to the avenue. Maybe Echagüe's being tailed, I thought. I turned around. Imagining they were marking me might have been a fantasy. But not that they were following Echagüe.

I used to check to see if I was being watched, too, he said. At first, when Esteban was alive, I worried like you, Gómez.

The woodsy fragrance of the Botanical Garden was heavy in the drizzle. It was a comfort in the night. The sensation that somewhere there was life.

Echagüe walked slowly. We went into the Galeón, in front of the 23rd Precinct. Beyond suspicion, according to him. Nothing safer than this corner, he said. The precinct station was surrounded by a fence. Policemen with helmets and machine guns at the door. Parked police cars. The inevitable green Falcons.

We're harmless, Gómez, he said. And he adjusted the cast. Two old farts.

We walked into the coffee house. It was crowded. Lovers whispering secrets over two tiny cups. Old women dipping pastries into their tea. Plainclothes cops. Despite their lack of uniforms, their faces gave them away.

We ordered coffee.

A whiskey, too, Echagüe ordered.

We sat silently until the waiter brought us the coffee and the Criadores. After the first sip, Echagüe readjusted his cast, took a running start, and prepared to tell a story:

Look at this ring, Gómez.

He wore the ring on the hand that was poking out of the cast. It was a ring purchased at some hippie store. La Galería del Este, Plaza Francia, someplace like that.

Esteban bought it in Villa Gesell, he said.

The Echagües had a house in Villa Gesell. The house was on one of the boulevards. The back of it faced a sand dune. All you had to do was climb that dune to catch a view of the sea. It was on one of those nights that Esteban confessed his militancy to Paloma. They bought two rings at an artisan's stand. They got engaged on the beach, by the light of the moon. When he saw Esteban wearing the ring, he challenged him: Since when do free-love militants believe in those right-wing symbols?

Now I wear it, Echagüe said.

He twisted the ring around.

After Esteban was captured, he went on, it was hard for us to petition for habeas corpus. The lawyers are scared shitless. Inés kept meeting with the mothers. We used our connections. I got a recommendation at the archbishopric. A country priest received me. When I gave him Esteban's information, he paused for a moment, pushed his eyeglasses higher on his nose, retrieved some lists from his desk. You should see, Echagüe, the priest said to me. Lots of them are boys and girls from good families, people in good positions. Like yours. But they're confused. Young people have invaded the slums, invoking Christ, but also Che. It's one thing to grow closer to the Church and another to give out weapons in the slums. The priest continued browsing through his lists. No Echagüe, he said. Esteban wasn't listed. And his combat name? the priest asked, staring at me over the top of his glasses. Do you know his combat name, sir? he asked me. Some parents do, he said. When they're asked what their child is involved in, they say they don't know. But when the son or daughter loses contact with them, it turns out they know more than you might imagine. So they shouldn't come around now acting like little plaster saints, because they knew their darling boy or girl was involved in something. If they don't give me some facts to help me get oriented, how am I supposed to find out? I'm not God, just a humble servant. If a family loses sight of God, these are the consequences. There are hangmen and there are victims here, Father, I said. Which side are you on? I asked him. On God's side, he replied. And God? I asked, which side is He on? You're not a believer, he said to me. You raised your son as an atheist. That's why he became a subversive. I cut him off: Esteban is a political prisoner. What outraged me most about the priest was that he never dropped his phony country-boy smile. The priest tried to comfort me: I'll see what I can do, Echagüe. You and your wife should make an Act of Contrition. If your repentance is sincere, the Lord will work the miracle. You're not going to help your son by asking questions at police stations or marching around with those crazy women in Plaza de Mayo. The only thing you'll accomplish will be to annoy the military. And they—I'm telling you this because I know them—have lost patience with the Marxists. Tell me, Echagüe, did you ever think your son might be in Cuba?

Echagüe jiggled the nearly-melted ice cubes in his glass. His whiskey had gotten watery. He lit a Parisiennes. He continued:

I grabbed the priest by the collar. I started smacking him. He squealed like a girl. His mouth was bleeding. Two huge guys took me down. They dragged me to a little room. What a beating they gave me. Then the priest came. Believe me, Gómez, the old goat hadn't finished his sermon. That this wasn't the way to find my boy, that I was making things worse, that besides praying, Inés and I should get out of the country. That we should forget about our wayward son. Just as he had forgotten about us. For sure he was in Cuba, he said. That if God had taken him away, it was because we didn't know how to appreciate His blessing. Children are a blessing from the Lord, he said. But they can also be a curse. When someone doesn't take proper care of the Lord's fruit, the Lord punishes. You people were punished, Echagüe. But the Lord's mercy, which is infinite, comes down through me. I'm not vengeful. I understand your infinite pain. Look, since I have no desire for revenge, I won't let them throw you in jail because of your anger. Let's say it was an outburst justified by despair. If you and your wife donate all your belongings to the Church and leave the country, the Lord will find a way to reward your good deed. Think about this proposal you're receiving from the Lord with my intervention. Tomorrow, without fail, you and your wife come to see me. I'll give you the name of a legal office, we'll take care of the details, and then you'll leave the country.

When was all this? I asked.

It doesn't matter anymore when it was, Gómez. There's no more when. All the whens have died.

Echagüe touched the ring. I thought I saw him rubbing it, as if it held some magical power.

We decided to stay, Gómez. A few nights later, at daybreak, the bell rang at home. As usual, my wife thought it might be, if not Esteban, at least someone with news of him. We heard a car taking off, tires screeching. I went to the door. I opened it. There was a box wrapped in newspaper and tied with a string. A shoebox. I picked it up. Inés was afraid for me to open it. It might be a bomb, she said. If it came from the military, I told her, they would have already blown the house up. I cut the string and unwrapped the newspaper. And I lifted the lid. Whatever was inside was also wrapped in newspaper. It had dried bloodstains. And a piece of paper with a message. That we should stop fucking around. I unwrapped what was underneath the message. There they were, in a little plastic bag. I didn't need to see the ring to recognize his hands.

By now it was around eight o'clock. There were fewer people in the coffee house. Echagüe gestured to the waiter.

After that, the business with Inés. I had to check her into the hospital. Into a psychiatric clinic. Echagüe cleared his throat.

Can I buy you a whiskey, Professor?

I thanked him: Some other time.

Yesterday Paloma called, he said. From Barcelona. And I told her.

I crossed Santa Fe. I inhaled the fragrance of the Botanical Garden. A damp, cold fragrance. I turned on Las Heras. I saw an old woman in a black coat with a supermarket bag. She was taking out pieces of liver and throwing them between the railings. The cats emerged from the darkness and came over for the food. I stopped to watch her. The cats mewed madly, entangling themselves as they fought over the liver. The old woman threw more liver and spoke to them, as if in prayer. She didn't say Here, kitty, kitty, or pussycat. My children, she called them. It was a while before she realized that I was watching her. When the old woman finished tossing the bits of liver, the cats fought viciously over the innards. The old woman turned and asked me:

Do you have children?

No, I replied.

She looked at me.

You're lucky, she said.

The old woman searched for more liver in the bag. She threw it against the railings. The cats calmed down.

Do you have cats? She asked.

I didn't answer.

Cats are more grateful than children, she said. Cats come back. Children don't.

The old woman turned her back on me. And continued on her way.

I crossed over to the zoo. I started walking alongside the railings. Now the night and the drizzle had a savage odor. The shit of caged beasts. I heard a roar. Then another. I walked faster.

6 As soon as I entered the building, Ramón came out to intercept me. He'd been waiting for me, he said. Diana, I thought. I must have grown pale. But Ramón attributed it to the flu:

You shouldn't go out walking at night with that flu, Professor. You ought to go to bed and ask your niece to take care of you. Thermal undershirts, mulled wine with honey, and a good sweat. The next day you'll feel like a new man.

Thanks for your concern, Ramón, I said.

I don't know how to ask you, Professor, he began. I know that you've got a thousand things on your mind, and now, on top of it all, you've got your niece here. But Juancito is having trouble with English. The boy has reading problems, and besides, he has bad pronunciation. He needs extra practice—the teacher said so.

And then:

Do me a favor, Professor. Lend him a hand with his English.

The fact that Ramón, a union member of his organization, would ask me to help his kid with English brought back memories. I remembered Aníbal, a meat industry worker, a lover I had in the Mataderos district when the Peronist resistance was just getting started. Aníbal was a delegate at the meat-packing plant. One time I went to meet Aníbal at a bar on the corner of Directorio and Corvalán. It was a winter morning. Then the two of us went to the home of a couple of brothers. In the front part of the house was a barber shop where customers talked about soccer and boxing. Workers from the meat-packing plant, brick masons, laborers, and a Criollo who had tied up his nag in front of the store. At that barber shop, barbarity had degenerated into lesser forms of bravado. Soccer, for example. Auto racing. Sports had replaced the shiv. There was a kid who read comics and spoke English. Britwit, they called him. He was the son of one of the brothers. If memory serves, the kid was the son of the socialist brother. The other one was a Peronist. The brothers had loud arguments. That whole *We the Peronists / all united will stand* was an illusion as long as families were divided into Peronists and the opponents. The two brothers decided to settle their differences with fisticuffs. They put on boxing gloves. I remember the blood, the spectacle of blood. And that boy, Britwit, splashed by the blood. Now that Ramón was asking a favor of me, I remembered all that, while, in my apartment, a pregnant guerrilla girl was waiting for me, clutching an automatic and a grenade.

No problem at all, Ramón, I said. It'll be a pleasure to help the boy.

That night yet another surprise awaited me. My apartment was dark. The only light came from the flickering of a purple neon sign that filtered in through the balconies. The silence compounded the darkness. I was afraid to turn on the light.

Diana, I called out into the shadows.

I turned on the light. And I saw, resting on an ashtray between the teakettle and the *mate*, the note she had written me.

I still have it, says Professor Gómez. He feels around among his folders, chooses one with a black cover and metal rings. He opens it, searches among blank sheets, forms, clippings, and finally comes across an announcement. He opens the rings, which produce a dry sound. He closes them again.

Seeing that note again moves the Professor.

Look, he says. It's a child's handwriting, like a little girl's. Slightly tilted to the left.

Dear Uncle:

There will never be enough words to thank you for your solidarity, the warmth of these nights when a lethal coldness sweeps the streets. I took the dollars. First chance I get, I'll pay you back. You made me feel as cared for as when I was a little girl, but you must understand that I need to find my baby's father. Like the poet says: "I walk on what's left of the dead / without warmth or comfort from anyone / I go from my heart to my tasks." I will miss you.

With all my love and a big kiss from

Diana

7 I had caught another cold, Professor Gómez recalls. The flu medication and the cough syrup hadn't done me any good. And, on top of that, fever. Sometimes, in the teachers' lounge between classes, I curled up next to the Vulcan stove in a corner. The little mouse passed by close to me, not even stopping to cast a glance in my direction. Then I would pick up my pen and hunch over my notebook once more in an effort to ignore my colleagues' conversations. That's why the best thing to do was finish that little essay on Wilde and start writing another on absence. The fact that absence triggered a literary effort to thread together a large variety of poetic images about a romantic void didn't mean that all those variations had nothing to do with the main topic: Diana's departure. Even if she had chosen to leave voluntarily, it didn't mean that it couldn't become a disappearance at the next turn of a corner. In the journal I carried around for stretches at a time, there were visions of comfortless sunsets, sunrises as unbearable as they were interminable, and the drizzle, because the drizzle was always there. Like the cold. That cold trembled in my bones. Always the drizzle, always the cold, always. And this kind of repetition, the phrases hammering away at the same sorrow, were, more than a stylistic trait of my writing, a callus. Because a callus was forming over my heart.

Thanks to a recommendation by Raimundi, I was able to get a special leave of absence. Raimundi, the Philosophy teacher. He had an acquaintance, a quartermaster colonel and a gambler like him. The colonel's wife kept him on a short leash because he squandered at the poker table whatever he had stolen at the barracks. Because of that, gambling, the officer was a close buddy of his. According to Raimundi, the colonel's marriage was always on the brink of collapse. And if she put up with the short circuitry of each gambling debt, it wasn't so much because of the stigma that divorce represented for a military man, but rather because his wife worried about losing his pension when her husband retired. Or kicked the bucket. The fact that Raimundi knew a military officer came as no surprise. This society wouldn't be what it is if the military hadn't always been part of the great Argentine family. From politicians to writers, more than a few have made their way through a military academy. There's no family that doesn't have a relative or acquaintance in uniform. And this single clue, in my opinion, explains why the connection between a philosophy teacher and a man in uniform isn't so outlandish, and through that link, influence at the Ministry that could get me a leave of absence for an indefinite amount of time. With a medical report to justify it and all. It would be signed by a captain of the Cavalry and Veterinary Division, a supervisor of scholastic health who, according to Raimundi, owed some favors to his colonel friend.

I hesitated to accept Raimundi's reference. Finally I rejected it. I preferred to save it for a more critical situation, I told him.

Now, without Diana, time exasperated me. I hardly ever carried my journal. I jotted down metaphysical reflections in spiral-bound notebooks. What else—if you took up writing about absence—could you jot down in times like those without risking your hide. The concept of the soul and the infinite, with their aspirations to eternal transcendence, were less dangerous than concrete, earthly concerns. Every detail, therefore, became a growing obsession: that dripping faucet, a humidity stain, the smell of cold steak coming from the kitchen, swollen gums.

Not counting preparations for work: pencil points, the handwriting on a card, the typewriter key that kept getting caught on the ribbon. Also word derivations and etymologies, chasing from one dictionary to another, an encyclopedia entry, and so on. This use of time had me trapped in a corner. Now my customary paranoia was compounded by tripping in the gutters of solitude. After what had happened, I no longer felt like going out into the street and wandering around in search of a seminal discharge. The lack of desire didn't even bother me. I had accepted it as one accepts the law of gravity. And, in fact, the gravity of my situation was obvious. Those questions that tormented me at times became a pain that accompanied me everywhere. You could get used to the idea of somebody leaving or the death of a loved one, but not to her disappearance. I was sorry I hadn't asked Diana more about her parents. Maybe I could have found a trail to follow there. Because, in spite of the terror, sometimes an unexpected spurt of intrigue that resembled anger came over me, telling me that if only I had a trail, I'd be able to take off and follow it to find her. But my illusion of anger never went beyond that. And it didn't take long to dissolve, leaving me mired in anxiety once more. The anxiety consisted of not knowing. I had grown accustomed to that anxiety. It had its secondary benefits: it protected me. That was how I convinced myself that it was best to close my eyes. And if I couldn't close them, it would be better to look the other way.

I had gotten stuck on that little essay. I was trying to start over, but couldn't. The history of English literature is Irish. I started to trace the etymology of the word banshee. According to my Appleton, it's a spirit whose wails predict a death in the family. I was pondering this when I pulled a chair over to the bookshelf and began leafing through the History of Ireland, a study in three thick volumes. Banshee, I muttered. Banshee. Banshee. It seemed like an invocation.

Then, the doorbell. I got out of the chair, and with my best medical professional's face, answered the door.

Ramón again:

No bills or taxes, he said. A letter. I looked at the sender. I recognized the woman's name. That neighbor of my mother's.

I suddenly felt dizzy. I needed to sit down. It took Ramón a while to understand what was wrong with me. He fretted:

Bad news, Professor? he asked.

My mother, I said.

I tried to phone. After a while I reached the neighbor. It was all over, she told me. She was already resting in the graveyard. My mother had planned it this way.

She said you taught those kids who won on those quiz shows, Sundays for Youth. You'll see my boy on the show one night, she said. He's got an important job. If I didn't tell you sooner, it was because she didn't want me to. Thank goodness death took her in her sleep.

My mother had no one to listen to her in that dying farmhouse by the cliffs, except that one neighbor, the nurse and midwife, the healer. My mother had died a few weeks back. Through the letter, the neighbor had fulfilled the deceased's wish: to let me know when everything was over. If she had written instead of calling me, it was because there was no longer any hurry. When I returned, my mother wanted me to find the store and the house tidy, clean, without signs of wear. According to the neighbor, my mother always stressed that I was a prince, accustomed to hobnobbing in fine places. She knew it saddened me to return to that place, and now that she was dead, her desire was to keep me from having to take care of anything but the inheritance. The only thing I needed to do was to show up at a notary's office in Carmen de Patagones and sign some papers.

Although hurrying made no sense at this point, Professor Gómez recalls, I managed to throw a change of clothing into a suitcase. Then I ran to catch a bus. It was quite a stretch to that place. As the afternoon burnished the bus window, I saw a scene in the countryside and wrote it down like this:

Chimango
making plans
While riding on a cavy

There was something more than mere poetic entertainment, a chance for me to play the Argentine Basho, in that scene, I told myself. I'll simply say this: what I wrote reflected my state of mind. The chimango, that bird of prey, represented anguish, and I was a poor cavy, trying to hide in a pasture. I had no escape. I could feel the chimango's presence, its descent plummeting upon me.

If there had been a hotel in the village, I would have spent the night in a room. I had no alternative, though, but to sleep in the house. I remembered the last time I'd been there, the wind twisting the TV antenna, my mother and I struggling to straighten it out. Not having seen her in the coffin, that fact that she had been unceremoniously buried, turned her into a ghostly presence, like the TV image when the wind twisted the antenna. She remained in every one of my movements. If I had seen her dead, I thought, I could accept her as dead. But not like this. And so my mother stayed alive. Somewhere. She appeared to me in profile, close by. I saw her everywhere. No sooner had I turned around, she vanished. I walked through the house and through the store. She had spent her whole existence there. Suddenly I had the impression that I, too, had never left. I wanted to cry, but my tears wouldn't come. I didn't even cry the next day, when, as the ice melted, I walked to the cemetery through the frost to find her grave. There were marble crosses and tombstones whose names and epitaphs had been smoothed flat by the sandy wind. At the back, toward the sea, was a new grave, with dark, fresh earth, the only one. I read her name on a wooden cross. But I didn't cry there, either.

8 I started walking. Walking, walking, and walking without a destination, sometimes zigzagging across the city and sometimes in a straight line, sometimes from north to south and vice-versa, and sometimes from east to west and back again. Office-filled skyscrapers, government ministries, department stores, shops, houses, warehouses, and infinite walls. Avenues of asphalt and streets of cobblestone. Parks, plazas, the boardwalk, the riverbanks, the shores of the Riachuelo. Train and bus terminals, slums. I walked ceaselessly, like a sleepwalker, lost in my own thoughts. I walked along, lost in myself. I felt no cramps, no fatigue. At times, yes, I shook with tremors. My chest pounded, about to burst; my neck contracted; I closed my mouth, clamping my teeth together. Suddenly it was dark; suddenly the sidewalks were made of uneven brick and the streets of earth, ditches, a rural settlement, patches of weeds, a wire fence, and in the distance, the dim lights of a potholed, deserted road, barely visible in the thickening mist. More than once walls blocked my way, the obstacle of a military operation, and even though every time I came across the repression they asked to see my papers, after checking my ID and studying my appearance, they let me go. And so I continued for a long time. Once I was stopped by a police car. The cops pushed me against a wall, frisked and interrogated me. I got off easy: they, too, let me go. Another time, early one morning, I was nearly run over by a green Falcon. Three guys got out, struck me on the collarbone with the butt of a rifle. They knocked me to the sidewalk. They went through my wallet, my documents. They were high. They kicked me in the kidneys. Unhinged, they argued among themselves. They took the pesos I had on me and then threw the wallet and the document in my face. I was lost. The bus stations and the slums. On those early mornings of mist and frost, I ran into street gangs, scary kids. Once a gang from Lugano got hold of me. They beat me, and later that morning I woke up in Salaberry Hospital. I was still alive. Apparently I didn't appear on death's agenda. Like that other time when I had a reaction to anesthesia in the Argerich Hospital. I didn't have a clue how I ended up at that hospital. A punch in the face had relieved me of three teeth. But I didn't remember a thing. I had to keep my mouth shut. And not just because of the pain. A doctor on duty, a Peruvian girl, told me, as she regulated my IV, that I was recovering from shock. Then she gave me a shot. Considering the symptoms, she said, what I had was wandering syndrome. A frequent condition these days, she said.

In the next bed, handcuffed, was a kid who couldn't have been more than fifteen. Dark, skinny, his face disfigured by blows, burns on his whole body, and his chest bandaged. Bullet wounds, I thought. The cuffs that fastened his hands and feet to the bars of the bed made him look even more like a little Criollo tied to a stake. He was a descendant of Martín Fierro and Moreyra, but also of Namuncurá. I couldn't stop staring at the poor thing.

The kid turned his head slightly toward me. His mug was black and blue from the blows he had received; his eyes were purple.

Don't ask, sir, he said. It's better not to know.

Part Three
THE HOOD

1 I was turning into skin and bone. And on top of that, the fear. Which intensified one afternoon, when, while rummaging through my box of index cards, I came across a bundle of letters in a plastic bag at the bottom. It was from a store in the Once district. The store had her name. The thought that Diana might have walked around there with this bundle of letters gave me chills. I also wondered why Diana had Mara's letters. One hypothesis was that the two of them had had one of their terrible arguments, and Mara had returned them to Diana, like lovers do when they feel their love is unrequited. Un. Requited. Now I paused at every paragraph, every phrase, every word.

Not only had Diana left herself open to Martín's spying on the letters, which would have been the least of it, but she had also compromised her *compañeros'* safety. I took notice of the return addresses. I thought of the successive places they had moved to in secret, an entire geography. There were many residences, always in different parts of Greater Buenos Aires, where Diana and Mara, superficial militants at first, taught reading in the slums, became part of the proletariat, moved to a neighborhood, and then, in syndicates and basic unions, functioned as Montoneras, recruiting combatants. So many return addresses, with such variety, suggested that they were false. By reading the letters, one could determine when Mara had left for Tucumán. And closer by, for Gran Rosario. The envelopes weren't addressed to Mara or Diana, but to Marta and Liliana. Mara was Marta, and Diana was Lili.

Reading the correspondence of those two involved much more than tracing the typical history of young militancy, marking a shift from left-wing reformism to revolutionary Peronism. Intensity, passion: that's what I'm talking about. The fact that Diana had lugged these letters around all that time revealed the density of her feelings. And the fact that, while the sound of a siren, the reverberation of gunshots, frightened screams, rose from the street, I stayed indoors, reading the tragedy of those two like the echo of a nineteenth century serial novel, says less about the two girls than about me. Even though I might have read those letters like a serial novel, it didn't escape me that the novelization of their romance was more real than my analysis of the texts as fictional fabric. They had lived the novel. I, on the other hand, was reading it. That is, my obsession was literature. A second-hand experience.

I asked myself why the hell the girl had hidden the bundle of letters in my library. My annoyance faded when I thought of a good reason: Diana was confident she would survive the terror, that she would save her hide, that she would return someday and pick up the thread of her lost time in her romantic correspondence. If she hadn't harbored that belief, I thought, Diana wouldn't have kept the correspondence.

I told myself that the healthiest thing to do would be to burn those letters, get rid of them, just as I had done with the one I took to Rosario. And yet, when I recalled those tiny pieces flying out the train window, I fell into a web of sadness. I was sure that that letter, the one from Martín to Mara, where he described his suspicions that someone else was stealing her love, now read, contextualized, and related to the correspondence of the two female lovers, would complete a puzzle. I had the feeling that there was literature in those letters, but also a mystery to be revealed. Of course: by submerging myself in those letters, I was reliving the love story of my two friends who had been massacred in the bombing. It had been exactly twenty-two years since their deaths. And now these letters brought them back to me. I began to take note of the thoughts this reading inspired in me. Not only did I not burn those letters. I changed the direction of my essay on absence.

Diana and Mara often resorted to subtext. Dear Friend, they would write, parodying the replies of lovelorn columns in women's magazines. Listen to the cry of your heart, they would write. The Cortázarian affectation of their style was touching, too. Reading it, you realized that the parody of cheesiness concealed—in addition to the fear of embarrassment—the certainty that love is always doomed to becoming kitsch, and when it overflows, it borders on melodrama. And therefore: Vallejo. Now they adopted a gaunt, rainy tone. A soft-boiled Buenos Aires was Paris in a downpour. But they soon recovered their sense of humor. After one of those spates of melodrama that spiraled into a fight, Mara gave Diana the Paul Anka record:

> Hold me, darling, hold me tight
> Squeeze me, baby, with-a all your might
> Oh, please, Diana
> Oh, please, Diana
> Oh, please, Diana

Diana didn't soften up right away. What was she trying to say with that tacky, imperialist crap, Diana asked her. Since neither of them could do without the other, they melted the ice in a few days. Always together; they were inseparable. They prepared for every midterm, every final, together. Since Mara lived in Morón, where her parents had a pasta place a few blocks from the cemetery, when she got out of class, she found it convenient to sleep over at Diana's house. Diana's parents had a store in Once and lived in an apartment on Calle Pasteur. "Sleeping over" was a ruse. They only managed to fall asleep after making love till they were soaked.

In some letters Mara called her Red. Popular wisdom's got it right, she wrote her: Redheads are the hottest. Mara had a mole on her cheek. Diana wrote a poem to that mole. Diana fell asleep sucking her thumb. Mara devoted an entire letter to describing how she slept. Mara liked to watch her sleep as she sucked her thumb; she would remove the thumb from her mouth and insert her own. Then she would suck Diana's damp finger.

When they tried to explain their feelings, they would veer off into a fevered prose, each one flaunting her psychological appreciation of the other. They used all sorts of verbs: project, internalize, experience. On other occasions they went in for poetic prose. What grew when they argued and distance came between them was a "Pizarnik-like desolation." Such literary girls, those two. Before they joined the guerrilla movement, one of them threatened the other with suicide. If one promised to throw herself under a train, the other, not to be outdone, would vow to slit her wrists.

In their letters, one ambition similar to that of all autobiographies stood out: to appear unique. The snares of the self. After an argument, each one would bring up a list of her own qualities and the lack of the same in the other. When they reproached each other for these defects, one of them, the slighted one, humbling herself and speculating, would spill over in a torrent of sublime kindness. One (predictably) imitated Alejandra Pizarnik, and the other (no less predictably) took on the role of Cortázar's La Maga. Sometimes they understood that in that imitation of the literary heroines of the moment, the gestures they mimicked were a caricature. Considering their respective origins, their class background (as people said in those days), there couldn't have been two more unlike individuals than those two. Alejandra, the sharp neurotic, and La Maga, the saccharine little fool.

They also theorized about what was happening to them. In a letter about the previous night, Diana writes to Mara: Pleasure is liberating. Ergo, it is revolutionary. And Mara replies: If Evita were still alive, she'd be a dyke. A quick story whose plot line develops from their first meeting in Latin class, the arrow wound of love at first sight while they studied Catullus, their first kiss the night when Mara went to Diana's apartment to study, tongues and declinations, caresses and verb endings. Just between us, says Professor Gómez, I like to think of those two making out in the shadows.

I could trace between the lines, uttering phrases, descriptions, redundancies, their initiation into Sapphic love, and shortly thereafter, into left-wing Peronist militancy, the inevitable discussion over whether or not to take on armed struggle. Initiation, I say. Here we should point out that their initiation was a joint one. Diana had gone out with a few boys, but she thought of herself as practically a virgin, and Mara, though she boasted of collecting guys and being familiar with all the hotels around the university, never imagined she could become a different Mara in her passion for another woman. What I mean to say: their initiation was mutual. It wasn't a case of one initiating the other. Diana, perhaps, was more elusive; she became bolder the moment when they were so close to one another and then eyes upon eyes, their breath, the kiss, the tongues. Diana, caressing Mara's neck, her hand warm and trembling, sliding down her neck. Mara, in turn, gently squeezing Diana's nipple, said: I love you. I adore you, Diana said to her. And they began to argue over which was stronger: to love or to adore. While they debated—and never resolved—the question, they couldn't live without one another. Everything they felt was superlative: totally in love, blazing hot, dripping wet, they wrote.

They met, along Corrientes, at El Colombiano, El Politeama, La Paz, El Paulista. Their favorite bar was El Colombiano. Around El Bajo, toward the south, they met at Bar Unión and the Anchor Inn. All those bars are mentioned again and again in their letters, making up the cartography and the setting for interminable conversations, sometimes with friends and *compañeros,* other times with boyfriends, because the two of them, intimidated by their love, tried to return, as Mara would say, to the straight path, to put their homosexuality behind them. When they climaxed, especially then, they were overcome by fright, by the uncontrollable. Their affair, they tried to convince themselves, had been no more than an initiation ritual while they were still defining their sexuality. And that made them feel calmer for a while.

And let's not even talk about jealousy. I saw you all lovey-dovey with that little twit from Sociology, Red, Mara accused her, angrily. Jealousy is awful: What right do you have, when you've slept with half the college, Diana replied. Then, the cruel argument. An envelope addressed to Diana contained all the torn-up pieces of a letter. It was a letter she had mailed to Mara. I picked up all the little pieces and reconstructed the text. Diana apologized; she admitted she had been sending mixed messages and recognized that even though she pretended to be so aloof, she was really very fucking possessive. Furious, Mara had torn up the letter, stuck the pieces into an envelope, and mailed them to Diana. The fact that it had been sent by certified mail proved that Mara had wanted to be sure her wrath would reach its destination. A few months went by without their seeing each other. But they suffered what Diana called a relapse. Diana theorized: There is no woman who at some point in her youth didn't experience a homosexual relationship. And the reply came in the following letter: You think that a person forgets afterward, Mara told her. Of course, Diana said. You forget it, like measles. The years go by and you forgot you ever had them. I'm crossing my fingers and hoping it's true, she said. Mara disagreed: Once you've felt it, it's forever. And if you acquired a taste for it, no dick will ever do you any good. In the envelope there was a black-and-white photo, a little blurry, of the two of them on a bike, riding along a dirt road beneath some poplars, wrapped in a play of light and shadow. The sun hits them full in the face. Diana is wearing a baseball cap and Mara, a straw hat. On the back of the photo Diana had written: Once you've felt it, it's forever. After these displays of love, Diana withdrew again. She was trying to distance herself. They needed to place a limit on the homosexual relationship, she wrote. The clinical nomenclature made the thing more rational. Forget about "Sapphic love." The term "Sapphic" made the whole business sound poetic, and she didn't want to pretend not to notice. Homosexual relationship, said Diana, lighting an unfiltered Particulares. Lesbos and Sappho, she maintained, covered up the sickness of this connection. To call what happened to her with Mara a homosexual relationship reassured her. As long as she could baptize that magnetism with a scientific name, she felt calmer: one could talk of an illness and a cure. Deviance, Mara wrote, paraphrasing Lenin. Bunk bed deviants is what we are. Diana, who had been in the Communist Youth Federation for a while, was sketching out a self-criticism in her bursts of remorse. And she managed to infuse Mara, who came from a tradition of catechism, First Communion, confirmation, parochial guidance, and Catholic Action, with doubt. There's a photo where you can see her, still a young girl, in a tournament, throwing a javelin. On the back, she wrote to Diana: I want to nail myself into your heart. Diana was moved by the inscription: My little lesbo, she wrote. And Mara: Keep the secret. It's all well and good to be a whore, Mara said. But a lesbo would be a tragedy for my folks at "La Bella Italia." Because that was the name of her parents' pasta place in Morón.

They'd find boyfriends soon, they told themselves when they had gotten past the guilt. They fought often, whenever their passion became unbearable. Any excuse was enough to make their correspondence go from change of opinion to polemic, from polemic to tantrum, and from tantrum to destructive fury. And now Diana was the one who tore Mara's letter to bits, stuck the pieces in an envelope, and sent it off to her opponent. I wondered what kind of researcher I was, reconstructing those letters with Scotch tape. If my goal was literary criticism, I needed to accept that every critic is a detective. The critic always starts out with a suspicion. And doesn't stop till he proves it right. My hypothesis was that they had kept their mad desire on too loose a leash. Even when they stopped, the hiatus didn't last very long. Besides, it was increasingly hard for them to admit that militancy demands an ideological chastity belt of its *compañeras*. There was no greater chastity than coupledom. A male partner, of course. *Compañeros* and *compañeras*, like Quakers, were supposed to form couples within the same faith. For a while they would hold back. A time that was never longer than a week, because they would cross paths in a corridor at the university, at an assembly, buying class notes.

At those moments of crisis, Diana thought that the most suitable thing would be to take some more time for herself, become stoic. The greater the pleasure, she calculated, the greater the pain. By depriving herself of pleasure, she reasoned, she also limited the pain. Besides, she wrote, pain questions things. Pleasure, on the other hand, is egotistical and only thinks about reproducing satisfaction. It was only a few short centimeters from there to becoming a complacent bourgeoisie.

What terrifies you, my little Jew girl, is guilt, Mara retorted in a jerky handwriting. Spinoza fucked you guys up good.

Diana ground out her cigarette in the bottom of the cup and wrote:

Spinoza, my ass. This horniness distracts us from our path, Mara. It throws us off course.

In another letter, Mara asked her:

Are you talking about the revolutionary path?

And Diana replied:

Homosexuality is a bourgeois sickness.

Sometimes I wonder what the revolutionary path really is, Mara wrote. Considering how similar Stalinism and Peronism are. A state of proletarian children, a state of Justicialist children. The health of the historical subject consists of giving birth to brawny little workers like the ones Carpani painted. I wonder if what upsets the *compañeros* is discovering that we have a clitoris.

You want it all, Diana replied. All of it. Be realistic.

I am. I demand the impossible.

You're greedy.

It's a family trait. The pasta place.

Those were their arguments when they fell into contradiction, as they also called the feeling that was burning them up. All those arguments were really just one, and they had a Maoist title: Regarding Contradiction. Because when they were overcome with guilt, their affair turned into a bourgeois contradiction. As I said, sometimes one of them was the tormented one. And then the other, fearing a breakup, would do the impossible to keep from ending it. It hurt them to realize that they couldn't end it. The revolutionary path, like taking holy orders, required abnegation. Possibly the one who had fewer problems with dedication to militancy, precisely because of her religious education, was Mara. Diana, despite an ostensibly more open upbringing, rooted in Positivism, which included a sexual education, was the one who reproached herself most for having fallen in love, and just as she questioned their passion, she tended to bring up their political differences at every militancy meeting. For Mara, the revolutionary path ran parallel to mystical asceticism. Diana faltered in the face of dogmatism: the revolutionaries' cassock was a denim shirt. Their cross, a machine gun.

I liked looking at them in that photo I found in one of the letters, finding out what each one was like. A beach photo in Villa Gesell, dated January of '69. Mara, curvy and round, in a floral bikini. Diana, skinny and angular, in a one-piece. Mara has long black hair, windblown. Diana, a very short haircut. They embrace as if dancing a tango, glued to one another. They embrace and look toward the camera. They embrace and, cheek to cheek, blow a kiss to the photographer, who, as I would later learn through the letters, is Martín. Behind the two of them are sand dunes. The landscape looks like a desert.

In fact, Martín did take that photo of the pair. According to the letters, at a campsite. Diana was already dating Martín. And she had introduced him to Mara. The truth is that, even though Diana had started going out with Martín, she hadn't managed to get Mara off her mind. It tortured Diana to find herself alone with Mara. And Mara, in turn, who had all her *compañeros* in the organization turned on, couldn't find a single one who could make her forget Diana.

Brutal, those letters in which Mara tells her what she thinks of her hookup with Martín. Mara uses every variation possible to refer to the male member. She boasts of knowing more about penises than her friend does. Don't be smart with me, don't tell me that now you've discovered the noble virtues of the dick. You'll never find a dick that suits you, honey, she writes. Because you're just as much of a dyke as I am, she says. It doesn't change a thing that you suck dick once in a while, not one thing. No dick will ever fill the hole I left in you, Mara writes angrily. Because that hole isn't just in your pussy—it's in your soul. Diana rebels, takes on a calm, understanding tone. She understands her jealousy, she says. But it's true, she writes to Mara: she's fallen in love with Martín. One afternoon Mara runs into Diana at the department library. Diana is seated, studying. Mara surprises her from behind. She hands her a letter: Tell me you get as wet with the sailor as you do with me and I'll leave you alone. Diana considers that the best reply is silence. But Mara understands her silence as a confirmation of her suspicions: Diana isn't really into that boy. Later on Diana writes her that she's made a decision. She doesn't explain. No explanation is necessary: she's talking about firearms.

I immersed myself in reading that correspondence, an activity that was rather a re-reading, always a re-reading, because I went over and over the letters, trying to make sure not one of the many meanings I was beginning to find in them would escape me. The bewitchment that love story held for me was identical to that of a female epistolary novel. Each letter was a chapter of the serial, a new episode, and not only in the literary sense. The bodies' surrender to a growing vertigo that stemmed from the body and stimulated the writing, was always necessary and urgent. It was what connected each letter, like a fragment of an intimate diary.

It's such a risk to write a diary, to confess. At times when confessions are drawn out with electricity, the sincerity of a diary can be dangerous. Sometimes one of them would jot down: It's going to rain. Because the notations often degenerated into meteorology, weather conditions as a sign of their state of mind. At other times both women's writing was encoded in metaphysics. There were letters in which paranoia was so great that they were seized with the obsession of narrating tiny details: the shimmer of the rain at night, umbrellas in the street, reflections in the puddles. There was an interruption in the correspondence. But that interruption didn't signal a dilution of their feelings. From back here, Diana wrote her: Right now I'm getting fed up with this life. Rain seems to pursue them everywhere. It was raining in Buenos Aires, and it was also raining in Rosario. Between one storm and another, the writing of those two sounded desperate. No matter how much they may have realized that a letter, like a journal, is nothing but a fiction one arms oneself with, they deceived themselves, promising each other they'd get together. What Mara wrote now was neither uncontrolled passion nor the dogmatic strength of a revolutionary epic. They were the letters of someone trapped: Last night I peed in my sleep, like when I was a little girl, she wrote. And the only things she could talk about were the stains on a wall, the clatter of a downpour on the roof, a dirt road in El Gran Rosario, where she was now hiding, not knowing till when. It's raining here, too, Diana wrote back from Munro.

The writing in those letters, when read as a journal, was at once a confession and a sinkhole. I descended more than a few times into the authors' inferno. I was after a hidden cache: acquaintances were referred to by their initials. But that trove wasn't forthcoming: I warned you that B. was a little whore, one scolded. She fucks her way to the top. It was also possible to read different points of view in the letters: S. isn't much better, the other continued; you should've seen him at that meeting of the organization, ranting against fags. He says fags should be shot. We're not fags, we're not druggies, we're Montoneros and soldiers of FAR. In the next letter there was a reference to a *compañera* called H.; from the writing you could deduce that she was a girl. I think Martín's hot for you, Diana ventures in one letter. And Mara replies: If I screw Martín, I'll find out how he does it with you. Days later, Diana asks her: With which of the two of us do you like it better? Mara responds: Guess. And Diana, in turn: Fuck all the pricks you like, but no one else's pussy but mine. According to Mara, Diana had a filthy mouth. And according to Diana, Mara was pretentious.

The correspondence, a diary for two hands, had its share of initiation talk, the vagaries of a presumably innocent *I*, naïve and unsuspecting: the author, that fabricated *I*, is always discovering or "revealing" something. Like all texts about initiation, about learning, it narrates a lesson, and consequently the writing turns pedagogical in the worse sense: moralistic. One might ask why it's so embarrassing to reread someone else's diary. If you never learn from someone else's experience, you derive very little from your own, which is almost always embarrassing. In a diary, one writes of embarrassment, resentment, victimization disguised as purity. A paradigm of negation, people who write diaries never draw any conclusions other than the ones that help them confirm their presumed purity and assuage their consciences. Those who write diaries shrug off their responsibility and always blame someone else, who's always the source of their misfortune. Their pain, the result of deliberate bad faith, therefore requires a catharsis that will work like an exorcism. Thus we understand one characteristic of this kind of writing: its temporality, even though it may describe events from before, *now* is when I'm suffering. When I can no longer tolerate what I'm suffering. The compulsion: urgency, unloading, and release. Another *a posteriori* reflection: if you go back and read the past, you have the feeling that someone else lived those experiences. The letters, that diary, covered a little more than five years. And yet reading them was like decoding papyrus in a morgue.

It was still drizzling at daybreak. The inevitable siren in the deserted streets. Absence and loss were the same thing. One was the equivalent of the other. And both of them had been institutionalized. I asked myself which was better—having thus far avoided being blown to bits or continuing in my role as witness, listening, reading, gathering information. And so, in my search for an explanation of the facts, my guilt wouldn't leave me in peace. Survivor's guilt, the guilt of someone with memory, the guilt of someone who has memory but also an awareness that in order to keep on going, it's necessary to forget.

Now, as I relate this, I ask myself who's speaking. I speak for the dead. So, which voice is mine. I am a chorus, I tell myself. Maybe what irked me most was this awareness that I was going to forget, that one fine day I would forget and wouldn't remember a thing anymore. Because at that time I believed it was necessary to forget in order to live. This awareness of forgetting was the thing that wouldn't leave me in peace.

And I opened one of the envelopes again, unfolded the Manila paper, spread the letter out on the desk, and concentrated on the handwriting, using a magnifying glass. In handwriting there is always truth.

2 One morning, before the alarm clock went off, the telephone summoned me out of bed. It was still dark. I waited for a muscle spasm to pass. I took a breath before picking up.

It was De Franco. He was worried, he told me. I glanced at the clock: a little after seven. The way things were starting to look with Azucena, he said. We have to get together, Gómez, he said. I need your opinion. He apologized for his anxiety, for calling me so early, but he wanted to be sure I wouldn't be busy that night. We have to talk. I think I've said it before: other people's pain distracts you from your own. Azucena distracted him from himself. And De Franco, in turn, distracted me from my woes.

That night, when I went downstairs to the street, a southeaster was whipping the city. The temperature kept dropping. Storm clouds moved in from the river, making the pitch-black city even darker. I walked along quickly, my gaze fixed on the cobblestones that passed beneath my footsteps.

The cold was so intense that De Franco waited for me still huddled in his overcoat, at a table in back. Before him were a notepad, a blue Bic, a cup of coffee, and the usual glass of gin. He was smoking and writing in the notepad, but not a poem. Prose.

Some meditations, Gómez, he said. I want to write a little essay on how to write a love poem. It's an essay that favors beauty over sentiment and its improvisations. Falling in love like a kid is no guarantee of the quality of the verses.

I hadn't heard from De Franco since that night when he told me about the *supernatural* events at the chalet in Villa Ballester. It seemed to me that De Franco was trying to downplay the nervousness of his phone call, that he was embarrassed about his anxiety, about having set up this meeting with me. He now regretted, I thought, what he had needed to tell me so urgently. It also seemed to me that he looked more defeated. No matter how hard I tried to divert my attention to his notepad, he wasn't going to make it easy.

I decided to plunge right into the reason for his call.

Azucena? I asked.

Gabrielito, he replied.

He folded the notepad and stuck it in a pocket of his overcoat. His deliberateness exasperated me. As I was already his confidant, his nerves had quieted down. He looked all around, searching for the waiter and waved him over. When the waiter was standing ceremoniously next to the table, De Franco ordered:

Two gins.

What I wanted was for De Franco to tell me about the boy once and for all. But it was obvious that I would have to adapt to his pace. When he told a story, as I've already mentioned, De Franco relived the event, and, in evoking it, he reconstructed the most trivial situations. It was also a matter of telling himself the story to convince himself that what he experienced had been real. Nevertheless, in his more recent tales, it seemed to me that his starring role had been reduced: if there was someone important in the story that he was trying to bring out, it wasn't himself. Nor was it Azucena and her husband. The kid, I thought. What mattered to De Franco, I confirmed, was the kid:

We spoke with him, De Franco spat out. Or rather, Azucena did.

In a dream, I said. Again.

No, Gómez. For real.

179

A psychic, De Franco said. She connected him with us.

De Franco went on to explain:

In circumstances like this, Gómez, when it's a matter of *supernatural* events, any recourse is valid. What do you have against the occult sciences?

I didn't answer.

Up till now, De Franco had been an object of pity, an emotion that included anticipated self-pity. Because now I was toying with the notion of how I would feel at his age if I hadn't found anyone to take notice of me. And so I felt a pleasurable kindness when I agreed to be his confidant: it made me feel better than what I was. The *supernatural* events disturbed me less than senile dementia. In De Franco, I was starting to find a developing alienation. But let's get to what De Franco told me that night.

A southeaster wasn't going to scare off Azucena. The least of her concerns were the wind and cold. I'm boiling, she had told De Franco. Azucena had left dinner prepared for Pedrito, some boiled meat, vegetables, stewed fruit. A neighbor would take care of him while she was gone. And please don't forget his medication, Azucena pleaded. Stuck to the refrigerator door with a magnet, she had left a list of his medicines and a schedule.

Then Azucena put on a wrap, De Franco put on his overcoat, and before leaving, she kissed Pedrito on the forehead. De Franco patted him on the back:

Be strong, *compañero*, he said to him.

And he felt like he wasn't saying it to the paraplegic in the wheelchair. He was saying it to himself.

I can picture them: Azucena and De Franco, waiting for a bus in the drizzle. The bus would take them to General Paz. Then they would take another one west. And then one more, Azucena said, which would leave them at the side of a road. From there they would have to take another bus to Hornos, a small town before Las Heras. At the bus stop they had a spat: Azucena wanted to make the whole trip by bus. De Franco was opposed.

I can picture them, the professor says. The two of them walking along, shrouded in the southeaster. De Franco trying to put his arm around her shoulder and Azucena shrugging him off. She didn't like anyone's arm around her shoulder. They weren't youngsters anymore. It looks ridiculous, she said, two old folks acting like young snots.

The train was more comfortable, De Franco said. The bus is faster, Azucena grumbled. De Franco said that the train was cheaper. Azucena argued with him. According to the neighbor, the bus was faster.

The neighbor who was caring for Pedrito, Azucena told him, had been consulting Doña Lidia for a long time. She had cured her shingles. Because her shingles was an affliction that had been brought on by witchcraft by someone close to her. Not only had Doña Lidia cured this neighbor of shingles. One Saturday, when the neighbor's daughter-in-law was ironing a dress to wear to a wedding, she was electrocuted. That was how the neighbor realized that it was her daughter-in-law who had caused her harm. Doña Lidia had great powers, according to Azucena. De Franco kept insisting on the train. And he finally convinced her.

The whole trip by train. A train from Villa Ballester to Retiro. At Retiro, a subway train, a combination of subway lines to Plaza Once. There, in Miserere, the train to Moreno, getting off at Merlo, where they would transfer to another train, the branch that goes toward Las Heras. They argued for a long time: De Franco loved trains. They lent the trip an air of adventure, he thought. Life looked different from the window of a train, he said.

How that girl suffers, said De Franco. Don't say anything, Gómez. I know what you're thinking. That I'm attracted to the novelistic part of the situation, that it gives me an illusion of latter-day Romanticism.

You can also remind me that Gabrielito isn't my son, even though he bears my name. If you're thinking of it that way, you're wrong. Gabrielito isn't my son, but he could have been.

3 That afternoon at the station, Azucena and De Franco were the only two passengers to get off the train, with its four broken-down, grimy cars. Hornos, a station with a single platform, in the middle of the countryside. The wind was colder now, or at least so it seemed to De Franco. He would never stop regretting, not only the impulse that made him accompany Azucena that afternoon, but all his impulses. His whole life long. When he went over his imaginary autobiography, he found that impulses had been a constant. He liked the word *impulse*. But the same word that could light up a poem could turn out to be fatal when applied to life. When a person writes his autobiography, he thought, he should be aware of this business of impulses in poetry and in life. Its consequences, fortunate in the first case, were always ill-fated in the second.

The station remained behind them. He and Azucena walked along a row of bricks placed on the dirt. The bricks threaded around the crossing guard's box and his pre-fab dwelling. In a nearby field, a cow and a horse grew bored. As they left the station and headed into the elements, they followed a road parallel to the rails and crossed a small soccer field. Azucena had a paper with directions to Doña Lidia's house, but De Franco, straight and tall, almost a full step ahead of her, was the one to take the initiative. Lagging a few steps behind him, Azucena concentrated on the little map that her neighbor had made for her and gave De Franco instructions.

It has to be past that general store, Azucena said.

And De Franco:

All right, leave it to me. With one finger on the little map, he asked himself: Shouldn't it be over there?

And so they continued arguing till, at a break in the road, they saw that the sky had been darkening: they were lost. And no one around to ask.

Leave it to me, said De Franco.

They looked for the road; they waved down a pickup truck that had stopped a few meters ahead. The man behind the wheel was a local who smelled like a corral. De Franco vaguely recalled an ode to the countryside by Girondo. But this wasn't the time to bring it to mind. Can I give you a lift, the local had asked. It's real close by. And then: Make yourselves comfortable. The three of them rode squashed together in the cab. A few drops began to glisten on the windshield.

It wasn't a long ride. The local stopped just short of a bog. I didn't wanna get you all muddy, the local said to them. Then the donkey won't pull for me, he said. Doña Lidia's house was that one behind the grove of trees, he pointed out. The house must be just a shell, De Franco thought. He noticed a few cars: new, luxurious models.

Even high-class people come to see Doña Lidia, the local said. Because Doña Lidia talks with the spirits, lots of people come. For their missing folks and for the dead. Because missing and dead aren't the same thing.

Azucena agreed. Then De Franco thought that if the guy hadn't brought them right up to the house, it probably wasn't so much to avoid getting muddy as it was on account of a superstitious fear of that place.

It's a fact that night falls earlier in winter, De Franco said to me. But that afternoon it seemed to me that night had come on even sooner, Gómez. There were red streaks in the sky.

The house, as De Franco described it, might have been the shell of a ranch house from the late 1800s. The wind shook the eucalyptus trees above the corrugated tin roofs. A windmill turned incessantly. The walls surrounding the property, once a barricade, had degenerated into a pile of worn bricks. There was a knocker on one of the doors. De Franco banged it three times. You could hear some dogs barking, as well as the cackling of hens. After an endless moment in the drizzle, just when Azucena, soaked through, had anxiously started asking him to knock again, a voice came from inside.

I'm coming, screeched an annoyed, high-pitched voice.

You'd never have guessed, Gómez, that the voice belonged to a dwarf. Seriously, Gómez. Doña Lidia's assistant was a dwarf. Bald and lame, besides. He wore a military jacket with gold buttons. But not so much a military uniform, though; if you looked at it closely, that jacket could've been a bellboy's outfit. A bellboy in cloth sandals, that is. The dwarf shooed the dogs away, a real pack of feral dogs. They didn't stop growling till the dwarf yelled at them a few times. Warily, the dwarf asked us if we had arranged in advance for an audience. Audience, I remember he said. Azucena mentioned the neighbor as a reference, and added that she had phoned the day before and a spoken to someone named Lindor.

At your service, said the dwarf.

We walked by a well. And then, preceding us along the veranda, the dwarf asked:

First time you've consulted Mamá?

First time, Azucena said.

Mamá is in great demand today, the dwarf observed. People are in bad shape. I'm afraid she's going to get sick on me. She's strong, but the consultations sap all her energy.

The dwarf led them to an enormous room heated by a brazier. In addition, there was an aluminum pitcher that filled the atmosphere with the scent of eucalyptus buds. There were a few leatherette armchairs and some curved Viennese chairs. But there was no place to sit—such was the number of men, women, and children who were waiting. They

185

came in all ages. De Franco didn't have to look at a certain guy twice to determine that he must have been an important character. There were also some nattily dressed types and two TV starlets. He later found out from Azucena that those two starlets were in a soap opera. But among those waiting, the majority were poor, sick folks wearing the expressions of the hopeless. Some had a vacant gaze, while others stared at a fixed point. Some muttered unintelligible phrases, while others shook their heads, denying their fate. De Franco and Azucena saw an old man with Parkinson's and, next to him, a fat woman with varicose veins. Although those belonging to a higher social status tried to avoid coming into contact with the needy, they all looked like family. That expression like a prisoner's when visiting hours are over, the eyes of a dying man who doesn't want to be left alone. All of them were desperate to save themselves or save someone else. One old man sitting in a corner had an amputated leg. And beside him, a pair of dilapidated crutches.

When he saw De Franco and Azucena walk in, the amputee nudged a boy who was sitting beside him. Get up and give your seat to the lady, he ordered. Azucena said no, really, she was fine just the way she was. You could see how affected she was by sitting next to the amputee. But she couldn't refuse the offer. The dwarf left, and De Franco remained standing to one side of the door. For a few seconds he felt like running away, just like on that stormy night in Villa Ballester.

The dwarf returned with a tray and two steaming cups. He extended the tray first to Azucena and then to him. It was an herbal tea, a brew De Franco found undrinkable: he thought he could taste lemon verbena, rue, and valerian, but there was another flavor that eluded him and was similar to onion.

The dwarf smiled at them.

To cleanse yourselves, he said. This infusion purifies.

The brew was disgusting and nauseated him. As he was impressionable, De Franco thought that the tea must have had hypnotic effects. He drank it, looking at Azucena out of the corner of his eye. Suddenly it occurred to him to ask himself how he had gotten to that point. He remembered when Azucena was his student in the department, a magnificent girl, as he had called her in his poems. He thought about her life and about his own. He thought that both their destinies had already been written the first time he laid eyes on the girl.

Among those waiting were women who told stories of Doña Lidia's curative prowess. Not to mention her telepathic powers. That psychic had a direct line to the Beyond, she did! There, where free will, science, and religion failed, was where her work began.

The dwarf peeked into the room again.

Zamudio family.

The old Parkinson's victim, the amputee, the fat woman with varicosities, and the boy who had given his seat to Azucena all followed the dwarf. The two starlets grumbled. The fops muttered, annoyed. The pompous ass protested that he was there first, that Doña Lidia couldn't dither with his time like that. The man was the perfect image of a has-been playboy: graying hair, tanned. When he moved he gave off a fragrance. He wore a blue jacket, a cream-colored polo shirt, and gray pants, and he had on suede shoes. He rebuked the dwarf. Touching his watch with his index finger, he said:

My time is very valuable.

Mamá sees people in order of their suffering, Lindor replied soberly. It was clear that the dwarf enjoyed the power Doña Lidia had bestowed on him. More than her valet or her secretary, he was her foreman.

De Franco looked at Azucena. Azucena returned a bovine glance. De Franco took her hands. He caressed them. And while he caressed them, he wondered how many times those hands had brought him pleasure. Not only that, but also how many times those hands had prepared his food, how many times they might have combed his hair, and how many times they had come together in a prayer for his life. De Franco felt exhausted. Then he looked at the graying playboy, who was now uneasily jiggling his car keys.

Leukemia, the man said. My daughter has leukemia.

The man was ready to cry.

The two starlets didn't take their eyes off him. That air of an aging leading man impressed them. The kind of Don Juan with status who can lead any unwary girl off to bed, he thought. The fact that the man's daughter was suffering from that incurable blood disease didn't affect De Franco as much as recalling that he himself was already aging when he seduced Azucena, his student. He chided himself for this moralistic preconception about the guy. Then the man, checking his watch again, mumbled:

I'm not going to make the meeting at the shipyard.

4 De Franco paused to summon the waiter and order another round of coffee and gin. The congestion was causing him problems; he coughed. He must have caught that cold in the country, he said. He also said that at a certain age you need a woman to keep your feet warm on winter nights. At a certain age, he said, like ours. De Franco took his time getting back to the story, and when he picked up the thread again, he recalled how the scent of eucalyptus clung to his clothing.

Then he described the woman:

A milky-skinned giant, De Franco said. As soon as you walked into the place, curled up in a black armchair, at a little table covered in black oilcloth, her white presence, almost phosphorescent, overwhelmed you with its elephantine dimensions. She was of an indefinable age, somewhere over sixty. Her white hair in a bun, pale, with a few freckles on her face. Maybe she was around seventy. Dressed all in white—her shawl, her woolen dress, stockings, and shoes—all white, Doña Lidia was an imposing figure in that office, tenuously illuminated by a lamp shaped like a candle. And this ambiance didn't smell as much of eucalyptus as of a mixture of incense and camphor. De Franco thought he could make out a table, a telescope, shelves with bottles, droppers, and test tubes. He could see portraits hanging on the walls: one of them was the Blessed Ceferino. He also saw some powders and weeds in various boxes, classified and labeled, a pharmacopeia that intrigued him. Maybe among those bottles there might be some cure for his congestion, he considered. But he thought it would be rude to ask. He and Azucena walked slowly toward the woman. Doña Lidia appeared to be dozing. But she wasn't:

The unhappiness in the universe is immense, said Doña Lidia. But faith cures everything. Have a seat and join hands.

No matter how much De Franco might have wanted to keep his agnosticism intact, his poetic sensibility got the better of him and he turned suggestible. Azucena's hand was cold and damp.

What brings you here, the psychic asked. Illness or a person?

A person, Azucena said.

Tell me his name. The whole name.

Doña Lidia jotted down the name, made a few calculations, and after completing a numerological exercise, smacked her lips.

Relative? asked Doña Lidia.

My son, Azucena replied.

Your son is a spiritual creature, Doña Lidia remarked to both of them. An idealist.

Azucena didn't clarify that the son was hers alone. And that pleased De Franco.

The boy's energy is more cosmic than earthly. A celestial force. What's going on with him? the woman asked.

She didn't give them time to reply. She herself responded.

Disappeared, said Doña Lidia.

Maybe you can . . . Azucena began.

The woman cut her off. What was he involved in?

The woman studied each of them with severe shrewdness. She riveted her gaze on Azucena and then on De Franco. It wasn't an interrogation, De Franco would recall later, as he told me about it:

She wasn't pressing us, Gómez. But she was scrutinizing us. You didn't have to be a visionary to confirm what was happening to us. Kids don't disappear because the bogeyman comes and takes them away, godammit. Azucena and I couldn't have been the only parents to seek help from a psychic. Witchcraft, the Tarot, the stars—any racket will do to give parents back their lost hope. The old folks go back home clutching a religious stamp, a talisman, a prayer, but at the first corner they come to, a green Falcon passes and wipes out their illusion.

To De Franco it seemed like an eternity went by while Doña Lidia studied them.

Gabriel, De Franco heard. Azucena had pronounced her son's name.

He's a good boy, Azucena told her. An idealist.

In the beginning everything was one, said Doña Lidia, closing her eyes. But then the one became legion. All young people are idealists. It's a bad time for spiritualists. There are evil magicians in the government. They're powerful.

I want to know where he is, Azucena said. If he's alive.

The plan is always found in the name, said Doña Lidia. The archangel.

My name is Gabriel, muttered De Franco.

Doña Lidia put out her cigarette:

In the name of the Father, she said, crossing herself. Karma comes before the Father. Past lives have an influence. Karma. And now Doña Lidia uttered a prayer, crossing herself. Azucena crossed herself too. And she jabbed De Franco with her elbow so that he would do the same.

To accept gain as well as loss, muttered the gypsy. Men become confused when they search. In the name of the Father, the woman crossed herself again. All those who have a body, suffer. In the name of the Son. And wherever there is searching, there is suffering. And of the Holy Spirit. Amen.

Azucena nodded.

Now give me your hand, my child, Doña Lidia said.

And to De Franco:

You too. The energy will come together. Don't talk to me. Let me concentrate.

What happened next, Gómez, De Franco started to tell me, would remain forever in his mind just like the other night in Villa Ballester. The giant took a deep breath. De Franco felt as if she was sucking out all the air in the room. He felt short of breath himself. Doña Lidia's breathing was a deep bellows. When she expelled the air from her lungs, she seemed to be emitting a warm, damp current of air that enfolded everything around her with her minty breath. Suddenly the breath turned into a repulsive vapor. At the same time, the pressure of the woman's hands became more intense. De Franco feared for his finger bones, imagining he would never again hold a ballpoint pen, write a poem. He wanted to pry his hand loose, but he was too embarrassed. He turned toward Azucena, terrified.

The giant's eyes were rolled up in her head, and Azucena was tipped backward. Beads of sweat dotted Doña Lidia's forehead. After a huge belch, she finally spoke, but not in her own voice:

Mamá, the giant said in a little baby voice. Mamá, Mamita.

Gabrielito, whispered Azucena. It's you.

The giant bucked, tugging on Azucena and De Franco's hands. In her trance Doña Lidia seemed as though she was trying to stand up, but she nearly fell over backwards. Azucena and De Franco held her up. Doña Lidia shook her head no, like an interrogation victim. She started shaking from side to side. Her convulsions came from electrical charges. De Franco pushed Azucena away. Doña Lidia uttered a few hoarse groans. Then a rale. It must have been then that the dwarf entered and came to the giant's aid.

Here I am, Madrecita, he said, climbing on top of her.

He grasped her face, gave her mouth-to-mouth respiration, and after slapping her, he turned to the couple and ordered:

Help me with her bra.

While Azucena and De Franco tried to figure out how to lay the giant down, Lindor kept whispering:

I'm here, Madrecita. It's all right.

Doña Lidia, still agitated, gradually regained consciousness. Then, as Azucena and De Franco lifted her by her armpits, she settled back down in her chair. She gestured to Lindor. The dwarf removed her shoes and brought her some slippers. They, too, were white. There was terror in the woman's eyes. De Franco embraced Azucena, but she rebuffed him and knelt before the woman, seizing her hands. Azucena wanted to know, De Franco recalled. But Doña Lidia, stunned, kept refusing. Less vehemently now, but still refusing.

My madrecita needs to rest, the dwarf said. Come back another day.

I want to know, Azucena said. Gabrielito.

Doña Lidia, with tears in her eyes, held Azucena's head in her hands. To see that giant crying like a baby, Gómez, it just broke your heart. A few minutes before, she had been in a trance. And now she was sniffling.

Bring me the syrup, Lindor, the woman groaned. And fasten my bra, *che.*

Right away, Madrecita, the dwarf said obediently.

I told you, my dear, the giant tried to calm Azucena. To look for truth is to suffer. There are places I can't enter. I don't have the power. You think I know everything. I didn't study with Mandrake. Don't ask me for the impossible, said Doña Lidia. I can't and I don't know. The evil magicians.

One more time, Azucena begged. I want to hear him.

Lindor returned with a glass. But it wasn't syrup. De Franco realized that it was cognac. Doña Lidia quaffed it with a single sip.

Tell me, Azucena pleaded. Where are they keeping him.

I can't, dear. My body won't let me.

Why, Azucena asked. Why can't you bring him here.

I can't see his face clearly, Doña Lidia said. I can't, because of the hood. Maybe it's not even him.

Azucena didn't understand. And neither could De Franco. At first.

Doña Lidia stood up and kissed Azucena on the forehead.

God be with you, my dear.

And then, turning to the dwarf:

Walk these people out, Lindor, she ordered him. Don't charge them.

Azucena rummaged in her handbag, took out her coin purse. But Doña Lidia stood firm.

Not one cent, dear.

Let's go, Lindor commanded.

It was hard for De Franco to drag Azucena out of the house. As they crossed the waiting room, De Franco noted that the number of visitors had grown. He wondered how much time had passed since they walked into the consultation room. It was obvious that during their consultation, he and Azucena had been transported, suspended in a cosmic zone. Among those waiting were three or four small children playing dice on the carpet. De Franco imagined that those children playing dice amid the suffering had some hidden meaning that escaped him. They, too, raised their eyes to watch them pass through.

De Franco and Azucena walked behind the dwarf. Night had fallen. The dogs followed them to the entrance of the property. If they hurried, the dwarf said, they could catch the last train to Merlo. They mustn't miss it, he told them. Now the southeaster was twisting the foliage of the eucalyptus trees. And then, in a reproachful tone:

You exhausted my madrecita's energy, he protested. The doctors warned her not to see clients so many hours in a row. You think you're the only ones who have a problem. Lots of people come here, just like you. A whole bunch of them, because of their children. And they wear out my madrecita. She tries to guide them, but she can't. The evil eye is one thing, and even cancer, all well and good, but she can't work with this business of the disappeared. She barely makes it to the threshold. The evil magicians won't let her through. Besides, you've got to understand, every so often the Falcons come poking around here. Don't get us involved.

194

5 There's always a limit. No matter how far we might plan to go, both on earth and in philosophy, there's always a limit. The Great Wall of China or El Cañadón de la Mosca: a limit imposed by nature, but also by human beings. A point beyond which you just can't go in certain situations, whether because of physical or intellectual risk, curiosity, or the need for answers, an explanation that can justify our journey, until, as I say, we run into the edge of a cliff or a wall. Regardless, you can't think about the limit while you're busy investigating. Maybe it's also a good idea not to build up your expectations too much. In that search, sometimes there are stretches where, through disorientation or cowardice, you stop till you can regain your spirit and start walking again. I'm referring to the investigation I found myself in without wanting to get too involved. For example, I was trying to find out how the story of Azucena and De Franco played out. Somehow, as the poet's confessor, I could play dumb and deny the fascination that Azucena's search awoke in me. It's not my story, I said to myself. It wasn't my story, true, but insofar as I, as the reader of that story, was concerned about how it would develop, there was also a search of my own whose meaning eluded me. The same thing happened to me with Diana, the fascination with finding out what had become of her. The letters, my access to her private life, to her love affair with Mara, the epistolary novel they had started—the whole tale needed a conclusion, and as long as I had no more news of Diana, it would remain unfinished. Sometimes I told myself that I wasn't just a reader, that my habit of passing through other people's lives must have a meaning: to complete a story in which, no matter how much I may have considered myself a witness, I wasn't really, not so much. A witness is involved, too. A word for the times, if ever there was one: committed.

Many times I wonder why I had been so interested in those lives, in documenting them through their testimonies, writings, clues; in rummaging through their stories, inserting myself in each and every tiny corner of their secrets. Why, I also wondered, hadn't I devoted myself with similar zeal to investigating my mother's past, the man who had emptied himself into her and then fled. There was and is an answer. I focused on others, using them as a mirror. But the mirror was often cloudy, the vision fuzzy, and many times the image that others reflected back to me was distorted according to each one's tragedy. Mine, by comparison, was a lesser tragedy: kidnapping and disappearance had not yet kicked down my door. On the other hand, this was a danger I preferred not to think about. And yet, it lay in wait all the time.

6 You didn't have to be a genius to figure out that the bag from the boutique with Diana's name was from her father's shop on Calle Pasteur. I looked up the address in one of the first letters. The sender was from the building on whose ground floor the shop was located. I started walking by the show window. One morning I saw the storekeeper, an elderly, hunched redhead, come out of the store and walk into the building next door. The façade was of black marble and had an iron door with glass and bronze railings. It was right next to the Argentine-Israeli Mutual Association. Sometimes I walked by the door and other times along the sidewalk in front. As I came closer, I slowed my pace and looked at the plaque with the number. Considering that numbers have meaning in Kaballah studies, where there's a number corresponding to every word, I wondered if the number of that building contained a hidden meaning. At the same time, numbers had been the identity that the Nazis branded onto their prisoners in the concentration camps. I couldn't ignore these digressions. They had a function: to muffle my fear of facing the situation and entering the building once and for all. There was always a policeman at the AMIA. I had scoped out some of the uniformed guards. I walked right by them without looking at them, playing the fool.

I took me a while to look inside the building. I started to come by on certain mornings, when the custodian came out to empty buckets of water on the street. That was a good opportunity to slip inside: while the custodian had his back to the entrance and was hosing down the sidewalk, I could sneak right in. If the guy stopped me, I could whip up some excuse: a fifty-something with glasses and a mustache, decked out in an overcoat, suit, and tie and who walked erectly and confidently, would never arouse suspicion. I had also considered other possibilities. To pass myself off as an inspector from a government agency. And so days went by, and I still hadn't summoned the courage necessary to enter that building, take the elevator up, and ring the doorbell of that apartment where Diana's parents still lived. If I wanted to have news of her, I said to myself, they were the ones I'd have to see. If they *had* any news, that is.

I also wondered, if I should actually see those old people, how to introduce myself. What would I say, I wondered. What would I tell them. How to explain that I knew their daughter, about whom they possibly had no information, the information I was seeking: to know what had become of her. Maybe Diana wasn't one of the disappeared, I said to myself. Maybe Diana was safe; maybe she had managed to cross the border into Brazil. For sure Victoria was about to be born. Or maybe she had been born already. I was sure the baby would be a girl. This conviction about the birth of the baby was, more than anything, a hunch that was trying to latch onto a certainty: Diana was safe. But I had no access to any fact that might allow me to confirm my hunch. My conjectures fed on fear. But that fear didn't allow me to go beyond speculating. I kept wondering how to introduce myself to her parents, how to explain my visit to them, how to get them to trust me and to tell me what they knew, if, in fact, they knew anything. When paranoia and fatalism take over daily existence, we are all suspect, and, at the same time, we suspect everyone else. I had come up with two stories to explain my presence to Diana's parents: the first, imaginary, consisted of pretending that I had been one of her teachers, that before dropping out of school, she had confided to me her decision to join the armed struggle. But this story had too many holes. Diana's parents would peg me as an impostor; they would imagine I was a plainclothes cop. The second story, the truth, presented its own complications: telling them how I had met Martín, how Martín had brought Diana to me, how she had taken refuge in my apartment until, at a moment when I was briefly distracted, she went away with her pregnancy and that woven bag in which she carried a grenade and a gun. That wasn't the kind of news her parents would expect, but at least, I consoled myself, it wasn't the story of her capture or her death. But then again, this story, the real one, had its complication. What would happen, I asked myself, if I gave them those love letters. A dirty trick, I replied to myself. The only thing these poor old folks need is to find out that their daughter had turned out to be not only a guerrilla, but also a dyke.

And so I continued on my way.

7 When it wasn't drizzling, there was a fierce, lacerating wind. In those days, on those nights, memory dug deeper all the time. Whenever I peeled an apple, I remembered her. In those days, on those nights, I wondered what she had felt during the years I was away. When my mother was alive, I didn't miss her like I do now. I knew she was there. I knew she was thinking of me. And the fact that she was thinking of me made me feel alive. The distance separating us had meaning: according to her, I was fulfilling a dream, I was someone, because my mother was convinced that, with my degree and a job, I was someone. Now, on these days, these nights, but more at night, I was broken up with grief. I could describe what a son feels when he misses his mother. But not what a mother feels when she misses her son. Especially if she has no idea where he is. I wondered if I would be capable of bearing such uncertainty. I tried to understand. But in these times understanding is no consolation. Not for the absent one and not for the one who misses him. Absence had never been so like death than on these days, these nights.

8 As I pass by that building again, always just about to enter, but lacking the nerve to do so, I wonder if the apartment might be under surveillance, if there might be cops posted upstairs, in the corridor, at both sides of the elevator, on the staircase. I must come to terms with my cowardice, I tell myself. Terror is the great justification I have at hand. The military have rendered daily life suspicious. And they've turned neighbors into spies. When we're all potential spies, we're all suspicious: I mustn't be ashamed of fear. But fear is shameful. And fear keeps us locked up.

And yet, when I think about those mothers who, with their white kerchiefs and the names of their disappeared children, march round and round Plaza de Mayo every Thursday, I can't forgive my cowardice. Esteban wasn't my son, I tell myself. Neither was Martín. I hardly knew Diana. And whatever I did find out about her, her secret, a secret more hidden than her participation in the armed struggle, I realize, was through those letters. I'd never even laid eyes on Mara. And just like with Diana, whatever I managed to learn about her was through their correspondence. Those letters were nothing but literature, I told myself. Feminine literature. Epistolary literature. It was the novelistic form they had lent to their passion to dramatize its secrecy. In the romantic correspondence between those two, beyond their erotic details, you could read their fantasies and frustrations in the face of a reality that stigmatized them. Neither the revolutionary catechism nor the armed forces' social re-education program provided that degree of passion.

Once again, as I lose myself in these thoughts, I wonder why I have to get involved in this mess when none of these kids—because for me they'll keep on being kids—when none of them, I say, were my flesh and blood.

9 One morning around that time, Ramón confronted me. He wanted to know if I'd forgotten about Juancito. He was having more and more trouble with English, he told me. According to him, the teacher at the institute where he sent Juancito had told him that the boy was easily distracted, that he didn't concentrate. I apologized to Ramón. My niece's visit and the disruption caused by my illness were a good excuse.

It's not good to be alone all the time, Professor, he said. Just look at me: since that old nag left me, if I didn't have Juancito, I would've gone nuts. She probably thinks that by her leaving me, the boy would screw up my life. But she did me the greatest favor ever. Because the good part about having a kid is that it takes a person's mind off the idea of suicide. Excuse me for butting into your personal life, Professor, but what you need is some company.

Don't get upset, I said. Send the boy to me.

And so it was that on certain afternoons, when school let out, Juancito began coming for his English tutoring. When a person is on the downswing, he can even develop affection for a flea. That's what happened to me with that pudgy little brat. So he won't have to break his hump like me, the father had said. So he'll have a future. And when Ramón said "future," there was an echo: I thought of Diana, of her unborn child. Ramón went on: So he'll study one of those fields that make money. Business administration, for example. So he can become an executive in an important company. That's what Ramón told me he wanted for Juancito. I was prepared to lend Juancito a hand. But Juancito wasn't just thick—he was a kid utterly devoid of self-confidence. His lack of confidence, I thought, was the same thing the Indians must have felt high in the hills, as they watched the troops below who had come to slit their throats or shoot them. Juancito brought me back to the origins of my own blood. I was condemned to being a half-breed till the day I died. And it was better if I simply assumed that destiny, not so much as an act of fatalism as of history, a condition imposed by class. What Juancito was giving me was a genuine lesson in my own identity.

You're not concentrating, boy, I said to him. What are you thinking about.

Juancito didn't flush or turn red: he went brown.

The sky is red, he muttered in English.

Juancito, now thoroughly bewildered, stared intently at his reader. I saw how his chubby fingers grasped the pencil.

I summoned my patience one more time.

I won't tell anybody. You can be honest with me, Juancito. What are you thinking about all the time.

About Raphael, Juancito replied timidly. When I'm older I want to be like Raphael.

Juancito turned an even darker shade of brown. I understood: he regretted the confession and was afraid of reprisals.

You can relax, I said. I won't say anything to your father.

And then:

Well, yes, maybe the best thing would be not to tell your father you want to be like Raphael.

I told my dad, he confessed.

How did he react, I asked.

He smacked me one, Juancito said. You wanna be like Leo Dan, fine, he told me. But like Rap-hael, never.

The *ph* sounds like *f,* I said.

I wanted to put that conversation aside. It broke my heart to see Juancito like that, so contrite. My concern didn't escape Juancito's attention, either. He tried to shift my mood:

Wanna see me do my Raphael impression? he asked.

Juancito went all out doing his number. He gave it everything he had. How could I stop him. He didn't even give me time to accept. He turned the chair backwards and moved toward the center of the room. He pushed the coffee table to one side and stood on the rug.

Then he wet his lips with saliva, fixed his hair to resemble the way Raphael wore his, picked up an imaginary microphone, pulled it close, shut his eyes, took a fleeting pause, and let loose:

> *I am the one*
> *Who pursues you every night*
> *I am the one*

I couldn't interrupt him. Then the phone rang. When I picked up I could hear heavy breathing, and in the background an auto repair shop, a radio, shouting.

When I hung up and turned around, Juancito was standing on the rug, waiting, hanging on my opinion, hoping I would congratulate him.

And so I did.

10 That night Walter came back. It was nearly midnight. It hadn't been too long since we'd last seen one another, but it seemed like years to me. His hair was longer, a shadow of beard. He was wearing a different black leather jacket. A new, expensive one. His breath smelled of alcohol. And he had a more querulous tone.

What are you staring at?

You surprised me, I said. It's been so long.

Don't act like an idiot.

I was overcome by fear. I felt dizzy. I tried to blow it off:

You want some coffee?

A whiskey, Walter said.

He went directly to the kitchen, opened the pantry, and took out the bottle of Smuggler's. He didn't look for ice. He drank it straight. Half a glass. I poured myself one, also. I needed it. I hoped that the whiskey would control my shaking. Then, without putting away the bottle, he returned to the living room. He took off his jacket.

It's strange you didn't split, he said.

Because? I asked.

More than one professor has messed up young people. They sent them to the front, and now they play innocent.

I don't know what you're talking about.

Walter took off his shoulder holster and laid the .45 on the table. He pulled out a pack of cigarettes and stuck one in his mouth. Then, with the same hand, he grabbed the lighter, a gold one, and struck it.

If you only knew who this Dupont guy is, he said. A financier for the Montoneros.

Each one of his gestures was rehearsed. He seemed more and more ashamed of having been hot for me. But guilt accomplishes nothing. Guilt turns us into moralists. And regret doesn't redeem us from pulling dirty tricks.

I stared at the .45 on the table. Walter followed my gaze. We had gone through this kind of situation before. A single slip on his part would be enough to let me grab the weapon. And then what, I asked myself. I'd shoot, assuming I had the courage to do it. And if I eliminated him, what would I do with the body. Killing is never the problem, I thought. The problem is what to do with the stiff.

Want me to cook something? I asked. It's not good for you to drink on an empty stomach.

Fags oughta have kids, he said. You'd be a good mother, Gómez.

He poured himself another whiskey.

I called you from work.

Lots of work? I asked. You don't look good.

What happened with Evangelina fucked up my life.

Women are a problem, I smiled.

Smile again and I'll knock your teeth out, he said. Evangelina was my little girl.

Sorry, I said. I didn't mean anything.

Evangelina, the youngest, he said. The one who was a little saint. The one who'd had open heart surgery. It didn't do a damn thing. She died. Just like Beti, she was. A miniature Beti. You don't know what we went through. Beti wanted to kill herself. Even though we have two other kids. I'm not saying that's a consolation, but two kids are two kids. Two handsome boys, you should see them. I told her we should try again, I could get her pregnant again. Why not try for a little girl, I told her. She closed her legs on me, Beti. I want my little doll, she said over and over. I want God to bring her back to me. I even thought I

207

could find her a little girl baby. I could find her one that looked just like Evangelina. But there was no way. Beti fell apart on me. I had to take her to a psychiatrist. She was mute all day long. I had to watch her all the time so she wouldn't do herself in. I had to get the boys out of the house, send them to some relatives. Just as well I did. I sent them off to Venado Tuerto. Because Beti threw herself under a train. Ever since then I haven't slept. No sooner do I close my eyes than I see Evangelina. And when I try to hug her, she's not there anymore. And I have to take a bus to go see her. I buy the ticket. But when I try to get on the bus, I can't find the ticket, and the drivers won't let me on. Other times, when I get to the station, the bus is already leaving. And it takes off, just like that.

Walter fell silent. His eyes were on mine, but he couldn't see me through the tears. I gave him my handkerchief. The same one on which my mother had embroidered my initials. The same one I had given Diana when she was crying in that same chair.

Tell me if what happened is fair, Gómez. All day long I kill myself working. All day long. Tell me why God did this to us. Why God destroyed my home like this, huh?

God doesn't exist, I was about to tell him. His misfortune gave me a sick pleasure. If I considered myself better than him, I shouldn't lower myself to the pleasure his suffering brought me.

Walter stood up. He stumbled as he did.

And he almost toppled over.

I held him up. It was a clumsy maneuver. He slipped his arm around my shoulder. Or something like it. The two of us nearly fell over together.

He rearranged the holster, the weapon. He put on the jacket. Then, the door slamming shut. And the echo of the elevator.

I picked up the handkerchief. And I washed it in the bathroom.

11 I remember the light in those days. Whenever I go through my papers and find, in a journal, a magazine, photos of that time, the city in those images is always flooded with winter light. You may tell me that it's just my impression, but that's not true. There's a grayness, the gray of drizzle and cold, blurring outlines, as if they were about to disappear in a night that's always on the verge of falling.

Although we never resign ourselves to the idea of the finite, we end up accepting it. I know that in those days it seemed easier to accept. What wasn't so easy to accept, however, was the uncertainty. *Chau*, if I've seen you before, I don't remember. Parting wasn't the same as forgetting. Saying goodbye to someone meant remembering all the time. Because in that constant remembering there lurked all the darkness that terror forced you to imagine. That black thing was always there. It was a cold sweat, dark and sticky. And it wasn't death, either. It was worse than death. A disappearance wasn't the same thing as a death. The gruesomeness of death, of earth, the dark earth, worms, decomposition of the flesh—all that corruption of matter was something you tried not to think about—but deep down, since it had its own logic, the logic of nature, its irrefutable truth, you ended up accepting it, and once you did, it allowed you to forget that sooner or later you yourself would become that rot, that nothingness. But the other thing, all the stuff that surrounded death yet wasn't death, but rather, like I say, worse than death, was always there, like your own shadow. And a person can't get rid of his shadow.

One morning I woke up, looked around, and imagined I wasn't there. I looked at my clothes on the chair—shirt, tie, pants, shoes, socks, the books on the floor, the notebook, last night's glass of whiskey, and then, when I stood up and walked from one end of the apartment to the other, I took note of everything just like a ghost would. I had turned invisible and I was an absence. I wondered what I was like when I wore those clothes, smoked that ground-out cigarette in the ashtray, underlined in that book, and now, standing up, not altogether alert, as I poured myself a cup of tea, the same thing: this was the cup I used when I was here, and this view through the window, the buildings, the antennas, the sky, the gray sky, the sky I used to see when I was here and was myself and not this sensation I was having now, the sensation of a subjective camera, incorporeal. I remember that I thought: If I'm not here, it's because I'm an absence. The sensation became entangled with the feeling of death, the dead man who comes back and sees how life goes on without him, but it wasn't death. What that sensation had in common with death was absence. It was more the idea of absence than of death. But if there was an absence without a demonstrable death, I thought, then I was one of the disappeared. And when I had this thought, it dawned on me: All this stuff that's happening to me, including my horrible insomnia, I said to myself, is the result of Diana's leaving.

There were times when my essay on absence seemed unbearable. On the one hand, I couldn't give up writing. And on the other, I felt like I was repeating myself. If my words, my sentences, were repeating themselves, it was because there were certain words I couldn't pronounce, and my vocabulary had shrunk. I wondered if the monotony I seemed to notice in what I had written might not have been the foreseeable result of what happens when a person tries not to call things by their names, when they overdo the subtlety, which in this case was not as attributable to deliberate ambiguity as to fear. To call things by their names was to risk one's hide.

When I couldn't stand writing anymore, I would go down to the street, into the night, the explosion. The excitement of the chase always ended up with the consolation of a sad fuck.

One morning as I was returning home, I was startled by a voice behind me.

"Don't turn around, Professor," Martín ordered. "Be cool and keep walking. And go into the building."

I opened the door and Martín slipped in quickly. I was shocked by his elegance. Overcoat, suit, tie, short hair, and a trimmed, military style mustache. I recalled his father. After my friends had been massacred in the bombing, after the "Liberating Revolution" had attacked the seat of power and taken over the country, destroyed by his wife's death in the bombing that he himself had launched, his father was named director of a public agency. His wife, Delia's, book was in my hands. As well as a bundle of letters, the Sapphic correspondence between the author and her lover. I hadn't planned to give the novel to the Captain, but the letters, yes. Even more than revenge, it struck me as an act of poetic justice. I relished the idea of throwing an exchange of letters in his face that, even more than proving him a cuckold, revealed exactly what kind of cuckold he was.

I remember meeting with the Captain at a bar on Avenida de Mayo. I remember how he thought of me as a blackmailer: name a price, he said. I remember that it was humiliation, more than anger, that prompted me to say to him: She was your wife, not mine. I got up and left. I left him alone with the letters. From the corner across the street, protected by a flower kiosk, I could see what he was doing. As he left the bar, he threw the letters into a trash can. I waited for him to go away before scooping up those letters, which I still have.

Professor Gómez falls silent and pours himself a glass of cold tea as the hush and calm of the night begin to spread. He looks around; he seems to be listening to shadows. Then he reflects:

I think I've already told this story, he says. I'm repeating myself, as usual. History repeats itself, like the tango says. The past returns. It always returns. Low tide, high tide. But the second *mise-en-scène* is different. The tide brings in something else. For a moment I thought it wasn't the son, but the father, who was standing before me.

You're your old man, I was about to say.

But I bit my tongue.

12 Martín couldn't bear the idea that Diana hadn't waited for him. He shook his head from side to side. He collapsed into the chair.

I brought the whiskey. I put the bottle and two glasses on the coffee table.

Martín was staring at the ashtray containing the butts Walter had put out there. I picked up the ashtray and took it into the kitchen. I was afraid. But I regained my composure, telling myself that Walter wasn't the type to show up two nights in a row.

She couldn't stand being locked up here anymore, I said. She waited for me to leave the apartment and then she took off.

I found the note Diana had written me and handed it to Martín.

He lowered his head, took a swig.

The story, their story, all of it together, had come down on his head with the void Diana had left. It might've been the whiskey that loosened his tongue, but it wasn't just the whiskey. Martín needed to talk. He needed to tell someone. Urgently, like someone who's kept a secret bottled up for a long time. They had lied to him about the story, his own and others'. And he, in turn, had lied. It seemed to me he wasn't talking about what he knew, just as a writer, even when he believes he's writing about what he knows, no sooner sits down and takes paper and pen in hand than he starts to realize that, in fact, one always writes about what one doesn't know, that writing a story, just like telling one, means finding cracks in it, fissures that resemble those deep gashes formed by an earthquake. Martín spoke, quietly, seriously. It also seemed to me that I wasn't the one he was telling his story to. He was telling it to himself. At the same time, he was trying to convince himself that it had been true and that he had lived it. Telling it to himself made it more real.

As Martín told me about the romance, Professor Gómez said, I tried to fit together those scenes I had read about earlier in the correspondence between the two women in love. I tried to place each episode in the timeline I had created while reading the letters. Managing to connect the episodes in successive chapters didn't surprise me as much as did the virile frankness of the guilty macho who now could not forgive himself for both his betrayal of his *compañera* and his absence. For a moment I thought that if not for Diana's departure and the risks she faced, Martín would never have blamed himself for cheating on his girl.

13 I've just come from seeing my father, Martín said.

More than seven years had gone by since he'd left the villa in Cogh-lan. Everything was the way he remembered it.

The memorabilia, a half-burned flag, the naval stamps, the galleon replicas, battleships, corvettes, and torpedo boats. Everything in its place, but all of it coated in dust. He wondered how old the Captain must be now. Over sixty, he calculated. Martín saw the family photos. The portraits framed in wood and silver. He stopped to study a picture of his mother, still single, mounted on a sorrel horse on a ranch. Beyond that, another photo: his mother smiling, with the frigate *Sarmiento* in the background. There were his parents, as newlyweds. There they were in another photo with their baby. In yet another, he, at age twelve, in his first naval uniform. Martín didn't remember that his father had developed so many photos. He wondered how the Captain could wander among the pictures of his victims. Maybe his father, hidden away at the villa, had fulfilled an intimate self-flagellation ritual, a daily exercise of penitence in pursuit of expiation. But there was another possibility, one that, knowing him, seemed more real: by living alongside the images of his victims, they had ceased to be victims. Possibly just a pretext, like Homer's characters, for the delight of the gods. His father was the type to think that way, he said to himself. This was the sort of irony he appreciated. The Navy, a classy branch of the military. We don't stink of shit. Martín understood: time had convinced his father that his victims weren't victims. When he launched the bombs on Plaza de Mayo that afternoon, he had simply gone there to meet his destiny.

In his double-breasted blue blazer with its gold buttons, his white shirt, and the kerchief around his neck, like the captain of an imaginary cruise ship, his father was a ghost that blindly conserved his style in a decadent, spectral atmosphere. Martín had hoped to retain some memory that would force him to unsheathe a filial greeting. But he didn't have any. No memory at all. His good memories were of his mother, and all of them were from outside that villa. For example, when his mother took him and a friend downtown to a movie one afternoon. Martín remembered her friend's name. Lía, he uttered. I remember her name was Lía, Professor. And she was a journalist, I think. I also remembered just now, that same time, the two women in love, a movie theater on Lavalle, the darkened auditorium, the kid in an English schoolboy uniform sitting between the two of them, and how behind his back and on top of the headrest of the seat he occupied between them, their fingers intertwined.

I'm sorry if you've forgotten something, the Captain greeted him sarcastically. I threw out all your things.

His father hadn't changed, either. If anything, he had grown harder.

Now that you people are retreating, the Captain went on, you're sorry.

I didn't come to ask forgiveness, Martín said. Or to forgive you, either.

I don't know what you're talking about.

Martín lowered his eyes. He didn't like doing it. It infuriated him that his father might interpret his gesture as an act of cowardice. He's not my father, he thought. He recovered and looked at him: I'm not his son, he thought. But no matter how hard he tried to distance himself from this man, the same blood ran through his veins. I deny your blood, Martín thought. If we were to face each other in combat, I wouldn't hesitate to shoot, he thought. Nor would he have hesitated

216

to give the order to fire if he had to. With no mercy. Pity demeans us, his father used to say. It's either the half-breed hordes or us. And we won. Martín was about to say to him, mentally using the familiar *vos*: If I had to shoot you, I'd do it. *Tirar contra vos*. It embarrassed him to say *vos* when rehearsing that sentence; it was too soft; it eliminated the distance. In effect, if the formal *usted* had any advantage, it was that of detachment. *Usted* was a ditch lying between them.

I had to talk to him, Professor, said Martín.

I kept feeling as though Martín wasn't saying this to me. He was saying it to himself, trying to convince himself. Just as he had tried to convince himself before, that night, at the villa in Coghlan, that he wouldn't fall apart when he rang the doorbell.

We're both military men, he said to the Captain.

You're wrong, *che*. You're not a military man. You're a little crook with delusions of grandeur.

Please, said Martín. An armistice.

What are you looking for, the Captain asked. For me to understand? To admit that what you did was just a childish rebellion? We soldiers aren't here to understand, but to act. Men of action. We'd rather make our mistakes in action. Not like you people, idiotic tools of the Soviets that go around claiming to be Peronists. Give me a break. And shacked up with a Jew, besides.

I could've drawn my 9 millimeter and pulled the trigger, Professor. Not that I didn't want to. It would've been so easy. Nobody would've been sorry. The people's justice. A single shot. I could've picked up the automatic and, with a steady hand, fired a shot into his forehead. A clean, straight shot. His body would've fallen backward. The impact would've shoved him against his relics. One shell, just one, would've been enough to avenge the innocents. But I needed to be cool. I had come to negotiate. Tactics and strategies. But I was burning with curiosity. How could he have known about my relationship with Red. I had never discussed her with him. Not even on those evenings before

I left. Those evenings when we had such strong arguments about the revolution. Banditry by morons, he called it. The armed forces will act like they did in Algeria, he told me. And he'd been right about that. In the end, the repressive measures were those of the OAS. But now I had to know:

How do you know about my *compañera*.

Naval intelligence, he replied. Or do you take us for idiots.

She's pregnant.

The Captain clenched his teeth. Martín thought that his father was swallowing his bile. He took a few steps backward. He turned his back on his son, breathing heavily. A controlled panting. Instead of containing himself, Martin thought, he would have rather seen his father slam his fist against a wall, throw an ashtray at a painting, break something. But that wouldn't have been like his father. The Captain detested stridency. He might have been deranged, but his derangement consisted of stiffness, formality. The Captain treated him like a subordinate. A naval officer is a man of honor, he used to repeat when Martín was a kid. A gentleman. Someone who never loses his style. We're a blond weapon, young man, you know what I mean. And you are one of us. One of us, Martín recalled. That was how that Captain talked to him when he was a boy.

But Martín hadn't turned out to be one of us. All he needed to do was to look at his profile in the mirror, the *lumpen* appearance he had acquired lately: messy hair, a beard, the dirty shirt. If a guerrilla fighter was supposed to blend in with the middle class, by changing his hideout, moving all the time, sleeping in a basement today, in a shed tomorrow, hiding in a freight car, always fleeing while his comrades fell like flies, he would soon end up looking like a vagrant. His father must have been disgusted with his appearance. As he grew older, the Captain's derision had matured along with him.

If they catch us, I said, we know what we're in for. I'm just asking you one favor, I said to him. Save the baby.

Your mother was pregnant, too, the Captain said. If it was a girl, we were going to call it Marina.

14 I couldn't just stand there listening to him. But I didn't want to give him the satisfaction of an outburst. I thought of Diana. I thought of her swollen belly. I kept my cool. We were still testing one another out.

In a war there have to be codes, I said to him. I'm asking you to save your granddaughter.

And why not the Jew?

I had to contain myself, Martín said. The old man was trying to wound me. He knew how. Where it hurt the most.

My *compañera* is a combatant, I said. She accepted the commitment to die fighting. But if they take her alive, we both know what they'll do to her. I'm not asking you to save my *compañera*. I'm asking you to save what she's carrying of your blood. Maybe that will save you from hatred . . .

I don't believe in salvation, you know. We Navy men aren't candle-suckers like those Army fools.

The Captain took his time before asking:

Why didn't you think about it before you knocked her up, he said. What more do you want of me.

Nothing more.

And now I can ask you a favor? he said to me.

He was dismissing me with his gaze:

Go take a bath, he said in that sarcastic tone. You stink. Clean yourself up, change your clothes. You can find some decent clothes in my bedroom.

I have to go now, the Captain said. I have a dinner with some friends. Take your time, but when I get back, I'm hoping not to find you here. Before, you were the one to abandon this house. Now I'm the one throwing you out.

He turned his back on me and walked toward the door. I watched him walk away. I thought I was seeing him for the last time, Professor. I would have loved to spit on his offer, but I was in no condition to reject it.

I hadn't bathed in a long time. I shaved. I used his cologne. Even though I was clean now, I felt dirtier than ever. I went into the bedroom. On the nightstand he had another photo of my mother. I didn't want to think anymore. I opened the closet, chose something from his wardrobe, put on this suit, this overcoat, and took these glasses from a drawer. I found the Ballester Molina among his shirts. I remember how as a kid I used to admire that weapon. I dreamed that one day he would let me fire it. He never did. And now I had it right there, at my disposal. I considered stealing it. I picked it up. Looking at myself in the mirror, I was suddenly aware of it: our physical resemblance. I looked like his younger brother. I left the pistol where it was, closed the drawer, walked away from the mirror, stuck my automatic in my waistband, kept the pill, left, split, bye-bye.

I swear, Professor, I thought it would be harder for me to ask the old man for such a favor. I needed to forgive him, I think. I was giving him an opportunity. When I left the house, I refused to look back. I had to hurry to avoid running into him. I wouldn't have been able to bear seeing him again. But I did.

Three Falcons were turning the corner and coming toward me. I had gotten about half a block away from the house. The shade of the trees covered me. I pulled out the 9 millimeter, hid behind a tree trunk.

From the darkness I watched the three Falcons go by. I saw them stop in front of the villa. I saw them get out of the cars. I recognized them: they had been with me at the Naval Academy. The old man got out last.

He had ratted me out.

I managed to escape among the shadows, turn the corner, and reach Avenida de los Incas.

15 Sometimes Raimundi, the one from Philosophy, emerged from his racing magazine to seek me out. Sometimes his racetrack stories distracted me for a while. His favorite was one that had happened to him in Rome.

In those days I was young and had traveled to Rome to study at a seminary, he told me. I became interested in St. Augustine. I had gotten a scholarship from a Catholic university. But I squandered my lire gambling in the Trastevere. If I kept it up, I'd have to go home early. I resisted as long as I could. But one afternoon I was overcome by temptation. And I went to the horses. There was this horse named Fedor. With a name like that I couldn't lose. He turned out to be a useless nag. And here I am. Use your head, Gómez. Luck is everything. Especially these days.

That afternoon we were alone in the faculty lounge between classes. Raimundi had frittered away a family fortune on gambling. A casino chip, a card, a number in the football lottery, or a favorite at the track— it was all the same to him. Rumor had it there was a file on him at the Ministry for having been caught placing bets with his Logic students at the Nacional San Martín track.

I'm telling you with all my philosophy background, Raimundi would say. Sure, you won't take me seriously because I'm into luck. The only thing that counts in this life is luck. Believe me, it even matters for the kids who've gotten involved in political shit. For example, that student of yours who was kidnapped a few months ago. He had no luck. The kid bet and lost. Whether they picked him up or not depended on a bunch of circumstances. Today, more than ever, history bears me out. To stay alive and kicking is a matter of chance.

It's not as simple as that, Raimundi, I said.

Just follow my argument about chance, Gómez. My theory is confirmed by the military forces in power. Why do some people escape and others don't. You can't tell me that in every roundup the only ones captured are those involved in politics. No, my dear friend. It could happen to anybody. Whether or not our name shows up in an acquaintance's datebook. The individual and the whole. Everything has to do with the individual. And we have to do with the whole. They take the target alive or they don't. If they take him alive, either he dies along the way or he makes it to the grill alive. If the target swallows the cyanide, he escapes. He escapes and so do we. If they don't give the target enough time to swallow the cyanide, they give him the *picana* and the *submarino*. And here we have two possibilities: either he rats you out or he doesn't. You don't have a fucking thing to do with any of it, but for sure, the dude uses you as a wild card. First he rats you out to buy time and so that his buddies who really *are* militants can escape. It could even happen to me, and I'm no player in the game of politics. We're all in Death's datebook. And don't tell me that story of the medieval knight who challenged Death to a game of chess in order to save the lives of a circus troupe. Total bullshit. Death doesn't play chess. Death tosses dice.

Then Raimundi glanced around the teachers' lounge, as if someone else might have heard us, and whispered conspiratorially:

Just between us, Gómez, confidentially. You can't hide your sympathy for the dissidents from me. Don't be afraid; I'm no blabbermouth. But be careful: your fear is obvious.

Raimundi passed me the newspaper: I'll leave you the copy of *Clarín*, Gómez.

Then I saw the photos and the article. I was dumbstruck.

Raimundi must have noticed my reaction:

It's enough to browse through the papers. They're sawing off our legs, Gómez. Remember. Crutches. Bet on the crutches.

Seeing his picture in the paper took me back to the past. The kid in his olive-green English prep-school uniform, so poised for his age, what was then known as a sensible child. Martín, sitting calmly at the Richmond, sharing the table with his mother and her lover, both women madly in love but intimidated by the boy's presence. Delia thought that bringing her son along on certain dates with Lía would dispel suspicions about the nature of their relationship, but it was a risk, anyway. He saw Martín sitting between them in a movie theater on Lavalle, while behind the boy's seat, they held hands. He saw him on another afternoon, very self-assured, walking along Avenida Santa Fe holding his mother's arm as she went to meet her lover. Even though Martín didn't reach his mother's shoulder, he held her arm as if he were already a naval cadet on parade. That afternoon on Santa Fe was just months before Delia and Lía were to die beneath the Naval Air Force bombs and a mere couple of years before Martín ceased to be a boy and became Cadet Ulrich. I saw Martín again, now a full-grown man, though with the vanity of youth, just as I had found him a few months earlier beneath the arcades of the Banco Hipotecario, before the ring of Mothers. I saw him with his bushy Mexican mustache, his cable-knit sweater, his sheepskin jacket, his jeans, and suede boots. I thought about his three changes of uniform: the English prep-school uniform, the National Academy cadet's uniform, and the civil uniform of the Montoneros. Once more, just like back in '55 when my friends died in the bombing, no matter how hard I tried to exorcize my pain by writing, literature didn't cure me. Literature was a hideout.

Tell me what kind of poetry there is in this *Clarín* article:

SUBVERSIVE CELL DISMANTLED

Rosario. (Télam.). Following an intense intelligence operation in Greater Rosario, military forces located a house in which a subversive cell was operating. In the early morning hours, when the occupants put up resistance to the raid, a heavy exchange of gunfire ensued, continuing till dawn, and resulted in the deaths of two subversive elements identified as Martín Ulrich, aka Cacho, and María Laura Campodónico, aka Marta. In the basement of the dwelling a clandestine printing press and a large quantity of weapons and explosives were found.

The one in the photo was Martín. And she, the girl, María Laura, must have been Mara. She was pretty. Very.

I asked Raimundi if his offer of a special leave of absence was still good. He could make it happen whenever I wanted, he told me. I just needed to let him know. The time had come, I said. Then I went to the director's office. Once more I asked for sick leave. This time it would be for an unspecified period. Outside, the street awaited me. And what awaited me, once more, was terror. Terror and drizzle.

16 One morning I got up, put on two sweaters, one of them right over my undershirt, but under my shirt and tie, and the other on top of them, slipped on my sport coat and overcoat, and took a bus to the Once neighborhood and then the train, heading west. It was drizzling, as usual, and when it wasn't, a polar wind sliced my face and penetrated my bones. Even though I was wearing two pairs of socks, my feet were frozen. I couldn't wait to get off the train and start walking to try to warm up a little. From the Morón cemetery, it was quite a few blocks to the return address on Mara's first letters. When I finally got off the train, as I passed the flower stands at the cemetery; it seemed to me that the fragrance of the roses, carnations, jasmine, wasn't a fragrance: it was the frozen air of funeral parlors. Bringing a bouquet to the dead, I thought, was a way to beautify reality, the reality beneath the tomb-stones and their vases, the subterranean world, underneath the earth, the flesh that detaches from skeletons, decomposition. Those who were able to place a bouquet on a grave at least had the certainty that their dead were there. The remains of their loved ones rested one meter below the surface. I asked a young flower vendor for the address I was looking for. He gave me a series of complicated directions. A woman from another flower stand came over and tried to orient me, but her directions weren't any clearer. I thanked them, picked up my pace, and continued walking along the cemetery wall.

I walked for some time, heading for a neighborhood where the streets were improved. On both sides of the street were ditches. The cross streets were of unpaved dirt. And beyond them were open fields.

There are some neighborhoods in the provinces that still retain a small-town character. Anyone who goes there and isn't from those parts is an outsider. And an outsider is always suspect. I was feeling foreign enough in the world without causing suspicion in this neighborhood. A police van pulled up alongside me. I forced myself to walk straight ahead, arrogantly.

A neighbor woman coming along with her shopping bag looked at the police van and then at me. The same thing happened with some kids who were chasing a ball on the corner. They stopped, looked at the van, and looked at me. And the same thing occurred again, I realized in those few seconds, because they were seconds, with certain neighbors: an old woman sweeping, some girls coming out of a kiosk: they all looked at me. When the van faded in the distance and turned down a side street, I took a breath. I was about to turn around, go back to the station, hop on the first train. But I pulled myself together.

I saw the sign with the word "Italia." The rest of the name was tarnished, rusted, and almost illegible: "La Bella." The store was no longer a pasta shop, but a shabby general store. I thought of a joke Mara had written to Diana about the importance of *fusilli* in combat, even though the name of that pasta had nothing to do with Falcons or fusillades. In that letter, Mara told Diana about her fights with her father. The Dago maintained that Perón was Il Duce. His daughter was crazy if she thought Perón was a communist. Perón was going to give the commies that same thing he gave the Blackshirts: castor oil. The father had been a Blackshirt. He knew what he was talking about.

The woman behind the counter of the general store was a shriveled Italian in her sixties. I knew right away that she was Mara's mother. She was waiting on some laborers, slicing cheeses and mortadella for them on the machine. The woman and the laborers all looked at me. *Qué tal,*

I greeted them. *Qué tal*, they replied. The woman didn't greet me. She looked me over between cutting chunks of feta. She had pale blue eyes.

What do you want? the woman asked.

Go ahead and help them, I said. I'm in no hurry.

Are you an inspector? she asked. Another inspector from the city was here last week.

I want cigarettes, I said.

We don't sell cigarettes.

Criollita crackers, then, I said. I'll wait my turn.

She and the workers scrutinized me. Then the men turned their backs to me. I couldn't stop staring at a black-and-white photo of a young woman, in a silver frame on a shelf, next to a Bagley almanac. The picture had a few bay leaves and a little religious image between the glass and the frame. And the young woman was Mara. It couldn't have been anyone else. She must have been no more than fifteen in the photo, but you could still see a budding physical development in her, a bust like those of Italian movie starlets of the 60s. I compared that photo to the one I'd seen in the newspaper.

The laborers left with their cheese, mortadella, and some bread. Looking mistrustful, the woman put the crackers on the counter. I tried to engage her in conversation.

There was a pasta shop here, I said.

There was, she said. Before.

That girl, I said.

What about her.

I'm just saying. She's beautiful.

You didn't come here to buy.

I'm not a cop, I said.

Then you're one of them. One of the ones that filled up her head.

The woman grabbed a knife lying next to a block of Gruyère.

You people filled up my little girl's head. You killed her.

I started to back away.

You're mistaken, I said.

You people ruined this house, she shouted. And she turned toward the curtain that separated the shop from the area in back.

The old man emerged from the back room. An old Italian guy, but tough. Bald; veined, callused hands. Now the woman was shouting in dialect and the old man was glaring at me. He snatched the knife from the woman and started to walk around the counter.

I didn't stick around and wait. I went out to the street, trying not to run. I had to stay calm. But the old man was coming up behind me. The corner seemed farther and farther away.

The woman shouted: Murderer.

And then:

Police, she shouted.

Fermati, paisano di merda, the old man yelled. He was panting, chasing me with the knife: *Che ti amasso.*

Some neighbors came out into the street. Then I ran. Two, three blocks, I ran. I turned at each corner, in a frenzied zigzag. I saw a bus approaching and waved it down. And as soon as the bus stopped, I jumped on the running board and grabbed on tight. I couldn't catch my breath; I had a stitch in my chest. I sat down in the last seat and looked back.

I got off the bus before it arrived at the train station. My undershirt was clinging to my back. I searched for my return ticket to Once. Standing on the platform, I looked to both sides. Men, women, employees, some nuns, laborers with little bags slung over their shoulders, students with folders. On the opposite platform was a girl with Lennon-style glasses and a baby in her arms, a backpack, and a woven tote bag.

The train to Once was pulling into the station when three guys surrounded the girl. Before the train could get between the two platforms, they grabbed her. The girl screamed, but one of the guys covered her mouth. The other grabbed the baby, and the third one, the tote bag. They forced her mouth open, struck her on the back of the head, in the stomach. The baby was crying. She spat till she vomited. They dragged her off. The guy carrying the baby stuck it under his arm. After that I didn't see anything else. The train prevented me from seeing. The doors opened and I got on.

We passengers avoided making eye contact. No one had seen anything. Maybe I hadn't, either. The train picked up speed.

Sitting next to me was an over-the-hill, bleached blonde. She smelled of cheap cologne. She was chewing gum. I lowered my eyes. She wore a black coat with leather elbow patches and a purple corduroy skirt. She had on shapeless, high-heeled shoes, and there was a run in one of her stockings. She was clutching her handbag and flipping through a copy of *Para ti*.

It's ugly out there, she said. You got scared.

Her informality disconcerted me. I nodded.

You're not mixed up in that stuff, she probed.

Not at all, I said. I'm a teacher.

What do you teach.

Literature.

How wonderful. I love to read. Romantic novels. Daphne Du Maurier. Although with my husband and the kids, I don't have time. He was fired from Ford. He was lucky they didn't haul him off with the union reps. Poor guy goes out every day with the want ads. All he can find is gigs in little auto repair places. And he's falling apart on me. I'd like to have more time to read. I've got my idealistic side. But you gotta eat, right? And if I don't bring anything home to fill the basket, we're screwed. That's why I go downtown every day. Romanticism is fine in novels, but life's something else. I can't make stew from a novel. It's not the same thing as osso bucco. I gotta be practical. And sacrifice.

Just to say something, I replied:

A sensitive soul.

Then she moved her leg closer to mine:

You look pale. For a few pesos we can work something out, she said. Whatever you can manage. And it'll help you get over your fright, papi.

17 The southeaster was coming in for the long haul. The wind was a hoarse uproar. From my nocturnal hideaway I heard the gale-force whistling, an abrupt door slamming, branches creaking, the lash of a loose cable, explosions of broken glass, a piece of sheet metal flying. This was the music of my insomnia.

The endless, icy whistling reached my bed. On top of the old sweater I wore another, equally old, black cable-knit sweater, raveled at the elbows. I had warmed the bedroom with a little electric heater and taken the letters to bed with me. I had filed them in chronological order. I jotted down my thoughts in a notebook. In a short time, I calculated, I would finish my essay on absence. I didn't harbor too many illusions of getting it published, but I was confident that sooner or later someone would value the work and appreciate my subliminal metaphysics.

Even though I didn't express blind confidence in posterity, sometimes I permitted myself the illusion that my essay on that correspondence would eventually see the light of day. Then, in that final dissemination of my work, it would become clear that my poetics contained political implications. Although at present it was impossible to publish such a piece of work, it gave me hope to imagine that someday the dictatorship would be over. At some future time this secret document, conceived in secret and in terror by a humble teacher of literature, would be salvaged. Let us acknowledge this: nobody writes without the hope of being read. And, in this case, published. In any event, I exercised caution: every time I finished reading the letters and taking notes, I hid the file and the little notebook.

It didn't escape me that there was another search contained in my interest in those letters. In addition to the story of lesbian love, there was a novel here. Martín's. A novel about his family. Up to the point where Martín, so clever that he had imagined he was cheating on Diana, turned out to be the real cuckold in this triangle. Reacting to a Freudian paradigm, he was repeating a story, his father's, the cuckolded naval officer who had bombed the Plaza as his pregnant wife and her female lover crossed it on their way to the port to escape from the country. I remembered the letter Martín had given me to take to Rosario, in which he wrote to Mara of his suspicion that someone else had won her heart. And I wondered how Martín would have reacted if he had discovered that it wasn't a male "someone," but a female, his own pregnant *compañera*. I wondered exactly how much of a coincidence it was that this nice, well-raised boy from the English prep-school whom I knew so well had unconsciously been looking for his lesbian mother in Diana. I detested this psych-textbook interpretation, but I couldn't dismiss it. My reasoning was pure determinism, I admit it. To what extent, I asked myself, was this reductive logic, with it fatalism, dictated by terror.

I was overcome by drowsiness; my eyelids were heavy. But after a while I woke up, startled into consciousness by associations that branched out in endless notes. My handwriting had turned into hieroglyphics. Soon I began writing on any scrap of paper I happened to have at hand: a napkin at a bar, a dry cleaner's receipt, a utility bill. A gramophone, that's what I had become. Even when I fell asleep, just like what happens to chess players, who keep on playing feverish games after they close their eyes, I dreamed I was writing. Everything I read could be interpreted from different points of view. But none of them totally convinced me. Each interpretation required a series of notes beforehand that would allow me to sketch a hypothesis. I couldn't stop interpreting how each word would be read. But that mania for interpreting everything didn't only include books. Little by little it took over reality: soon I was unable to leave the most ordinary, banal gesture alone. This grew worse at bedtime: from the shape of a shadow on the wall to the wrinkle in a sheet, everything was language that had to be submitted to an arsenal of criticism.

I started to become convinced that language was everything. But deep down I knew: taking refuge in language hardly freed one from danger. Which, in turn, implied another danger: madness. If all the hypotheses offered by a reading were questionable, the mother of all questions was one, just one, the most devious: Was I myself, I wondered. How was it possible to get any sleep after such mental gymnastics? Every so often I would get up, walk to the bathroom barefoot, and look at myself in the mirror: checking myself every so often became an obsession, seeing if that face corresponded with the image I had of myself. I started to get up more and more frequently. Eventually I began spending interminable stretches in front of the mirror. Till my feet froze. As a result, I slept less every night and then, during the day, I nodded off, dreaming brief dreams that turned into hallucinations, like that time I heard those two women talking. They dictated to me. And I wrote it down.

My breakfast consisted of tea and Criollita crackers. At noon I had some broth made from bouillon cubes and spread paté on the Criollitas. For dessert, an apple. At night, for dinner, I duplicated the lunch menu. I was turning into a fakir. And though all this time seemed eternal to me, it lasted barely a week.

One night I picked up my essay on absence, bundled up warmly, and went downstairs to the shop across the street, a sort of bookstore, photocopy joint, and kiosk combined. It was run by a young couple with two awful twins. A pair of ink-stained Tom and Jerrys. They were about to close, the woman told me. They'd have the photocopies for me the next day. Impossible to get them any sooner. I felt ridiculous, demanding that they have them ready that same day. Just a couple of millimeters separated ridiculous from suspicious. What I least wanted was to seem suspicious. With all the work Tom and Jerry gave the couple, they probably weren't even interested in my file, I told myself. I also thought that if I went back home with the original, for sure I would go back to my crazed note-taking. All right, I would come back the next day for the photocopies, as soon as they opened. I returned to my apartment, took a Valium, and went to bed.

The next morning dawned to a black sky, the wind still whistled in the streets, papers, leaves, and trash piled up, heads stayed down and lapels went up. It was early. I couldn't wait for the shop to open so I could pick up my photocopies. As soon as I stepped out onto the balcony I saw two green Falcons and an Army truck. Then some police cars, a dark blue police van. Some plainclothes guys got out of the Falcons, armed with Ithacas. They swooped down on the place. A captain in a helmet, pistol in hand, jumped out of the truck. The soldiers surrounded the store. They dragged out everyone who was inside. First the customers, though there weren't many. Then the owners, the couple and the little twins. The plainclothes officers pushed the couple toward the Falcons. The kids, crying, were dispatched to the military truck. They lined the others up against the wall. They frisked them for weapons, seized their documents. They threw a fat guy to the ground, pointing guns at him. The guy was crying. They kicked him in the belly. I saw how the guy threw up. Except for the family and the fat guy, they let everyone go. Some soldiers carried off everything there was in the store, from the photocopier to the metal shelves, not forgetting, of course, the merchandise that had occupied one corner up front. Cartons of cigarettes, candy, toys. When they had finished emptying it all out, a police car arrived. The Army left. A cop was left in charge. He was a dark-skinned type with a mustache. He rubbed his hands together and tapped his feet against the chill. The temperature kept dropping.

In my misery I felt the anguish of vanity, what someone who has lost his masterwork feels, assuming that my little essay on absence was that. Deep down I grieved for my essay's bad luck and imagined that it had been my masterwork only because I had lost it forever. There were more significant losses all around me.

And more profound absences.

18 In those days my phone was tapped. In the background you could hear the sounds of an auto repair shop and that Palito Ortega song, *La felicidad.* The screaming, too. Walter, I thought. But I had no way of calling him back. That lasted a few weeks.

I didn't have the energy to go to Entel and ask for repairs. I imagined that if I filed a request, the repair would require a file, an investigation. Better not to subject my life to any investigation. I decided to wait. Every so often I picked up the receiver. Same thing: that song, those screams. The most advisable thing for my mental health was exercise: to start walking again. I began wandering through the city once more, getting lost. I walked till my legs couldn't take it anymore. There were times when I even got as far as Nuestra Señora de Pompeya church. My walks usually ended up at some church: for example, Nuestra Señora de los Remedios, on the other side of Parque Avellaneda. More than obsessive wandering syndrome, what I did was a pilgrimage. Maybe I was waiting for a miracle, but I didn't know what kind.

Till early one morning, on a Tuesday, the phone started ringing again. From the Burn Institute, a nurse told me. De Franco had been admitted two days earlier and was just beginning to regain partial consciousness. He could now receive visitors. He had asked for me. No one else, the nurse said. I was the only loved one the patient claimed to have. That *loved one* thing really got to me. Please, she urged me, you need to come. Because the poor man can't find peace. My visit would soothe him.

De Franco was the Mummy. All bandaged except his mouth and eyes. Or rather, one eye. I addressed that eye:

Don't overtax yourself, De Franco. I thought I saw a glimmer in that eye.

I don't have much time left, he said.

According to De Franco, after the consultation with the psychic, Azucena was overwhelmed by negligence. Whatever flirtatiousness remained began to dissolve. First she stopped bathing for a few days. She no longer dyed her gray roots. The neglect included the chalet. Once so obsessed with the decorative details of her home, she no longer bothered to adjust a picture, sweep the corners, or change the water in the vases, where the scent of rotting flowers filled the entire house. The garden suffered from the same abandonment. Grass and weeds encroached on the flagstone path. Not to mention Pedro's deterioration. It wasn't that Azucena forgot to change his diapers. It was that she no longer cared. The husband, in his wheelchair, traversed the house from one end to another, reeking. De Franco wanted to vanish, but his guilt kept him there: after all, Gabrielito was sort of his son, too. A gentleman like him couldn't back down under those circumstances.

Besides, at this age, Gómez, he said to me, it's not so easy to find a chick.

De Franco had gotten used to spending Saturday nights at Villa Ballester. Azucena insisted that he stay till Sunday. De Franco knew that even if she didn't admit it, her insistence was due to her fear of being alone. Now she only talked about Gabrielito.

A lampshade, Azucena said to me one night, related De Franco. They've turned my Gabrielito into a lampshade.

And she continued to stick pins in Videla's photos. As usual, she would then slip them under the door of the sealed room.

Another time Azucena got the idea into her head that they had bound Bibles with her son's skin.

I'm going to check out all the *santerías* in the city till I find him, she told De Franco. I know I'll find him in God's book.

De Franco remained silent. And stared at the sky. With this gray, drizzly weather, what he feared most was that a terrible storm would erupt, leading to a repetition of the tragedy of that night when the thunderclaps had driven the invalid crazy and provoked Azucena's delirium, even though De Franco wasn't altogether convinced that it really had been a delirium. He couldn't forget the bluish light twinkling under the door of the sealed room, the door handle turning without explanation.

That night Azucena drugged Pedrito, tied him up, got into her nightgown, and went to bed. De Franco put on a shirt that used to be Pedrito's. She turned her back and he put his arms around her. They heard a police siren. Far, very far away. Then, silence. A silence barely cut by the passing of a car, a gust of wind, a dog barking.

Stay till tomorrow and I'll make you some goulash, Azucena said.

Okay, said De Franco.

He fell asleep clinging to Azucena, inhaling the dense scent of the nape of her neck. She hadn't bathed or washed her hair, but she did apply perfume. And that heavy perfume, mixed with the odor of recent sex, gave De Franco the comforting feeling of animal heat. He fell asleep thinking that nothing in life mattered more than a dish of food and a lay. Not much more. He slipped into drowsiness. But his rest didn't last long.

More than the heat of the flames, it was Pedrito's frantic laughter that woke them. Pedrito was applauding and laughing his head off. The fire consumed the entrance to the home, the dining room, the kitchen, and the sealed room. Pedrito had managed to untie himself, climb into the wheelchair, and set fire to the pile of newspapers and magazines Azucena collected. The house was on fire. It was too late, and not just to put out the flames. Also to escape. When they opened the bedroom door, a wave of heat suffocated them. The most intense, raging fire scorched them. From the sealed room, came children's voices, an infantile chorus:

Can you see, can you see,
It's the glorious J. P.

When he heard those screams, Pedrito started babbling the Peronist March. He sang and spun around in his wheelchair. He had a plastic fuel can in his lap. He propelled himself toward them at full speed. De Franco managed to close the door. The crash of the invalid and his wheelchair against the door coincided with the explosion of the fuel. Azucena cursed herself for having barred the windows. Flames were also rising on the other side of the door, the outside. There was a blast at the doorway: the fuel can Pedrito was carrying. If they wanted to escape, they had no alternative than to pass through the flames. De Franco had an idea: they wrapped themselves in the blankets.

When I got to the street, on fire, I realized I was alone, Gómez. I'll never know if Azucena was trapped by the flames or by the past.

Sometimes they're the same thing, I was about to reply.

De Franco's single eye dripped fat tears. I took out my handkerchief.

That night they took him back to intensive care. I went home to my apartment. In the morning another nurse phoned.

De Franco had died at dawn.

19 I thought of my mother, I thought of Esteban, of Martín and Mara. Since it was unavoidable, I thought of Diana. I couldn't stop thinking about her. If she hadn't gotten in touch with me again, I thought, there were two probable explanations: either she'd been kidnapped, or else she had managed to flee the country. And both explanations justified her silence. If they hadn't come for me yet, I thought, it was either because Diana hadn't given me up under torture, or, if she was safe, she hadn't called me so as not to get me in trouble. But I was anxious. In fact, in the absence of news, for me Diana had become one of the disappeared. Her features and habits were now taking on a physical presence in my memory. The same thing happened with the memory of my mother. Sometimes I recognized her gestures in my own. Other times, when I didn't recognize myself in them, I wondered if those gestures might be from my father, that unknown quantity.

If I really wanted to know about Diana, I reflected, I simply had to visit the apartment on Calle Pasteur where, with luck, her parents would still be living, and again, with luck, they might know something about their daughter. With luck, I repeated. It's just that luck probably held more sway in those days than ever before. Luck and superstition. Because when terror infects the body, it's followed immediately by prayers, religious stamps, candles, a string of garlic, a little red ribbon. Let him who is free of magical thinking throw the first amulet.

I spent a long time deliberating whether it would be better to go there in the morning, in the afternoon, or at night, during the week or on the weekend. The calculus of my fear, in fact, was circular and became an excuse for postponing my visit. It was a Saturday afternoon, as I recall. Night was descending over the city. Finally I put on my raincoat and walked out into the street. A heavy drizzle was falling. I glanced at the sky: A thick, dun sheet. No sooner did I hit the street than I felt the terror attack my weakened legs. I walked against the wind, hoping that by whipping against me, it might clear my thoughts. But every time a green Falcon passed by, I felt like I was about to vomit up my guts. Maybe if I hurried, I could warm up, I told myself. And so I picked up my pace. I worried that haste might make me look suspicious. I was about to cross Sarmiento when I stopped to let another Falcon go by. Suddenly I saw green Falcons wherever I looked. I was walking through a city whose cars were all green Falcons, all of them with three guys inside, their arms sticking out the windows, with their Ithacas and their pistols aiming in both directions. The Falcons left clots on the asphalt, the blood marks of their bloody tires. I tried to walk hugging the wall: there were no doors to let me in or to hide behind. The buildings had no doors. Only windows. But even those began at the second-floor level. Behind each window, entire families with little blue and white flags applauded and celebrated the parade of the green Falcons. You could hear the echo of a march in the wind. It was the Peronist March. I leaned against a wall. I felt something warm and sticky on the palms of my hands, on my fingers. The wall was gushing blood.

20 Diana's parents looked older in the somnolent shadows of the apartment. Bernardo and Clara had covered the mirrors with white sheets. If we don't see ourselves reflected in mirrors, we don't exist. The old man must have noticed how I felt about mirrors.

The woman offered me tea with lemon in a heavy glass. They were testing me out, I recall. Especially the old guy, Bernardo. Where and when had I met his daughter, he wanted to know, what sort of relationship did we have, why was I so interested in finding out about her now. The military had already ransacked the apartment, he said. Early one morning. They had surrounded the block. They kicked the door in, turned everything upside down. They weren't in uniform, but you could tell they were military. Sell the store and go back to Israel, they advised them. They would be closer to their daughter in Israel, because surely Diana was training with the Palestinians.

Bernardo kept testing me. What did I teach, he asked. What had Diana studied with me. He didn't let up: Was it true that Diana had been my favorite Literature student when I was teaching in the department? He wanted to know her favorite authors. I figured, as I would later confirm, that the old folks had already gone through this: someone who came to see them, and with the explanation that they had information about their daughter, extorted money from them. Some guy had visited them a few times, asking for money in exchange for information.

He had also asked them for clothes to take to the place where she was being detained. A naval facility, he told them. Because the Army had handed her over to the Navy. He couldn't give them more information. A rehab farm for male and female political prisoners, he said. Then Clara made up a little bag of clothing: jeans, socks, a heavy sweater, underwear, and a copy of *War and Peace*. Money, too, everything she had in the safe in the apartment. A few days later, Bernardo said, as he was walking along that same block, in front of a construction site, among the garbage in a dump truck, he saw some clothes: it was the clothing Clara had given the NCO. Among that same garbage was also the Tolstoy book. That guy never returned. And they'd had no more news of Diana.

I'm not a cop, I said.

The old folks looked at me. Clara lowered her eyes. Bernardo held my gaze. I asked myself what those eyes saw in me—if they saw the person who had sheltered their daughter or the fag who'd been turned on by a cop.

I stared back at him.

If Diana were free, I thought, that business about the guy would never have happened. So then it was clear that Diana had been captured. And, as was the case with so many young men and women, they might never hear of her again.

I looked at the sheet-draped mirrors. As I said, not seeing my reflection, I felt like a ghost. And those two old folks were ghosts, as well.

Come, Bernardo beckoned. I followed him toward a little room that faced the courtyard. Diana's bedroom. All of it a library. I focused on one bookshelf. It was filled with books of Russian literature.

Again I felt his eyes on me. Bernardo had his back to the window. I saw myself reflected in the glass. Now I existed. But this didn't bring me any peace.

The truth, he said. Tell me the truth.

He spoke without anger, without rage. His strength came from his gaze. I will never forget that gaze, the professor recalls. It seems easy to define a gaze literally. Anyone can plug in adjectives and think they're being faithful in describing a state of mind.

What truth, I asked him.

Yours, he said.

The old man took the copy of *War and Peace* from the library. The cover was half torn off. He shook off a layer of dust. That was the book he had picked up from the street.

My daughter hated English literature, he said. Read this passage she underlined:

> *It was clear and frosty. Above the dirty, ill-lit streets, above the black roofs, stretched the dark starry sky. Only looking up at the sky did Pierre cease to feel how sordid and humiliating were all mundane things compared with the heights to which his soul had just been raised. At the entrance to the Arbat Square an immense expanse of dark starry sky presented itself to his eyes. Almost in the center of it, above the Prechistenka Boulevard, surrounded and sprinkled on all sides by stars but distinguished from them all by its nearness to the earth, its white light, and its long uplifted tail, shone the enormous and brilliant comet of 1812—the comet which was said to portend all kinds of woes and the end of the world. In Pierre, however, that comet with its long luminous tail aroused no feeling of fear. On the contrary he gazed joyfully, his eyes moist with tears, at this bright comet which, having traveled in its orbit with inconceivable velocity through immeasurable space, seemed suddenly—like an arrow piercing the earth—to remain fixed in a chosen spot, vigorously holding its tail erect, shining and displaying its white light amid countless other scintillating stars.*

And then, studying me carefully, he asked:
Who are you.
I couldn't hold his gaze anymore.

21 One morning there was a shimmer of sunlight on the balcony windows. I turned on Radio Nacional: they were playing Mozart. Nothing wrong with a Mozart concerto to start the day. I started walking around the apartment, conducting an imaginary orchestra. I even felt better physically. I felt *allegro*.

But then the phone rang. Again, terror.

The voice sounded distant. It was a young woman's voice.

It's Paloma, she said. Paloma. I'm calling you from a phone booth.

I managed to repeat her name. She was calling from Barcelona. I didn't know whether to keep on being terrified or return to my previous joyous state.

I wanted to thank you, Professor, Paloma said. Thanks to you, I'm alive. If it hadn't been for you . . . I love you very much. That's what I wanted to tell you. I've got to get off now. I love you very much.

I hadn't done a lot that morning. Or rather, I didn't think I'd done anything. That call brought me back to myself. Suddenly I felt like I was making a decision, that nothing could spoil the feeling Paloma's phone call had given me.

Spring was in the air. Soon it would be Teacher's Day. And shortly after that, Student's Day. I felt like returning to school, returning to my classes. If I prolonged my leave of absence, I thought, I'd still be a prisoner of my shadows. Life went on. And I was alive.

I showered, shaved. After a warm bath and a shave, I looked much better. I was ready to go on. It was necessary to go on. If I was alive, I said to myself, I had to resist. I used to like the verb *to resist*; I still do. A survivor is someone who resists. I stepped out onto the balcony. The sun was a miracle.

I was just going to go to the school. I gulped down a cup of tea. For the first time in a long while I didn't need a raincoat to go outdoors.

I hesitated before buying a copy of *Clarín*. The newspaper was always a source of bitterness. Opening it meant risking that death would take me by surprise just when I was starting to recover my spirits. Death is part of life, I said to myself, not the other way around. A spring-like optimism flooded my soul.

The article was on page three. In a joint Army-police operation in La Paternal district, three police officers had lost their lives in a confrontation with guerrillas. The subversive delinquents, members of a cell operating in the vicinity, had been liquidated. There were photos of the police officers. *Fallen in the Line of Duty, Departmental Heroes*, I read. There would be a tribute to them. I immediately recognized one of the heroes. It was a strange sensation, a murky joy. It resembled happiness. But it wasn't happiness, because I was ashamed to feel what I was feeling. I was rejoicing over a death. Walter's death. This was an unnatural kind of happiness, I reflected. Bearing in mind the secretiveness of our relationship, the secret would now remain sealed forever. No one would ever know that I had once been turned on by a cop. Now I was clean. Spotless. That death gave me back a kind of purity. But the sensation was growing filthy. It was a chickenshit's happiness.

I threw away the copy of *Clarín*. As I did, I recalled how the Captain had reacted when I gave him those letters. Filth, the Captain had called those letters. And he had tossed them into the trash. I was no better than the Captain, I thought. The abrupt way in which I had gotten rid of the paper, as if by throwing it away I could get rid of evidence that incriminated me.

Who was I, I wondered. The guy who was elated by Paloma's phone call, or the one who had been turned on by Walter. I also wondered if Paloma would still love me if she found out about my affair with Walter. I was no better than my colleagues, either, those who shared the teachers' lounge with me. The Ortegosa woman from History. Iturbide, the guy from Anatomy. Raimundi, from Philosophy. Literature wasn't a subject that could be rated above History, Anatomy, or Philosophy. Maybe literature, in its pretension, confused history with the activity of bodies and the conclusions that could be drawn from their behavior. Literature didn't explain: it inquired. It didn't cure: at best, it relieved. But this didn't redeem it. Just as it didn't redeem my return to teaching, to the classroom, the students. To resist, I thought. That was what it meant to survive: to resist.

I took the book out of my briefcase. I stood in front of the class. Once more I read:

On ne tue point les idées.

Epilogue

AND THE WORLD KEEPS TURNING

The following year, during the World Cup and at the height of the dictatorship's publicity campaign, Sergio succeeded in getting his cancer-ridden old man to assign him power of attorney. Then, with the help of Rodolfo, the radiologist, he murdered him. And Gina, too. When the police burst into his office, Rodolfo tried to kill himself by jumping out a window, but so ineptly that he landed on the metal roof of a rotisserie joint and they hauled him off to the slammer. They found Sergio, starving and delirious, in the shell of an abandoned ranch in Pergamino.

A few years later, during the Falklands War, another murder took me by surprise. Its notoriety was eclipsed by the imminence of defeat. We were winning. And then suddenly they kicked our asses. The English brought in Gurkhas, rumor had it. They fucked the kids and then slit their throats. There was a perverse pleasure in the telling of it. Like following some other crime story that wasn't about the war. The Falklands War buried the public's interest in Ramón. A man who beats his son to death was nothing in a country that sends its own people to the slaughterhouse. One afternoon Ramón caught Juancito in front of a mirror, dressed in his mother's clothes. Ramón testified that his hand had slipped with the beating. How could he possibly have wanted to kill his own son? It was an overreaction. Later, in the Caceros jail, he devoted himself to studying the Bible and writing to all the people who had harmed him. He admitted he had been guilty of intimidating the apartment residents by burning hair and hanging up toads. He also confessed to having denounced Del Solar to an Army acquaintance by telling him that a subversive was living in the building.

In '83, when the military leaders' trials began, the courtrooms overflowed with journalists. There was no room for a flea. As the testimonies unfolded and the victims—men and women, young and old—continued to testify, as the weeks went by, the sessions started losing their audience. By the end, there were very few journalists in attendance. Terror had become a bore.

During the sessions, Iturbide, the Anatomy teacher, had to give up his post. He was accused of participating in torture sessions at a secret military prison. His victims identified him as the doctor who answered to the nickname "Dr. Mengele." He was a beneficiary of the Due Obedience and Full Stop laws. The latest I heard of Iturbide had to do with a public protest by H.I.J.O.S. militants in front of his home in Villa Devoto.

Raimundi, the guy from Philosophy, ended up testing his plan: to break the bank at roulette in Mar del Plata. He didn't beat it, but he did come out loaded with cash after a lucky streak. With the dough I collected, I'm retiring, Gómez, he told me. And I'm taking that little trip to the Black Forest. The House of Being, get it? I get it, I replied. But I didn't say what I was thinking: money was burning a hole in his pocket. Before he left, that friend of his, the Colonel, invited him to a poker game in a security agency belonging to some other friends. Raimundi lost. Everything. And more. The guys he got into debt with were hard-core. I'm dead meat, Gómez, he said to me before vanishing from the school and from the places he used to frequent.

The Ortegosa woman wasn't any luckier. In 2001, her savings in dollars were frozen in the economic freeze, *el corralito*. She died of a heart attack, banging on the steel plates protecting Citibank.

2 One afternoon, as I stood at the bar at Florida Garden, drinking coffee, a bald, slender, elegant guy with a salon tan came over to greet me. Kind of old to be wearing an earring. He must have been around fifty, the age I was when I fell in love with him. Niqui remembered those days. Now he understood me, he said. A boy had made his life hell, just as he had done to me at a certain point. The boy broke his heart, he said. And that hurt him more than AIDS. Besides, life had played another dirty trick on him: he worked as a graphic designer at a lab that manufactured Viagra. Niqui was the creative director responsible for packaging, brochures, and promotions.

I saw Bodhi again, that ethereal, spiritual boy, at Parque Lezica. It was hard for me to connect that mass of flesh with its shaved head and olive green combat gear with the lithe, fragile youth who went by "Siddhartha" and bought books at the Kier. Now Bodhi was an obese skinhead who sold Nazi literature at a stand at the fair. He had a bat on the table and a Rottweiler chained to a tree.

How could I ever forget Lutz. No, I haven't forgotten him. Exploiting his knowledge of the occult, he had created a sect in Corrientes that combined the devotional aspects of various religions that best suited his purposes. He used his magnetism and power to persuade the unwary to donate significant sums to the new faith and organized parties with minors. It came out in *Crónica*. When the parents of a fifteen-year-old girl, the guest of honor at one of these events, reported the sect's activities, Lutz tried to flee. The courts tried seven people who were apparently connected with the ritual murder of a twelve-year-old boy. In the homes of the accused they found skeletal remains and elements related to ritual practices. Lutz had been the mastermind of the crimes. José Alberto Lutz, pachydermic septuagenarian. The rituals included sexual practices and the decapitation of the victim, whose head was found elsewhere. According to the investigation, the defendants were part of a network of pedophilia, child prostitution, and drug trafficking. Lutz, seventy, obese, dressed like a priest, was detained by the prefecture on a boat crossing from Puerto Iguazú to Foz.

In his essay *The Occult Sciences in the City of Buenos Aires*, Roberto Arlt mentions that sort of grotesque character. No doubt Lutz belonged to the category of swindlers Arlt described. But considering the degree of psychological meltdown with which I came to him, the business about the Great Damage that he had described still struck me as a reasonable title for that disastrous period.

3 When democracy was restored, it was discovered that one of dictator Videla's children had been born with a cerebral malformation. He suffered from a lesser form of intellectual disability called idiocy. The son was an in-patient at Colonia Montes de Oca, more like a concentration camp than a clinic for the mentally disabled. The place had an evil aura of notoriety in police reports, due to its degrading treatment of patients as well as the sale of organs. Later Videla transferred the boy to a Bible school in Morón. Two French nuns worked there. As they did with the other patients, the sisters bathed the child, taught him to read, took him camping. When Videla was dictator, the two nuns, accused of being subversives, were arrested by the Navy. They were kidnapped and tortured at the Naval Mechanics' School. Domestic and foreign protests were hurled at Videla. The dictator played the great Pilate and washed his hands, claiming he couldn't do anything for the two sisters who had wiped his sick child's butt. Also among the disappeared, those nuns. So Videla had a sick son, I said to myself. If she had survived the fire, Azucena might have enjoyed knowing this fact. And her happiness would have been like what I felt when I heard about Walter's death. This feeling still torments me.

4 The repressive machinery of the dictatorship had, and still has, its connections firmly established under democracy. Consider, for example, that State crime, the AMIA assault, in which Diana's parents died. The explosion destroyed their apartment. The old folks died beneath the rubble.

5 I often wonder what my fate would have been if my essay on absence hadn't disappeared when the military raided the photocopy shop. There's nothing more foolish than imagining that the pages that one lost were transcendental. Because vanity has a way of swelling your head and making you think that the writing was brilliant and that your essence, that of a personal genius, was lost along with them. As my genius had resided there, in that lost essay, I was no longer anywhere else. Therefore I wouldn't write again. And I didn't. "How sly you are," my mother used to tell me. But, I wonder, up to what point does it make sense to cling to who you were before, knowing that you're always someone else. This person who lived to tell the tale is someone else. Yes, you're always someone else.

To lose something you've written can be a double loss. You lose the written record of what you've lived, and by losing the writing, it seems as if you've lost the lived experience. Let's rehash it: I had lost. Thinking about it, everything I hadn't been able to say in that essay on absence in an allegorical way, I've said now, plainly and simply.

Because you can't get away from history. Nobody can play the fool, no matter how hard he tries. I'm sorry if I'm running on. I'd like to soften the dogmatism, that defensive tone. What the hell, it fell to me to swallow this story. So don't try to change my tone.

I *am* this tone.

More than thirty years had to pass for me to have the courage to tell this tale. Some loose ends still remain, yes. I try to tie them up. And also, as before, fruitlessly, I try not to make literature. I try to relate the facts, record them.

I thought I had left them behind. But the story won't let go of me. When I reassembled it, a kind of melancholy invaded me. How, at that time, the worst of my life, no matter what you might think, was it possible for me to have felt so alive. I often ask myself if pain is necessary in order to appreciate life. I hesitate to reply that it's not.

My life then had a meaning. To put a student in a taxi, to give shelter to a pregnant girl. No heroism in those acts. I was propelled by the facts, I say to myself.

Look, here's the little aluminum foil figurine Diana left me. A ballerina.

6 When I tell it, as I've just done, I repeat to myself: It's not to anyone's detriment, but for everyone's good. Let each one draw his own conclusions.

As far as I'm concerned, the professor says, I've got no more chords left for this strumming. I feel like I'm fading. I've got only one favor to ask. Don't bury me in holy ground. Better to throw my ashes into the sea. But before that, while I'm saying goodbye, while I'm going, I'll leave the gate of this story open for those who want to come in.

7 I thought I saw Diana from a distance in San Telmo. It was on a Sunday morning at the Plaza Dorrego fair. I tried to elbow my way in through the crowd. When I finally got closer, I knew it wasn't her.

Another time I thought I saw her at the demonstration on March 24, 2006. It had been thirty years since the coup. Night was falling over Avenida de Mayo. She was walking along with the row of Mothers. At one point she turned, looking for someone. Diana, I shouted. In the din of singing and drumming, Diana couldn't hear me. It took me a while to reach her. And again, when I was at her side, I saw that it wasn't her.

This sensation of seeing her has happened to me a few times. And it wasn't her.

No, I never heard about Diana again.

Never.

And the world keeps turning.

ACKNOWLEDGMENTS

Ángela Pradelli, Cristian Domingo, Carlos Cottet, Eduardo Belgrano Rawson, Carolina Marcucci, Juan Boido, Rodrigo Fresán, Lucía Capozzo, Tomás James, Antonio Dal Masetto, Esther Cross, José Pablo Feinmann, María Seoane, Ernesto Mallo, María Laura Meradi, Esteban Seimandi, María Inés Krimer, Débora Mundani, Jorge Rodríguez Marino, Martha Berlín, Elisa Calabrese, Susana Rosano, Michele Guillemont, Juan Gómez, José Roza, Ricardo Arkader, Patricia Muñoz, Miguel Berger, Analía Belén, and Miguel Paz.

And to my sister Patricia.

Guillermo Saccomanno is the author of numerous novels and story collections, including *El buen dolor*, winner of the Premio Nacional de Literatura, and *77* and *Gesell Dome*, both of which won the Hammett Prize from the International Association of Crime Writers. He also received Seix Barral's Premio Biblioteca Breve de Novela for *El oficinista* and the Rodolfo Walsh Prize for nonfiction for *Un maestro*, as well as the Premio Democracia in 2014. Critics tend to compare his works to those of Dostoevsky, Tolstoy, and Faulkner.

Andrea G. Labinger has published numerous translations of Latin American fiction. She has been a finalist three times in the PEN USA competition. Her translation of Liliana Heker's *The End of the Story* (Biblioasis, 2012) was included in *World Literature Today*'s list of the "75 Notable Translations of the Year." *Gesell Dome*, Labinger's translation of Guillermo Saccomanno's *Cámara Gesell* (Open Letter Books, 2016), won a PEN/Heim Translation Award.

**OPEN
LETTER**

OPEN LETTER